The Chapman Books

Aaron J. French

Erik T. Johnson

Adam P. Lewis

The Chapman Books
Trade paperback ISBN: 978-1- 62898-004-2
eBook ISBN: 978-1- 62898-005-9

Cover design: Alan Davidson

Uncanny Books
810 West Knox St.
Durham, NC 27701
http://uncannybooks.com/

PREFACE

Greetings, my fellow fans and readers of all things hidden, strange, obfuscated, darkly fantastic, and obscure:

Several years ago I ran into Adam Lewis at a "Seekers of Haunted and Eldritch Places" convention being held in Savannah, Georgia, among the old brick buildings and teetering cathedrals of the city. He and I shared a drink in the downstairs hotel lobby, and although he seemed in good spirits, I could tell something troubled him.

After a while, and a few more drinks, he spilled it, revealing that an aunt living in the same town as the convention had passed away, naming Adam as the beneficiary. (That was how he was able to attend — because he was in the area going over the deceased aunt's estate.)

When I told him I was sorry to hear it, he claimed that really what bothered him was the thing he had found shoved in his aunt's attic, something long untouched and covered in years of dust: a box containing several perplexing items — ancient newspaper clippings, an ornate Bible belonging to a family called Chapman, a collection of photographs, and three brittle manuscripts (well, he called them manuscripts, but more accurately they were diaries of a kind).

The manuscripts, which he had picked through, detailed disturbing events regarding this Chapman family, including accounts of demon possession, ghosts coming back from the grave, house-bound hauntings, storybooks come to life, insanity, dementia, schizophrenia, even murder. Most disconcerting was that Adam had no idea why they would be in his aunt's possession or what they had to do with his family. Connections between the three manuscripts, if any, were scarce.

Adam seemed relieved to be able to tell me about the manuscripts, and invited me to see them. I had the feeling he didn't want to be the only one bearing the burden of their existence.

We spent the night rummaging through the items in the box. Along with the beautiful antique Bible, which was in pristine condition, the newspapers were from the mid- to late-1800s, yellowed around the edges, and stuck in decayed leather bound albums. They were from all over the South and recounted incidents involving the various medical doctors and Chapman families, most involving death, scandal, and weird reports of alleged occult activity. One 1872 issue of the *Atlanta Herald* outright claimed the Chapmans were practicing Satanists who sacrificed children in obscene rituals.

The problem was that the reports were conflicting and many took place in different states. Moreover, it was not clear whether these were different Chapman families, the same one, distant relatives, etc. The bulk of the articles portrayed the Chapman family as having mental problems, the children as invalids, and there were even statements from the several doctors who had treated them.

In one of the articles a doctor *named* Harold Chapman — which was the same name as the father in a few Chapman articles — had been denounced as a charlatan, charged with malpractice, and was being pursued by authorities. The bottom line was this: while interesting, the clippings sparked more questions than they answered, causing us to finally set them aside in confusion.

The handful of photographs, whether framed or ready to crumble, showed a collection of families, some named Chapman, some unnamed, dressed austerely and seated before the camera; some showed other families, similarly unnamed; and several showed male doctors, often holding up a stethoscope or a medical bag.

The three manuscripts were bound in individual leather folders. Adam had read through them already, and as he showed them to me, he summarized their contents. I flipped through the decaying pages and felt like I was in a movie, some unholy mix of David Lynch and Roman Polanski. The scribblings of ink were so ancient-looking, and yet so real, so authentic, and the creases of yellow, fibrous material reminded me of the lines in an elderly person's hands. I could imagine the authors pouring their hearts into them so many years ago, and I did a fast-forward to me holding them now, in this house — and something like *déjà vu* ensued.

They were written by three different authors, and each one told a different story, all quite unwholesome and horrific, yet all involved a variant of the Chapman family. The words flowed before my eyes as my fingers turned the pages. Adam regaled me with horrifying descriptions of each account, and by the time he had finished, I was certain some presence was in the house with us, some invisible guest listening to our conversation.

"I've been thinking this would make a good horror collection," Adam said. "Now you know why I invited you."

When this all became clear, I smiled. "Count me in," I said.

After we discussed the specifics of the project, I hailed a cab back to my hotel and was already formulating the Chapman story as narrative in my head. I returned home the following week and Adam and I set to work, communicating via Skype calls and emails.

It soon became clear that what we were attempting was a) confusing, b) difficult, and, c) totally weird. We needed an expert on all things confusing, difficult, and weird, and we immediately thought of Erik T. Johnson, well known to both of us as a master of the outré and un-sane. We brought the project to Erik's attention, and he replied that this was right up his alley. He joined our team as a fellow author and "peculiarities consultant."

Adam, on the other hand, served as archivist, continually referring back to the three Chapman manuscripts as our novellas took shape. We spent the better part of two years hashing the whole thing out. What emerged was the book you hold in your hands, three authors' attempt to bring to life the forgotten ghosts of the past, to shape them as an artistic presentation.

We thank you for your purchase of *The Chapman Books* and we hope its horrors will find some closure with you.

Aaron J. French
February 2014
Tucson, Arizona

CHAPMAN ONE
THE STAIN
AARON J. FRENCH

The land around Orangeburg, South Carolina, at the end of the nineteenth century was known for its inhospitality. When the war was on, it was not safe to venture beyond the town limits for fear of coming across a regiment of Blues. Nowadays the threat had reverted to its original form: that of getting lost in the Shysword Forest.

There were lots of tales about folks going out into the wilderness for whatever reason and never finding their way back. More than once Stetson himself had answered such calls. It wasn't uncommon for one of the townsfolk to rush into his office blathering about someone with a spoiled limb whom they'd picked up along the road or by the Shysword Creek; drifters, a lot of them. Old veterans turned drunkards.

Dr. Stetson drove his motorcar along the winding dirt track, surveying the deep miles of forest. Pine, cedar, birch, mingling together in a network of branches, their trunks marching up and down the hills. Nets of oak and ivy covered the ground, giving way to thistles where the trunks lay fallen and moss-covered, moldering back into the earth.

His train for Albany wasn't due until five that afternoon. He'd allowed plenty of time. His brother lived in Columbia, and

Stetson planned on leaving his motorcar there while he was away. For the most part, Columbia had recovered from Sherman, but they still had a lot of work ahead of them.

In the seat beside him lay his suitcase with all of his clothes and toiletries. On top was his smaller, yet no less important, doctor's bag. On top of that, the strange telegram he had received two days ago.

Dr. Jasper Stetson
Terrible and uttermost horror has befallen us. You have always been my family's healer. I trust no other. Please come at once. The Chapman family needs you. I have wired money for a train.
Jane Chapman

He'd known Jane since she was a girl when her last name was still Bottington. He'd known her parents too: William and Genevieve Bottington. The Bottington Plantation was one of the most lucrative cotton plantations in town, right up till the war ended. William and Genevieve died soon after to consumption. Stetson had been their physician until their deaths and he'd always regretted his inability to save them.

They left everything to their daughter, Jane, who at the time was twenty-one years old. Not long after that she met the enigmatic Harold Chapman, a drifter turned carpetbagger who came to town a few years after the war. Jane hired Harold to look after the plantation. For a while it was just the two of them out there, which incited much gossip and scandal. Of course they fell in love, to the chagrin of the townsfolk, who collectively looked down and anything "Northern," carpetbaggers especially.

But Jane and Harold got married, sold the plantation, and left for New York. Stetson hadn't heard from her since, but the plantation was still there, owned by a man named Reginald Wheaton (though it had become more of a farm than a plantation). He had pretty much forgotten about Jane Bottington and Harold Chapman.

Until this telegram.

Surely there are better physicians in Manhattan, he'd thought. Yet he was flattered Jane remembered him after all these years.

Still, there was something menacing about her message.

That first line — *Terrible and uttermost horror has befallen us* — what did that mean? More consumption? He hoped not.

Pine and birch gave way to ash and cypress the farther he got from town. The loam was getting soggier. Soon all these cypresses would be standing in swamp water —

Something moved across the road and he squinted to get a better look.

A figure was walking along the shoulder. Perhaps a furlong yonder. A lumpy thing with a hunched back and long dangling arms. Dressed in a black suit, carrying a black and red umbrella, and wearing a battered chimneypot hat.

One of those veterans, prowling the wilds and drinking himself to death.

The vehicle bumped along, and his hands gripped the wheel tightly. He stared at the figure, unable to look away. Something was very wrong — *strange*, rather. Odd. Surreal. He was kind of fuzzy with a weird aura hovering about him, and his dark clothes seemed to swirl imperceptibly.

The motorcar gained on him.

I won't look. I'll keep my hands on the wheel, my face forward, and drive right on past.

But before he could stop himself, his head had swung to the right. He gaped at the figure. *God in Heaven…*

Fear brutalized his heart. His nerves exploded, driving a chill into his bones.

The wanderer, whose drunken shuffle awarded him less than fifteen feet per minute, turned his head too at the exact same moment and stared into the cab. The red and black umbrella twirled above his head. Stetson saw a grotesque, pig-like hoof gripping the handle.

The wanderer's face was also uncannily piggish, with round, smooth, fatty features and snout-like jowls. Sharp teeth jutted up and down from rubbery lips. Eyes, set to either side of a wide flat nose, looked black and glossy, with flies crawling over them.

Stetson thought maybe he was imagining the pig creature. But as the motorcar took the lead, the wanderer reached into his coat and withdrew a long, very crumpled piece of cardstock, and held it up for Stetson to see. Written in sloppy reddish ink (*or in blood,* Stetson thought) was the message *You Are Going To Die.* The pig creature displayed the sign proudly, baring his teeth.

Then Stetson moved ahead and the creature fell away to the side. Stetson craned his neck to peer over the back. The pigman had stopped and was standing eerily still, holding up the sign as he watched the motorcar pull away. The red and black umbrella spun slowly, resting on his shoulder.

Stetson turned back around—and the moment he did he screamed, slamming on the brakes. A deer stood eating berries from a strew of undergrowth scattered across the road. When it caught a glimpse of the motorcar, it bounded away.

Stetson's heart beat a mile a minute. He looked back again, but the road was empty. He turned around, taking a deep breath.

I must be losing my mind.

He opened his medical bag, fished out a sedative, and swallowed it dry. Then, after a few more breaths, he depressed the accelerator and continued down the road. He still had a five o'clock train to catch.

*   *   *

In Albany, a tall man picked him up at the train station.

"Are you Dr. Stetson?"

"I am."

"This way." He extended a hand for Stetson's suitcase.

"Who are you?"

The man bowed. "Forgive me. I am Reynolds. One of the Chapman family's assistants. Their driver. I've been instructed to take you to the estate."

Stetson surrendered his suitcase. "I like sticking close by this one," he said, indicating his doctor's bag.

Reynolds smiled, then turned and led them through the train station. Outside he made a beeline for the deluxe black Ford motorcar parked by the curb, opening the door for Stetson to climb in the back, then tossing the suitcase in after him. Reynolds installed himself behind the wheel and they were off.

The man spoke little. When Stetson tried plying him with questions about the illness at the Chapman house, he said only that it wasn't for him to discuss.

Not unusual, a servant wanting to abstain from gossiping. He respected the man's wishes and questioned him no more. He shifted his gaze to the window as they rolled through the streets of Albany. The motorcar passed between Colonial houses, buildings with triangle roofs, several nice churches whose steeples prodded the sky, and lots of pedestrians milling about: window-shopping, strolling, dinning; some carousing sailors.

To the east he glimpsed the waters of the Hudson, a dark gray snake weaving among the buildings. As they advanced through town he noticed several canals, some with low lift bridges, others with steamships piloting down them. Albany's atmosphere was one of transportation and commerce, much faster-paced than the Southern villages to which he was accustomed.

Fine weather too, but it was the middle of the day and he imagined by evening it would be chilly.

Reynolds took the road leading out of town and soon they were surrounded by dense pine thickets and bristling spruce branches. Stetson had been trying since South Carolina to forget the strange being he had encountered on the country road. But this lonely forest through which they passed had engendered images of piggish beasts groping their way out of the trees. It was all he could do not to panic.

Stetson eventually dozed. The landscape grew increasingly dark, until finally they arrived in another small village with dirt roads, several shops, and a grand courthouse erected in the town square. The sign above the archway said *Village of Roycepeake.*

Reynolds took a left and headed west into a fresh sea of pines and spruce. "Almost there now," he said.

Within ten minutes they rolled up to a redbrick retainer wall, where Reynolds got out, opened the gate, drove the motorcar through, then closed the gate again.

The house loomed on a grassy eminence, surrounded by towering maples. The front yard was arranged into a series of terraces, each set off by another smaller redbrick retainer wall, with a waterless stone fountain erected in the center.

Reynolds drove them alongside the house and parked the car in a covered building where several other motorcars were housed. He opened the door for Stetson, then retrieved his

5

suitcase.

Stetson followed the servant into the house. The foyer was luxuriously vast, with hardwood floors, glass tables, and even a pink divan draped by a sheet. They stepped down the hallway and arrived in a grand sitting room. Sofas, oak tables, desks, and bookcases, with a crystal chandelier hanging from the ceiling and a tasteful array of artwork. Such extravagance was beginning to make him uneasy, for he was not accustomed to it.

Jane Chapman was coming toward him across the Persian rugs, her arms outspread. "My dear Jasper," she said.

"I will leave your bag in the upstairs bedroom," Reynolds muttered, shuffling off.

Jane wrapped Stetson in an embrace. He yielded easily, letting himself be clutched, feeling the warmth of her body. He could smell the floral fragrance of her blond hair.

"I'm so glad you came." She was already sobbing, her voice restrained. "We've lost one. I couldn't stand to lose another. Why does God do this to people?"

"I came as soon as I could," he said, patting her on the back. She'd been a young lady last time he'd seen her. Now she was robust and middle-aged, with all the characteristics of a mature woman.

She wore a checkered foulard robe, trimmed around the skirt with blue ribbons, three bands of silk wrapping her chest, and an array of pearl jewelry dangling from ears and neck. She looked dazzling, though somewhat exhausted. Dark circles couched her eyes. Her skin was pale, and she had premature crow's feet.

"You look lovely, my dear," he said, holding her hands, "but tired, really, you ought to be in bed. Have you been drinking enough water?"

She shook her head. "I'm not the one who is ill."

"No? Then who? What do you mean, 'We've lost one?'"

She glanced away, demure; then she brightened, though her felicity was obviously an act. "What about you?" she said. "You look so distinguished! Of course, you always did. Even when Mama and Papa were alive. But you've gotten much handsomer."

"I've gotten nothing but older, dear," he said.

"How are things back home? Is the plantation still there?"

He nodded. "Operated by a fella named Reginald Wheaton. Not much cotton there now. Reginald deals in livestock."

Her brows knit as she considered this. Stetson marveled at the complexity with which her features could appear youthful and mature, womanly yet childlike.

"Please," he said, letting go of her hands, "you must fill me in. I've been dying to know if you are ill. I've racked my brains these past few days. Tell me, what is the meaning of *uttermost horror*? Why such words in a telegram?"

She was about to answer when a male voice boomed across the room. "The words were my choosing. I felt them apt to describe our situation."

Stetson peered around Jane and saw Harold Chapman standing at the far end of the room, a whiskey glass in one hand, a weatherbeaten book in the other. He was larger than Stetson recalled, his frame altogether more masculine and imposing, his head much squarer, his chin like a chiseled block. He had a streak of dark brown hair and his shoulders seemed to jut out to either side, pulling at the jacket of his burgundy suit. He looked very mature, grown up. A far cry from the estranged Northern army brat who had wandered into town all those years ago.

"Darling," Jane said. "Jasper has arrived like I told you he would. Our prayers have been answered."

Harold made a face. "That remains to be seen."

"Oh, don't mind my husband," she told Stetson. "He's been under a lot of stress."

"A lot of stress, and a lot of utter horror," he said, arriving and shaking Stetson's hand; he had a strong, commanding grip, which felt good to Stetson's nervous fingers.

He continued, "Stress doesn't justify the awful situation we find ourselves in ... and as for poor Maggie..."

A series of thumps came from overhead, and Harold glanced at the ceiling. Jane followed his gaze; when the *bump, bump, bump* repeated, she immediately burst into tears. Stetson tried to assist her but she shooed him away, taking a seat on one of the sofas and dabbing her eyes with a kerchief.

"Who is Maggie? Is she the one who is sick?"

Harold nodded. "Aye, Maggie. Our only daughter left now that Karen is gone."

Jane began sobbing louder.

Stetson lifted an eyebrow. "Karen—who's that?"

"Karen was our firstborn, our most lovely daughter. Brightest, prettiest, most charming daughter a father could hope for." Now tears welled in Harold's eyes. "She was getting ready to attend university. She wanted to be an intellectual, a writer even. I believe she was smart enough to succeed, too. But now…"

"Did Karen get sick?"

Harold wiped his eyes. "Aye. Well, no. Sick isn't the proper word for it. Illness, mayhap, but even that's misleading."

"What would you call it?" Stetson asked, setting his leather medical bag on a nearby table. His arm was growing tired.

"*Possession*," Harold blurted, eyes widening.

Stetson squinted. "What do you mean, 'possession?'"

"I mean *demons*, Mr. Stetson."

The doctor guffawed. Jane had looked up and was giving him her most pitiful and earnest appeal.

"You must be joking," he said.

"No joke," Harold replied. "Our family is under attack from a demonic presence. It's already taken Karen's life and now it vies for poor Maggie. But God help me if—"

Stetson shook his head. "I'm a doctor. I don't believe in the supernatural, and I'm also an Atheist, which means I don't believe in God, or the devil, or angels—or demons."

The driver, Reynolds, entered the room and crossed to Jane, kneeling beside her. He was shadowed by a bulky dark-haired woman dressed in a blue calico dress and cloth apron.

"Please, take her upstairs to her bed," Harold said to them, gesturing toward Jane. "She's had enough excitement for today."

"I'm fine," Jane said indignantly.

"You're not fine. The weariness is written on your face." He glanced at Stetson for support.

"I would agree," Stetson said. "Your appearance suggests overexertion. Fatigue. Rest, and plenty of water—that's my recommendation."

Jane allowed the servants to help her to her feet. "Yes. All right," she said, smiling at the doctor. "It is very good to see you again, Jasper."

"You as well, my dear."

"I can't thank you enough for coming."

"I'd still like to know why I'm here."

Jane shot a pleading glance at her husband. "I'll explain everything to him," he said, "and I'll show him to Maggie's room. You get some rest."

She nodded weakly, then vanished up the stairs.

"Tell me about these demons," Stetson said.

Harold sighed and his body seemed to deflate. "I don't know that it's *multiple* demons. Actually I think it's only one, same one what took Karen and now has a hold of Maggie. Almost like Karen whet its appetite. Like it's feeding on them, for Christ's sake."

Stetson noticed that the book Harold carried was the King James Version of the Holy Bible. "Are you a religious man, Mr. Chapman?" he asked.

Harold nodded. "I wasn't before, not at all. I was like you, an Atheist. If there was a God, I thought: why would He allow our brutal war to take place and rip the country in twain, dividing the good people?"

He looked away. "But having our oldest daughter taken by something as *obscene* as that creature. Well, I had no choice but to believe. But even that didn't save Karen. All the prayer in the world couldn't save her. It was her destiny to die. And I think God was testing me, like Job in the Bible."

The patterned bumping echoed along the ceiling and they looked up. For a moment Stetson thought he saw a face looking down at him through the wood. A little girl's face.

"How did your daughter die?" he asked.

"The demon, it … entered her, took over her body. It lived inside her, like a squirrel lives inside a tree. She wouldn't eat, wouldn't drink, wouldn't sleep. It sucked her dry, and eventually she perished, her soul depleted. When we found her corpse in the bed she looked like an old burlap sack: desiccated, thin. She was buried within a week."

"How long did it take to kill her?"

Harold thought a moment, then shrugged. "A month, I suppose. It happened quickly."

"Did she see a doctor?"

"Yes. We had our doctor from Roycepeake. He was up here until the end."

"What about his prognosis?"

"He wanted to say it was mental illness because he could detect nothing wrong with her physically — aside from the fact that she was starving and dehydrating herself. He said to hire a head doctor or perhaps have her taken to an asylum. So far as he's concerned, Karen committed suicide.

"But I refuse to believe that. Karen was a normal, intelligent woman, and always had been. She'd never shown signs of melancholia or psychosis, and she had such a bright future ahead of her — not to mention a loving family. What could motivate her to commit suicide?"

Stetson let the rhetorical question die. Then he said, "Did you?"

"What?"

"Hire a head doctor or have her taken to an asylum?"

"No! But … I was looking into it when she passed. It was too late. Honestly, though, I do not think it would've helped. You see, at first I did not understand what was happening. I thought some illness was making her say these crazy things — "

"What things?"

He spread his hands, exasperated. "Demons and devils, and all this blasphemous ranting. She claimed a strange pigman had visited her. Then later she claimed to *be* this pigman. None of it made sense."

Stetson's heart grew hard in his chest. "Excuse me, did you say pigman?"

Harold nodded. "Karen mentioned the pigman several times. Toward the end she claimed to be him. But I think she was talking about the demon possessing her. I believe the demon could speak *through* her. I've read up on the subject since her death. Demons are known to deliberately mislead and confuse mortals. Do you know the Bible passage?"

"What passage?"

Harold cleared his throat and quoted scripture sublimely from memory, or perhaps he was paraphrasing...

"Matthew 8:28-33: 'And when he was come to the other

side into the country of the Gergesenes, there met him two possessed with devils, coming out of the tombs, exceeding fierce, so that no man might pass by that way. And, behold, they cried out, saying, What have we to do with thee, Jesus, thou Son of God? art thou come hither to torment us before the time? And there was a good way off from them an herd of many swine feeding. So the devils besought him, saying, If thou cast us out, suffer us to go away into the herd of swine. And he said unto them, Go. And when they were come out, they went into the herd of swine: and, behold, the whole herd of swine ran violently down a steep place into the sea, and perished in the waters. And they that kept them fled, and went their ways into the city, and told everything, and what was befallen to the possessed of the devils.'"

Stetson forced the emotion he was experiencing back down into his unconscious. So he'd mentioned a pigman, and pigs—and now he was quoting Bible passages—so what? Stetson had had that hallucination by the road. Now he was having nightmares about pigmen. So what? This didn't prove anything.

"Are you all right, Doctor?" Harold asked.

"Yes, fine. Excellent recital. You were saying about Karen?"

Harold eyed him queerly, then continued. "I was saying that my daughter perished like an old dead tree, and there was nothing anyone could do about it, and now she's buried in Holy Royce Cemetery behind the church."

"What about your other daughter? She is ill?"

"Possessed," Harold corrected. "Maggie is only seven years old, and she is possessed by the same demonic being what had wrung the life out of poor Karen. I'll be damned if it's going to happen again. "

"When did she become sick?"

"A week ago."

"Tell me."

He sighed. "It started at Karen's funeral. Everyone was there. Her brittle corpse was on display for all to see. A lot of crying, Jane especially, and Pastor Reese quoted scripture to us. A dark day for the Chapmans. About halfway through the service, Maggie stood up from the pew, approached the coffin, but no one noticed her—not until she climbed into the coffin with Karen."

Stetson's eyes widened. "She climbed *into* the coffin?"

"Yes. That ain't all. She squatted on Karen's chest on her hands and knees and started oinking like a pig. She pummeled the corpse with her fists, making horrible snarling noises and guttural squeals. She was like a crazed animal."

"Jesus."

"Suddenly she lifted her skirts, removed her bottoms, and defecated right there inside the coffin. She was shouting *pig pen, pig pen*. I was horrified and humiliated. I snatched her from the coffin and marched right out of the church. Furious, I handed her off to Wendy and Reynolds and told them to take her straight home and get her cleaned up. Then I went back inside, helped restore Karen's corpse, and sat through the rest of the service. The pastor and the other attendees were mortified."

Stetson scratched his head. Not the worst he had ever heard, but still shocking. "Was that the start of it?"

"Yes. She's been in bed ever since, and gotten worse. I haven't called the doc, well because I know what he would say: call the head doctor. He thinks we're a bunch of lunatics. Who knows, maybe we are." He threw up his hands in despair.

"So Jane called me. And yet, if she is indeed possessed, why not contact your local minister?"

Harold scowled. "I wanted to do that, but Jane insisted on you. I suppose it doesn't matter *who* Maggie sees, so long as he cures her."

"Ah, now I understand," Stetson said. "Not only do I bring a fresh set of eyes, but I'm not connected with Roycepeake. Thus I cannot tarnish your reputation as a nice, sane, normal family. What about a genetic link? Have you considered that, Mr. Chapman? Jane's folks died from fluid in the lungs, but how about your family? Any history of mental illness or premature death on your side?"

Harold shifted his weight from foot to foot. "I don't see what that's got to do with anything. What is this word, 'genetic?'"

"Genetics is a brand new field of study in medicine. It's very exciting. It's the study of the genes of a person."

"Genes?"

"Genes are how living organisms inherit features from their ancestors. Children usually look like their parents, yes?

That's because they have inherited their parents' genes. They can also inherit ancestral deficiencies. Like illness."

"That's a wild theory," Harold said.

"No wilder than your demons. In my opinion genetics plays a large role in mental illness; oftentimes someone diagnosed as mentally deficient has another mentally deficient relative lurking in their past, and another in *their* past. You can usually trace these back, and that's why —"

Harold cut him off. "You are starting to sound like Doctor Miller from Roycepeake, do you know that? Do you think we're mad? Do you think little Maggie is crazy? The problem is with the demon, and until you come to terms with that, you're of no use to Maggie. You might as well put a bullet in her head yourself."

"Get a hold of yourself, man. Do you realize what you're saying?"

"I realize. But I don't give a damn."

"It's irrational."

"Damn your rationality. I'm trying to save my daughter."

Stetson met the man's eyes, refusing to look away, and they stared at each other. Stetson suddenly realized Harold was hiding something. *Could be a big deal; could be nothing.* "Can I see her now?" he said.

Harold spent another moment glowering, then softened his gaze. "Yes. It's best if you see for yourself. Then you will believe." He turned brusquely and headed out of the room and up the stairs.

Stetson retrieved his medical bag and followed after. He could already feel his neck hairs standing on end.

*   *   *

The squat brunette stood on the landing. Harold said to her, "I'm taking the doc into see Maggie. Have you checked on her today, Wendy?"

Wendy nodded, not meeting his eyes. "Yes, sir. I gave her some soup and tea this mornin'. I don't know that she ate much. She was laying on her side with her eyes closed. And that horrible breathing she does."

"Fine, fine," Harold said, reaching for the door at the end

of the hall. With his hand on the doorknob, he turned back to Stetson. "We moved her into Karen's old room because it has more space." He pointed across the hall toward another door. "That's her actual room, and next to it is David's."

"Who's David?"

"David is our son. He's almost ten years old, but he's out with the nanny presently."

"Has he been sick?"

"No. The demon has only infected our girls."

Harold opened the door and they stepped inside. The room was almost completely dark. Just a hint of light filtered in through the fabric of the closed curtains. The first thing he noticed was the smell—an unpleasant reek of vomit, body odor, and feces.

Harold opened the curtains, then the window. A breeze and an arch of sunlight fell into the room. "Forgive the smell," he said. "We cannot get it out no matter how hard we try."

The sunlight illuminated the ragged queen-sized bed, piled with pillows and blankets. In the center was a small form tucked away in the folds, with a mess of shaggy blond hair near the headboard.

"Maggie," Harold said. "You have a visitor."

The lump stirred.

"She stays cooped up in here?" Stetson asked, appalled. "Alone, in the dark?"

"We aren't the ones keeping it dark," Harold replied. "Whenever we open the curtains she immediately closes them."

"I don't understand."

Then the mound was rising, a corpse emerging from the soft soil of its grave, shedding layers of fabric as it ascended. What emerged was the bedraggled young girl dressed in cotton pajamas, sitting upright on the mattress, blinking sleepily.

"Daddy?" she said. "Who is this?"

"Don't let her fool you," Harold warned. "That voice is an act."

"Are you a maniac? She's just a little girl." Stetson crossed the room and sat at the edge of the bed. He saw Harold grow tense, but he ignored the man.

"I'm Doctor Stetson," he said. "I'm an old friend of your mother's, and I'm here to take a look at you."

The girl turned her head. When her gaze fell on him, a chill passed over his spine. Her skin was waxy, almost pinkish, and her cheeks looked abnormally round, like a chipmunk's. Her blond hair, tousled, seemed entwined inexplicably with dark streaks. Her nose was flat and yet her mouth appeared bloated, hanging greedily below a pair of obsidian eyes.

Christ, she almost looks like a pig.

"You're not our normal doctor," she said. There was a quality about her voice, too, which threw him off. She sounded like a grown man *imitating* a little girl's voice.

"That's right. I'm not," he said. "I come from the South, where your mommy and daddy used to live. I even knew your grandparents on your mama's side."

"I never met them," she said.

"Nice folks." He opened his medical bag, taking out his stethoscope and head mirror. He donned the latter, flipping the mirror down over his right eye.

"Let's have a look."

He bent toward her face, using the reflected sunlight to inspect her eyes, which appeared devoid of color, just lumpish black orbs. He peered into her ears, found usual traces of buildup, and then examined her nose and throat. Aside from the piggish quality, they appeared healthy. He did, however, notice a swelling in the tongue: a sign of dehydration.

He replaced the head mirror in the bag and donned his stethoscope; this he placed against her chest, surprised to hear an accelerated heart rate. He replaced the stethoscope and closed his bag.

His eyes flicked to the night stand where a bowl of soup and a tea mug stood untouched. "You're not eating or drinking," he said. "How come? Don't you feel thirsty? Hungry?"

She shook her head. "I don't need to eat or drink."

"'Course you do. Everyone does. That's how we keep our physical bodies healthy. If you don't eat or drink, you'll die."

"You don't understand. I have met the pigman on the road."

His blood went cold. *Shut your mouth,* he felt like screaming at her. *Don't you say another goddamned word.*

"She's in the preliminary phase of coming into contact

with the pigman," Harold said. "She doesn't believe she has *become* it yet."

Stetson forced himself to speak. "Where is this road?"

She blinked. "It's inside my head, in my mind. It's a bridge between two worlds, the road to the other side. Pigman is walking this road into our world."

"Karen said the same thing," Harold commented.

Stetson began to sweat. His palms felt clammy and he was shivering. It was not just the talk of the pigman; there was something else, something building in the air like electricity.

"You don't have to eat or drink because you've met this pigman?" he asked.

Maggie tittered. "I eat and drink of him. He sustains me as God sustained the Hebrews in the wilderness. But his will be a righteous food. The manna of God was just filth thrown down from Heaven." She gestured with contempt at the cold soup and tea. "The food and drink of this Earth are likewise filth. I have no use for them."

The Roycepeake doctor was right to suggest a head doctor, Stetson thought. He considered Jane Chapman but could recall no mental derangement; he also considered her mother, Genevieve Bottington, but again recalled nothing. And Jane's grandmother was before his time. So where did these mental illness genes come from?

Chapman.

The word thrummed in his mind.

Just because the women are the ones becoming ill does not mean the corrupted genes came from Jane.

Maggie suddenly flung herself at Stetson, flipping her hair wildly and lunging forward. She startled him, hooking him around the collar.

"What in God's name – "

She began throttling him—"There is no God here, only Pigman, and there is no name but his name!" Her voice had changed, was deeper, fuller like a man's. Her face was stretched open, swollen tongue darting between tiny pointed teeth. Her eyes burned like fire.

"He will walk in my shoes!" she screamed, jerking Stetson back and forth. *"And he'll rip me from this world, and then I'll cut all*

your throats with his butterfly blades!"

"Get her off me!" Stetson yelled.

Harold grabbed Maggie by the shoulders, but she held on. Her mouth was growing wider, the size of a black grapefruit, her repulsive tongue whipping out toward Stetson's face. It seemed to extend supernaturally, reaching a foot out of her mouth like a rubbery tentacle.

"You are going to die!" she shrieked.

Stetson pushed with all his might as Harold yanked on her from behind. At last she came free, disengaging with a suction-y sound. She tumbled back onto the bed and began rolling back and forth.

Stetson snatched his doctor's bag and marched out of the room. Harold followed, closing the door behind them.

Several heavy thumps sounded from the opposite side.

"She's just closed the window and curtains," Harold said.

Stetson flung the door back open, wanting to see for himself. The room was eclipsed by darkness, and in the shadows he discerned a squat figure standing beside the chest of drawers. It was Maggie. When she saw him she squealed like a pig and dove back underneath the bedcovers.

Stetson closed the door. He stood in the hall, panting. He turned and saw Wendy standing there on the landing, with Harold beside her.

"You're taking this well," he told them.

"We're veterans when it comes to demons," Harold replied.

"Demons," Stetson reiterated.

"You believe me now?"

"I need a drink. Something strong."

Harold nodded to Wendy: "Fix us two bourbons, please. We'll be down presently."

She bowed. "Yes, sir."

"This is only the beginning," he told Stetson. "You do realize that."

"I suppose I do."

"Contacting you was Jane's idea, not mine. I had no inclination to drag you into this."

"What's done is done. Let's get on with it."

17

Harold eyed him squarely, then gave a brisk nod. Together, they descended the stairs.

*   *   *

"I have seen the pigman," Stetson said.

He sat across from Harold in the vast dining room at a long rectangular table. Flowers and candles were set up. Light from several high windows streamed into the room. Evening was coming on.

Harold sipped his bourbon. "What does that mean?"

"Just what it says. On the way to the train station—I believe it was Tuesday morning—I saw a grotesque man dressed all in black walking alongside the road."

"And?"

"As I drove by he turned to look at me, and he bore a striking resemblance to a pig. I was quite horrified, naturally, but I kept driving and then tried to convince myself I had imagined it.

"Now all this talk of pigmen and demonic possession and meeting by the road... Christ, I don't know what to think about it. My pigman was also holding a sign that said I was going to die."

Harold flinched. "Karen said that all the time. Maggie does too. 'Course we never *do* die; it is always *them* dying." He was getting angry. His face had turned red. He drank his whiskey down.

"I won't say I believe you about the demon," Stetson said. "But you are on to something. According to the theory of genetics—"

"Here we go." Harold threw up his hands.

"—traits that include mental derangement and psychosis can be transferred from one host to the next."

"Host?"

"Yes, host is a carrier of the gene. In Maggie's case, a great-grandmother, grandmother, mother, etc. The corrupted gene is passed down through generations. It doesn't always manifest itself in the host, either, but can lay dormant. Waiting, biding its time, until eventually it instructs the body (or mind) to produce a certain feature and behave in a certain way."

"I'm sorry, Dr. Stetson, but I am a simple man, from the

country originally. I look at life through a lens of simplicity. Jane and I have acquired a considerable amount of capital—"

"From Jane's parents."

"Yes—from Jane's parents. What I'm getting at is that our financial status doesn't mean we take up with lofty theories. Myself especially. Science and medicine I know next to nothing about."

He got up, left the room, and came back presently carrying a large brown book, which he dropped on the table. "To my mind," he continued, "this is the only conceivable cause of what's happening."

Stetson glanced at the binding. The title was *Demonology and the Study of Possessions*. It was an old book. Quite worn from use.

"But don't you see?" he replied. "This gene theory is much like a possession. The host, in this case Maggie, is possessed by the corrupted gene. It is causing her to behave strangely and to invent wild fantasies."

Harold sighed. "Listen, Dr. Stetson. It has been a long day for us. I am weary, my wife is weary. You've just finished your traveling. Let us retire and meet in one hour for supper. After a good night sleep we can further our discussion."

Stetson nodded, and they sat for a while in silence, finishing the bourbon. Light from the windows increased with shades of purple, moving toward full-blown night. Shadows sprang up all over.

Reynolds, tall and laconic, entered the room.

"Ah, Reynolds," Harold said. "Show Dr. Stetson upstairs. Point out his nearest lavatory."

The tall man bowed and passed in front of the table. The doctor finished his drink and set the glass down, grabbing his medical bag.

"That was a fine Tennessee whiskey," he said. "Just what I needed."

Harold smiled. "Glad it served its purpose. See you presently for a good meal?"

"I look forward to it."

Stetson followed Reynolds out of the room.

19

Unpacking, getting himself situated, using the lavatory — this took all of forty-five minutes. Then Stetson returned downstairs at Reynolds's prompting.

In addition to the array of candles the sitting room and the dining room were both lit by two electro-powered chandeliers. Stetson gazed up at the magical handiwork of Mr. Thomas Edison.

There will soon be running electricity in every house, he thought. *Not just in affluent ones like this, or storefronts, restaurants, and theaters.* He mused on the rapid change of the times. The ending of the Civil War had paved the way for so much.

The dining room bustled with activity. Three female servants dressed in blue calico robes with white aprons hurried about ferrying fabulous-smelling food dishes. At the table sat the Chapmans — Jane, Harold, and their son, David. All except Maggie who was probably lying in the darkness upstairs.

"Welcome, Jasper," Jane said. Her aura beamed. She wore a fine black silk dress, her hair done up in curls. "Sit here," she said, indicating the seat beside her.

Stetson nodded. He sat down and glanced at Harold on the far side of the table, realizing the man was drunk.

"Glad you could join us, doc," Harold said bitterly, his words garbled.

"Don't mind him," Jane remarked. She directed Stetson's attention to the young boy. "This is our son, David. David, say hello to Dr. Jasper Stetson."

He had brown hair like his father's, and his face was a vacant mask of forgotten emotion. He seemed almost doll-like, at the very least subdued — especially for a boy of seven.

"Hello," David said, his eyes fixed on the glass of water set before him.

"Your mother has known Dr. Stetson since she was a little girl," Jane said.

David nodded.

Stetson looked at him. *He's scared. Not just scared. Terrified. He's completely shut himself off.*

"Nice to meet you, David," he said. Then he added, "So …

what do *you* think happened to your sister?"

David's eyes pricked up. "Which one?"

"Maggie, of course."

Stetson could feel the tension radiating out of the boy's parents. But for the moment they remained silent. Finally David said, "I believe the devil's got her. The devil got Karen too. He'll probably get me next."

Harold slammed his fist on the tabletop, startling them. One of the servant women nearly dropped her food tray. "This demon only goes after women," he said. "I told you that, boy." He shifted his unsteady gaze to Stetson. "What's the big idea, doc? You trying to scare him?"

"He looks scared already," Stetson replied.

"'Course he's scared. He's got one sister dead and another headin' that same way —"

"Enough, Harold," Jane said. Wendy and a dwarfish servant woman finished bringing out the dishes and began serving food from the sideboard. Dinner was a very appetizing smorgasbord of meats and vegetables.

"I'd like to get through one night without fighting," Jane continued, almost in tears. "It's fine that you're drunk, Harold. I don't blame you. But I'm exhausted. I don't want to hear your ugly thoughts."

He threw up his hands, but said nothing. He started eating, and David followed his lead. Father and son looked similar in pose, each eating glumly, hunched over the plate.

Jane turned to Stetson. "I know you're wondering why I called you here. It's true about the possession. If you don't believe it, fine. But I beg you to stay on and help however you can. We're desperate."

Her words had the effect of melting Stetson's cautious, business-only exterior. He placed his hand on top of hers. "Of course I'll stay on, Jane. You were like a daughter to me once. And I did see your folks through to the end. It would only be right, then, to see this through to the end."

She smiled. "Thank you, Jasper." They hugged. Harold abruptly shot up from the table, upsetting the chair behind him. David glanced up fearfully as his father stormed out of the room without a word.

"He's had too much to drink," Jane explained.

"Is this behavior typical?"

She looked away. "It's gotten worse since Karen. He used to drink ... oh, I don't know ... occasionally. But with everything that's happened, the stress has become too much for him. But he's a good man. I wouldn't have married him otherwise."

"I believe you."

"It's just that lately everything has turned utterly dreadful. Sometimes I think we've been cursed, that God despises us."

"I don't think so, my dear. But these are hard times. And your family's been hit extra hard. I know it's not easy."

"No, it isn't."

They fell silent as they finished their meal. David was the first to ask to be excused. Jane excused him, then she said she wanted to go and sit with him before bed, and so excused herself.

Stetson finished and headed upstairs, as the servants began extinguishing the candles and cleaning up the dishes.

*   *   *

He was in bed, half asleep. Or was he awake? He lay on his side and the room looked pitch dark, and when his eyes adjusted he could discern the shadowy outlines of furniture and doorways but everything was fuzzy. He felt immobilized, like he was glued to the mattress —

Now he stood in the middle of the room. Directly in front of his closet door. Just standing and staring.

Something was over to his left, by the door that led to the hallway. He had no idea what it was — or *who* it was. The presence had no shape, mass, or substance.

Suddenly the presence noticed him and was trying to get his attention. He felt strong rays of hatred and anger radiating out from it, flowing across the room like ethereal serpents. A force of pure and unadulterated evil assailed him. Then he was rushing toward it, was over by the door in half a second, yet he still saw nothing; he only sensed it. Yes, the outline of a figure was there, but this figure was indistinct.

He became so terrified that he tried running and that's when he realized he was dreaming. If not dreaming then lying in bed still with his mind elsewhere. He did his best to wake himself, to regain consciousness—

—And a moment later he found himself back in his body, in bed for real. He remembered the presence, his flight from it, and although he still couldn't move, he was able to force open his eyes.

He flinched involuntarily from the glimmering face that floated before him. A bluish aura shone, enveloping it. He was able to pick out features—eyes, nose, a yawning mouth. He tried to move but he was paralyzed.

Fear traveled through his body like an electric current, vibrating him. He stared up in horror at the pigman's glassy black eyes, flat nostrils, drooping ears, fleshy scalp, mouth of horrible teeth, and massive pink tongue—

He regained full control of his limbs and jerked himself back, uttering a curse. He entered into waking consciousness, which caused the leering pig face to dissolve back into the wavering air, as though into water. He lay very still, allowing the fear to wash back into him like an ocean tide. He glanced at the spot where the pig face had been but saw nothing; he glanced at the spot by the door where the presence had been, but also saw nothing; and he felt relieved that the room was empty, that he was alone. He rolled over on his back, staring at the ceiling.

The wood up there was arranged into a series of cross-sections, each running parallel to each other. He was on the second floor and there was a window to his right that looked out on the front yard. The curtains were drawn.

He heard the unmistakable sound of a female crying. He froze, straining his ears. Yes, he could hear it. Was it Jane?

No.

Maggie.

He listened. The crying seemed to be coming from everywhere at once. He wondered if anyone else could hear it.

Are they just going to leave her in there? His fear suddenly morphed into outrage, and he tossed the covers back and got to his feet, lit the lamp on the night stand, dressed in his robe, and carried it out into the hall.

The flames threw jigsaw shadows along the walls. He passed David's door and came Karen's old room, where Maggie stayed. The weeping was coming from inside.

Steeling himself, he turned the knob and entered. His lamp cut through the inky darkness like a fiery knife and illuminated a young girl, crouched and disheveled on the mattress. As soon as he came in her eyes darted to him, her pupils wide, soulless and black, with tears covering her face.

"I heard you crying," he whispered. She looked so dreadful, but he forced himself to keep calm. "Is everything all right?"

She shook her head. Her mouth had a long, elastic look; the tip of her swollen tongue was protruding. "I'm dying," she said. Then, raising her left arm, she signaled for him to come closer.

He sat on the edge of the bed, placing the lamp on the night stand, and instantly she lunged for him, wrapping her arms around his neck. He struggled, but she was abnormally strong. She wailed, throttling him, tossing her hair before her face. He heaved her lithe form and pushed her away, and at that moment she went very still and smoothed back her hair, her face becoming dark and expressionless.

Raising one bent arm she signaled him again but he shot up immediately and stood by the wall.

"You're jumpy," she said. "No need to be afraid."

"I'm not afraid," he said, lying.

She picked up on it, and, smirking, said, "If you're going to fix me, then fix me."

"I heard you crying."

She scoffed. "That wasn't me. That was the thing."

"The pigman?"

She chuckled. "Not the pigman. The little girl. The sacrifice. The one whom you desire to save."

"But you don't speak like a little girl."

"That's because I am *not* a little girl. I am her darker half, the one allowing the pigman to come through into this world."

Multiple personalities are hereditary – genetically passed on. Harold's bloodline could meet the criteria. "I don't understand," he said. "Aren't you Maggie Chapman?"

"I have no name. No personality. No soul. No worth. I am but a gateway. All humans are dualistic by nature. All have a

24

dominant self and a dormant self."

She grinned. "I am the dormant self, awakened. The part of her that moves in her dreams. I manifest myself in all the suffering she experiences, and yet she is always unaware of me."

A light bulb went off in Stetson's mind. "You're talking about her subconscious."

"I am talking about the soulless darkside of every human being, the part whose purpose is to facilitate the flow of spiritual wickedness. Some choose to call it evil. The Bible calls it evil."

"If you're not Maggie, but this gateway for evil," he said (and the corpselike girl nodded), "then why come after Maggie now? Why must evil be present at all?"

"I do not know the cause of everything," she said. "I am no philosopher. All I know is the present situation: that the Chapman bloodline has been chosen because of its wicked history. It is Maggie's time to bring forth her infant swine. She is its vessel in this world."

"What about Karen?"

"Karen was an early attempt, which failed. It won't happen again. The swineman will trod with earthly feet—these feet."

She leaned back, wiggling her toes and giggling. Then with the ease of a feline she leaned forward, hooking him around the neck. She vanished a portion of the wall behind her by waving her free hand. Light, a distinctly redolent smell (one of trees), and fresh air streamed into the room. She drew him toward the opening.

"No!" he cried, trying to resist. She overpowered him, employing some uncanny strength. She ferried him forward into the circular aperture, pushing him through the wall itself, into a blur of colors, scents, and sounds.

He closed his eyes. No matter how much he wanted to, he couldn't find a voice to scream. He felt like he was being torn apart and stretched open—like his world was being unmade.

*   *   *

The Chapman girl was beside him, small and innocent, holding his hand as they walked along a forested road.

He recognized this road: the one that led out of his hometown; the one where he had seen the pigman on his way to Columbia that day. But now he and Maggie headed down it, not toward Columbia, but in the opposite direction.

What if I see the pigman again? No … I don't want to see him. I want to wake up.

Near the outskirts of his hometown, Maggie turned down another dirt track, which no one ever used. Overgrown with vines and weeds, Stetson could remember seeing this track a thousand times, but there had never been a reason to venture down it.

So he followed her now as she let go of his hand, needing both her limbs to navigated the terrain. She pushed through clumps of ferns and hopped over fallen maple logs, dodging sandpits and boulders. Occasionally she turned to look at him, and he saw that her face wasn't malevolent or piggish; it seemed childlike once again.

They clambered through a frenzy of wilderness for hours. Eventually the sun began to set behind the trees, casting batwing shadows, and he saw a light in the distance and they emerged at last onto a flat piece of land dotted with wood buildings, one of them a large country house.

The light came from a porch lamp. Maggie crept around the side of the house, peering in through a back window. She signaled Stetson to do the same.

His eyes took a moment getting acclimated to the interior, which was lit by a single candle; the moment they adjusted, his heart jammed into his throat, and he lurched, sickened and nauseous. He was about to scream when Maggie slipped a hand over his mouth, shaking her head.

Keep silent.

Her voice rang in his head like thunder. She signaled him back toward the window, and, reluctantly, he returned.

Through the glass he spotted the outline of a woman hanging on the far wall with several lengths of chain. She was nude and her head looked down, covered over by her matted brown hair. Her body drooped in the restraints. Purple bruises and red welts checkered her skin, and a trickle of blood ran along her thigh.

A collection of flogging implements, including a leather

whip and a cat o'nine tails, lay strewn about the floor in front of her. Some had blood coating them. Among these were several bludgeoning instruments — a club, a blackjack, a truncheon.

Stetson's stomach turned. *Christ, someone has been using those on her.*

Maggie looked at him. *He beats them repeatedly for several days after he kidnaps them. And then he rapes them and leaves them hanging there all alone. He will come back later and do it all over again. He will kill them eventually and bury them behind the wood pile.*

She turned and pointed out a sagging mound of rotting wood near the edge of the trees.

He has done this many times, she continued, *and he will do it many more, until he finally goes insane. Then he will wander into the woods to die.*

Stetson sent his own thoughts out. *Who is he?*

She stared at him. A noise came from somewhere and they both jumped. It sounded like a door closing.

Time for us to leave.

She abandoned the window and started around the side of the house. He hurried after her. She moved cautiously, as if afraid that something was stalking her. When they came to the front, she veered toward the road, her small form silhouetted, backlit, and casting a tall shadow on the ground.

On impulse, he turned to face the porch lamp. He froze. Someone was there, seated in the rickety old rocking chair, doused in shadows, featureless, giving only the impression of a person. The figure rocked slowly.

He squinted, pushing through the fear building in his chest, ignoring the voice telling him to *run, run, get away as fast as you can* (was it his voice, or Maggie's voice?). As he focused on the figure, the air around the porch swirled to life, blurring into wiggly non-colors, mesmerizing, and he couldn't look away.

Reality seemed to burst, sending shards like glass in all directions, as the figure lunged to a standing position. Stetson realized it was a man. A big man in cotton trousers and a creased collared shirt, wearing a crumpled plantation hat on his head. He moved with unbelievable speed, cutting the distance between them like a bullet.

Abruptly he stood right next to Stetson and shouldered

into him, pushing him back, staring into his face with terrible blue eyes, his mouth a snarl of wickedness.

Stetson screamed as the man forced him to his knees. Movement exploded in his periphery and he saw Maggie's childlike profile, plumed in light, soaring toward him.

She arrived as the man's face funneled outward in a piggish snout, his gums sprouting a spiny nest of teeth, his eyes growing wider, wider…

Stetson's scream echoed louder throughout the trees.

*   *   *

He was awoken after dawn by Wendy, the brunette housemaid. He could scarcely recall much of what happened, aside from some terrible nightmares. But he did remember Maggie's sobbing. Had he gone to check on her? Maybe that part was a dream.

After breakfast, which all the Chapmans attended, Wendy escorted David to school and the rest of them headed onto the back verandah to enjoy coffee and talk. The calm summer day was blue and free of clouds. The backyard was slathered with manicured green grass, hemmed in on all sides by trees and closely-cropped hedges. The three of them sat in wood rocking chairs, around a table with a white sheet covering.

"I want to apologize," Harold said.

"For what?" Stetson replied. But he knew the answer.

Harold sighed. He looked tired, his face stubbly with a beard. "I was inconsiderate last night," he said. "You're a guest in our home, we invited you here."

He glanced at his wife, but Jane's face remained stolid, watching the swaying branches.

"I … had too much to drink," he finished. "It is a problem of mine. A devil thing. Always has been. Worse, recently." He sank into himself, brooding.

"I understand," Stetson said. And this was true. After the strange events he'd experienced yesterday, and the toll it was taking on his mental faculties, he had begun to see how this sort of thing wore at one's sanity — how it tore apart an otherwise rational mind. "I don't judge you," he added.

Harold looked up. "Thank you, sir."

Stetson nodded and sipped his coffee.

"Told you he was a respectable man," Jane said to her husband finally. "Jasper is going to help us. I know he is." She swung her pretty, troubled face at Stetson. "I have faith in him."

"You may be right, darling," Harold said.

They sat in silence, the leaves whispering about them.

Jane said, "What will you do?"

"First I am going into Roycepeake to speak with your old physician, the one who treated Karen."

"His name is Dr. Emerstein," she said. "I can give you his address." She reached into her handbag, extracted a business card, and gave it to him. "What will you ask?"

"Whatever comes to mind. The more I know about what is happening, the better chance I have of helping Maggie."

Harold rose from the table. "You can use the motorcar Reynolds picked you up in. I'll get the keys." He vanished into the house.

"How'd you sleep?" Jane asked.

A flood of images flashed through his head. He suddenly felt numb. "Fine," he muttered. Then — "I thought I heard Maggie sobbing during the night. But I can't remember if it was just a dream. Did you hear it?"

She frowned. "Can't say that I did. But it wouldn't surprise me. The poor girl is under the influence of a demonic spirit. I'm surprised she's not wailing all the time."

Stetson fought the urge to say something skeptical. He let it drop.

She continued, her voice crackling with emotion. "Oh, Jasper, it is all so terrible. Whenever I stop and think about it, it seems like too much, and I fear I can't go on. But then I tell myself that I must — for Maggie's sake. And for Karen's."

She turned to him. "The truth is I'm scared of her, Jasper. Of what's *inside* of her. I'll bet you think I'm cruel. That I'm an unfit mother because I stay as far away from that room as I can. But listen, whatever is in there is not my little girl."

"My god," Stetson said. "I didn't realize you felt so passionately about it. So tell me, who keeps Maggie cleaned and fed? Who checks on her and makes sure she hasn't dashed herself out the window?"

"The servants do. Wendy, mostly. She's a good woman. Balkanese, hard working. Harold looks in on Maggie too, if he's had enough to drink."

A gleam of fiery indignation lit her eyes. "Do not judge us, Jasper, we are frightened, can't you see that? We none of us know what to do. We're doing the best we can. Please don't give me that look."

"It's shocking, is all," he said.

She bowed. "I know. But soon you will understand. Nothing here is normal. In truth, it's all insane."

Uttermost horror has befallen us. The words from her telegram sounded in his head. No, not her words—Harold's.

He's done this many times, and he will do it many more, until finally he goes insane from what he's done. Then he will wander into the woods to die.

Now whose words were those? He tried but couldn't remember. A moment later the head of the Chapman household emerged on the verandah and gave Stetson the keys. "You know how to drive?"

"Oh yes. We're not as uncivilized as you Northerners might think down in the Carolinas."

Harold nodded, amused. Under his arm he carried the black leather bound book. He said, "Do you still believe Maggie's condition is genetic, as you say?"

"I do."

He handed Stetson the book. Its title—*Demonology and the Study of Possessions.* "Do me a favor, if you please," he said. "Read some of that book before you go to sleep tonight. I will rest better knowing you have at least considered an alternative theory."

"Of course," Stetson said, and stood. "Now, if you'll excuse me I'd like to get going into town."

He bid them adieu, pocketed the black leather book, and headed inside.

*   *   *

The doctor's office was on the second floor of a two-story wood building with glass windows. Downstairs was a general store.

Stetson parked the motorcar on the other side of the empty street (Roycepeake seemed to have many empty streets), and stood at the base of the staircase leading to the office. A few quaint townsfolk milled about in the general store; some more sat in chairs outside the store window; still more moved along the wood sidewalks. They didn't pay much attention to Stetson, although a few shot him a suspicious glance.

As he entered the small office with the medical plaques hanging on the walls, he uneasily noticed a free-standing human skeleton anatomy model lurking in the corner. He wasn't sure if it was actually grinning at him, with hollow eyes above a piggish snout, or if he'd simply imagined it.

The woman behind the desk, petite and bookish-looking, cleared her throat. "Can I help you?"

"My name is Dr. Jasper Stetson. I've recently assumed care of some of Dr. Emerstein's former patients — the Chapmans. I wish to speak to him about their medical history."

Her eyes glimmered behind her spectacles. "He is with a patient right now. But..." she flipped through a ledger on the desk, "...he is free after. Would you like to speak to him then?"

Stetson nodded. "I'll wait over here."

He moved to one of the waiting chairs, sat down. He could hardly ignore the overbearing presence of the skeleton model, a symbol of death dominating the room.

The secretary went back to her work. Not five minutes later the door on her left opened and a short bald man wearing a lab coat appeared with an elderly woman using a wooden cane.

"You just keep off that leg as much as possible, Miss Greenington," the man said, patting the woman's shoulder.

"Thank you, Doctor," she said.

His eyes found Stetson. "Another patient?"

"This is the Chapmans' new doctor," the secretary answered. "He's here to discuss their medical history."

Dr. Emerstein tensed. The lines in his forehead, leading up to the smooth surface of his crown, wrinkled, but finally he nodded, turning back to the woman. "Schedule an appointment with Alexia, Miss Greenington," he said, "and take care of that leg."

"I will," she said.

The doctor motioned to the open door. "Shall we?"

Stetson got up and followed him into the room. He was led past the examination table, past the metal sinks and trays housing a variety of medical implements, to a cushioned chair near the wall. The doctor sat upon the examination table with one knee up, the other anchored to the floor, hands enfolded in his lap.

"So," he said. "You're here to talk about Karen's death?"

"That's right. Also Maggie."

The doctor frowned. "What's Maggie got to do with it?"

He doesn't know. Does anybody know? "Maggie has whatever Karen had," he revealed.

The doctor leaned forward, his tone becoming less professional, more gossipy. "It's what that whole family's got. If you're saying Maggie Chapman has developed an acute psychosis and is now acting out internal fantasies and has begun to starve and dehydrate herself, well then I'd say she's putting on big sister's clothes."

Stetson expected he would say this. He replied, "That is what is happening. The little girl is becoming like a savage feral dog, caged in a room upstairs, starving herself. Very disturbing."

"Indeed. I watched Karen go the same way—and I watched as the rest of her family kept her at arm's length, not wanting to be near her—which is understandable given the intensity of Karen's psychosis. Still, it was unpleasant to watch. Rather than comfort the poor woman they dreamed up a cockamamie delusion about demonic possession. Karen, who'd become embittered by her family's refusal, played the role of being demonically possessed, combining it with her (at the time) severe mental illness, until eventually she just wasted away. Ugly and tragic, if you ask me. But that's the Chapmans."

"Sounds familiar," Stetson said.

"To what?"

"To what's happening with Maggie. The set of circumstances you have described fits her present situation."

"That's a shame. Poor Maggie is just a young girl. I think it's all a game, a horribly tragic deadly game. That's why Harold didn't send for me this time. He knows I won't play. I told him to get a head doctor. Are you a head doctor?"

32

Stetson chuckled. "Not that I recall."

"How did the Chapmans come by you?"

He explained his relationship to Jane and Jane's parents.

"I see," Dr. Emerstein said. "In a sense, then, you are their last resort. Because Jane knows you personally, she thinks she'll be able to convince you that Maggie is possessed."

Although he had anticipated this to some degree, Stetson was surprised by the amount of suspicion and mistrust the doctor held for the Chapmans. But he didn't want to let on that he found this surprising. He said merely, "That sounds about right."

"Good, so long as you're clear about it. Frankly, I wash my hands of the whole thing. She became delusional, her consciousness split into multiple personalities, so she starved herself — in other words, committed suicide — and her family stood by and watched it happen. Nothing else to say."

"Are you familiar with the theory of genetics?"

Dr. Emerstein smiled. "You're clever. I have read about that in some of the journals. It's an interesting idea. Applicable to the Chapman case, I suppose."

Stetson got to his feet. "That's all I needed to hear. Thanks very much for your time, Dr. Emerstein. I feel confident now about making my diagnosis."

They shook hands and Stetson headed for the door, but the doctor stopped him at the last minute. "There is one thing," he said.

"Yes?"

He frowned a little, thinking. "Well toward the end it got really bad with Karen. I literally begged Harold to call a head doctor, and though he said he would he kept resisting and putting it off. During the last few days I didn't come around. I only came that very last day, to pronounce the body."

"What happened?"

He seemed to grow pale as he spoke. "I was alone in that room — with Karen's corpse. I'd made up my mind that she was dead. The rest of the Chapmans were downstairs. There was only that servant woman in the hall. Karen had sprawled out on the floor, and as I attempted to lay her back in bed, I felt a strange sensation in my fingertips, like electricity, which seemed to come up from her flesh.

"I let go of her body and dropped it on the mattress, stepping back against the wall. Now, you may find it hard to believe, but remember that I remain a skeptic of this demonic possession business. However, being a man of truth, I must recount the facts as I have them.

"As I stood looking at her corpse, I heard an awful groaning sound, a belching, a stomach rumbling, and then her stomach began to swell. It grew until she appeared impregnated, and then just as suddenly her mouth opened with a horrible moan. It was followed by a cloud of coal-black dust, which plumed over her head like a volcanic eruption, dispersing into the surrounding walls and ceiling. After a few brief seconds, the cloud disappeared and the moaning ceased. But the air remained tinged thereafter with an abhorrent stench like rotting meat. Rotting *pork*, to be exact."

Stetson stared at him. "What do you suppose caused the cloud?"

The doctor shrugged. "Unclear. I got out of there directly, and I haven't given much thought to it since. But if I had to speculate, I might say that due to the prolonged exposure to desiccation and malnourishment, her internal organs had begun to rot prematurely. And once she died, her body finally expelled the buildup of decayed matter alongside the gasses. This buildup also accounts for the horrifically deep, gravelly voice she was able to generate toward the end of her life."

He paused, studying the anatomy diagram chart on the wall. Then finally he said, "At any rate, just thought you'd like to know. I'm sorry I can't give you an exact cause."

"Quite all right," Stetson said, "and thank you for telling me. It's another curious piece in the Chapman puzzle."

He said goodbye to the doctor and headed out of the office, tipping his hat to Alexia, the secretary, then making a beeline for the door. He did his best to ignore the grotesque man-size pig skeleton glaring at him from the corner.

*   *   *

When he arrived back at the house, it was late afternoon. The sun was standing over the trees in the west, preparing for its leap into oblivion. He saw a man working with a pair of shears in the front yard. It was Reynolds.

Stetson waved on his way up the stone path, but the other did not return the gesture; he seemed only to glower, pruning absently at a maple tree. Stetson noticed one of the motorcars missing from the parking garage.

The house was very quiet as he walked through the deserted sitting room and dining room and up the stairs. From the corner of his eye he noticed Maggie's door at the end of the hall cracked open. He resolved to investigate, but first he wanted to stow the demonic possession book Harold had given him on the shelf above his bed. He also needed a quick toilet.

Finally he returned to Maggie's room and was shocked to find it empty. The bed was still a mess of blankets, pillows, and sheets.

She might be hiding.

The thought sent a chill up his spine. But, mustering his courage, he checked in the closet, under the bed, behind the furniture. He found the fact that she was gone almost more distressing than if she had been there.

If she's gotten loose, I should find her.

Controlling his panic he crept back into the hall, peeking in the young boy David's room, which, he found, was similar to his own room: sparsely decorated, though with expensive pieces: bed, desk, table, chairs. Books and toys lay scattered about. The place looked eerily deserted. He closed the door.

He was heading toward the double doors at the other end of the hall when a sound poked out of the silence like a sprouting weed. He stopped, listened.

Maggie was calling.

"Jasper... Jasper..."

She called for him by his first name. Why this frightened him so much, he couldn't say. Only that he suddenly became conscious of a certain connection to her. He didn't like this feeling, this sense that there was no one in the world for this little girl, other than himself. It imparted a heavy responsibility. He dashed down the stairs, listening again for her voice.

"Jasper..."

The backyard.

He rushed through the dining room and threw open the French doors, barreling out onto the verandah. He stopped short of the railing just as his eyes touched upon something in the grass. It was Maggie, standing in the center of the backyard, the hedges surrounding her, the tall trees looming over her head. She wore her usual stained cotton pajamas, and her blond hair was a wild mess. She stood very still, almost like a statue, with a blank glassy look in her eyes, with the beginnings of a pig snout jutting above her wide, greasy mouth.

The sun sank suddenly into the trees. Like that it went from daytime to twilight. Without moving her head, the grotesque mouth opened. Words oozed out, *"Jasper... Jasper..."* They sounded lifeless, dead.

"Maggie?"

He stepped cautiously from the verandah onto the grass. His body went numb with fear, and he could sense a quiet inner storm of panic, but all this he deftly ignored, for it was his function to remain professional and uphold the role of physician.

Her icy gaze melted him. Her nose seemed to flatten then funnel out into her upper lip, creating the snout from which hung a fat pink tongue. When she spoke again, her voice was not her own.

"Are we alone?" the pigman asked.

He glanced at the house. "I think so. I don't know where the others went."

"That is not important." The snout wrapped around into a grin. "I didn't feel safe to reveal myself until they were gone."

He stood about ten feet away, with only the grass separating them. The breeze blew and the sun sank lower. The landscape darkened.

"What do you want?" he said.

Another repugnant grin from the pigman. "To eat your soul."

There was a thunderclap suddenly and the sky tore into pieces. It rent and shredded into a series of black-gray strips. Dark storm clouds appeared, roiling like water in a kettle, and streaks of lightning flashed in a zigzagging pattern.

He was about to retreat when he saw the first one drop like a hard stone from the sky in a direct vertical line. A fattish pink mound about the size of a bread loaf, accompanied by a whining squeal, slammed into the grass, exploding with fluid and blood.

He stared at it.

Another came. Then a tempest of the obscene and absurd and Stetson screamed as the pig fetuses rained down from the sky. They struck against the house, against the roof and the trees, splattering into cloud-bursts of guts and gore. A few struck his head, and they smarted, and he even heard their oinking cries.

He sought cover beneath the verandah. The roar of the pig rain was deafening, so intense that he thought the roof might collapse. He stared at Maggie, who now resembled a dwarf-sized pig standing upright. Her pajamas lay in a shredded pile on the grass before her, and she had raised a pair of hoofed limbs to the sky, like some kind of shaman commanding the weather. And down they fell, those thousands of miniature piglets, shrouded in a cacophony of hideous oinking.

Just as quickly as it began, the rain stopped and twilight returned. Everything grew still and silent. Stetson realized with a jolt that he no longer stood beneath the verandah, but was back in front of Maggie; she, similarly, had reverted to her original form — that of a sickly-looking young girl.

Am I dreaming?

Maggie looked at him, her blue eyes full of tears. She let out a single anguished sob and collapsed on the grass.

Sobering, Stetson scooped her up and ferried her into the house. He was met with shrieks of surprise. Jane, Wendy, and another servant woman stood before the dining table — Jane dressed very properly, with an array of purple linens wrapping her form, and wearing a feathered purple hat.

"What are you doing?" she cried.

Stetson rushed past the table, carrying Maggie like a bride. He headed for the stairs. "She was outside when I came back from Roycepeake," he shouted. "You left her unattended!"

"Wendy — help him," Jane ordered.

The plump woman shadowed him up the stairs, followed by Jane. Stetson barreled into the room, placing Maggie on the bed and wrapping her in a blanket. Her gaze was blank and her whole body shuddered uncontrollably.

"Bring some water," Stetson said.

"She won't drink it," Wendy replied.

"Do it!"

She glanced at Jane, who nodded, and then vanished into the hall. The Chapman woman was a marble statue of fear and angst—frozen. Looking at her, Stetson suddenly realized that she didn't want to be here but felt she had to be because Maggie was her daughter, or perhaps because she felt socially obligated. But he could tell the experience was sticking knives into her composure, tearing holes in it, ruining her superficial facade.

A resentment worm slithered into his thoughts.

"For Christ's sake, she's your daughter," he said.

Tears flooded her eyes. She took a step forward. "I know that, don't you think I know that?" She glanced at the bed, sobbing. The little form shook beneath the covers.

"Watch her," he said. "I need to get my bag."

Jane shot him a panicked look, something that begged him not to leave her alone, but he told her with his eyes to stay put, then headed for his room. He passed Wendy on the landing, carrying a glass of water. "Give it to her gently," he said, and she nodded as she passed.

He returned a moment later to find both women crouching by the head of the bed. Wendy was cradling Maggie's upper torso, while Jane attempted to pour some water between the girl's lips.

At least that's a reassuring picture.

He stepped in to do his examination, determining that her vitals were all high but she had a temperature, and her heart rate was accelerated, her respiratory rate too. Her body was in the throes of extreme shock. He administered a sedative to calm her, and within minutes she had fallen asleep.

"When's the last time she's eaten?" he asked Wendy.

The servant blinked at him. "She ate a little toast and jam this morning."

"Bring her some more."

"I do not think—"

"I don't give a damn what you think."

She got up solemnly and marched out.

Jane gave him a weary, exhausted look. "Can I leave now?"

"Don't you want to sit with your daughter?" He had not meant it to come out so bitingly, but after the experience in the backyard, his emotions were running rampant.

"It isn't *just* my daughter," she replied coolly. "That thing is in there."

He reached out and touched her hand, his tone almost apologetic. "I know."

She smiled. "Thank you, Jasper."

"Where were you?"

"Harold thought it would be a good idea for us to attend the evening prayer service at our church."

Stetson nodded, glancing at Maggie. "What about her?"

"We thought she would be fine. We've left her alone before and she's never gotten out of bed. We asked Reynolds to look after her."

He recalled seeing the tall man in the front yard, pruning trees that weren't entirely in need of pruning, as though he were occupying himself, and the look of revulsion he gave Stetson as he entered the house. *None of them wish to be anywhere near her, as though she carries the Black Death.*

"I see," he said. "Where is Harold now?"

She shrugged. "He disappeared into his study the moment we got home and closed the door. The service did not do for his morale what he had hoped."

I'll bet he's having a drink. He knew it was bitter, and he sighed and released his lingering resentment. He stood, taking Jane's hand. "Come, let's go and get ready for supper."

She bowed slightly and they exited the room, leaving the young girl asleep on the mattress.

*   *   *

Harold was absent at supper, which fit Stetson fine because the man's presence was beginning to weigh on him. He, Jane, and the young boy shared a nice meal together, getting in some good laughing and lively conversation. He told Jane all about his medical practice back home, and how it hadn't really changed over the years. Jane listened with gusto, and then proceeded, in turn, to recount the last few decades of her life.

Young David even joined in, taking up some of the evening with talk of his school and his friends. Without his father around, the boy seemed freer—though a dark cloud lingered over him. Stetson hated thinking about the effect this whole experience was having on him.

He retired to his bedroom once the wine started to gain hold. He was exhausted from the day. He considered looking in on Maggie but reckoned she was as much in need of rest as he, so instead he went straight to his room, disrobed, donned pajamas, and fell on the bed.

Then he recalled the book Harold gave him. He reached to the shelf over his head and retrieved it, examining the black front cover and the gold script of the title: *Demonology and the Study of Possessions.* He opened the pages and read for thirty minutes.

Some of it was interesting, especially sections pertaining to multiple personalities and how demonic possessions could be manifestations of such a disorder. The more outlandish passages, mostly where supernatural happenings were described, he glossed right over, thinking them fatuous. But he did take an interest in the resolution of such cases, more particularly where the cause of the disorder was traced back to a childhood trauma or a deranged relative. A few times during his reading, he felt his skin prickle with gooseflesh, as he imagined the horrifying scenes described. He recalled the strange hallucination he had suffered that afternoon—an image of bloody pig fetuses raining from the sky—and the whole thing left a tense feeling in his stomach.

As his eyes started to droop, he closed the book and replaced it on the shelf. He lay back, thinking. *Every one of those cases hinges upon the family surrounding the possessed, whether a distant relative involved in the occult or one afflicted with mental illness, or a member of the immediate family, most commonly an abusive parent, sibling, aunt or uncle. It always comes back to the family, and if what I believe is correct – that all cases of extreme mental illness within a family are genetically linked (the Chapmans included) – then these cases help to substantiate my argument. Notwithstanding their sensational accounts of roaring demons and hovering apparitions.*

He nodded, pleased with himself.

A moment later, he slept.

*   *   *

The dream pulled him through. Maggie floated above him, guiding him along, over trees and farmland, over rivers and ravines, down into the thick of the wilderness, where the decrepit log dwelling stood isolated, surrounded by a yard of dilapidated farm equipment. The two of them touched ground together, like a pair of falling angels.

We're back.

Maggie looked at him. She was wearing her light blue pajamas. Her small pale face, framed in blond locks, appeared so innocent, so pure. She was not speaking, only pointing. Toward the cabin and the dark man sitting on the porch in a rocking chair.

"He is here too," she said.

Stetson glanced at her. "Who is?"

Maggie pointed into the thick row of trees opposite the house. Stetson peered through the foliage to get a better look. When he saw what stood there, an intense fear flooded him.

Oh God.

Lurking in the trees was the pigman, concealed unless looked for, wearing the same ragged clothes and chimney pot that he'd worn alongside the road that day—though Stetson saw no sign of his black and red umbrella.

"We're all here," Maggie said.

"Can he hurt us?"

Maggie shrugged her shoulders. "That depends. He can't hurt our bodies, if that's what you mean. We're not in them." She started walking. "Come on. We have a very important meeting to attend."

They reached the porch and the man in the rocker rose to his feet, stepping from the shadows. He was very tall, gaunt, and wearing his farm-worked cotton pants, creased collared shirt, and crumpled plantation hat. He was thin and seemed to have a sharpness about him, as if he were the edge of a blade. "Where's my boy?" he said.

They turned toward a rustling on their left and saw the pigman stalking out of the trees, lumbering across the grass. He came beside the porch and stood eerily silent. The creature carried a dark cloud of energy about him, barely visible, but which radiated out from his bulky appearance.

"Where's my boy?" the man repeated.

The pigman turned his head, assessing him. When he spoke, his voice was almost too guttural to be understood.

"The boy is now grown, Elrod Chapman," he said. *"He has a boy of his own. But we have a hold of the bloodline here, with the daughter."* He gestured with a hoofed limb toward Maggie Chapman.

The man—Elrod Chapman, presumably—looked the young girl up and down. Then he spat a mouthful of tobacco juice. "Why not the boy?"

"The son is forbidden," the pigman said. *"One of the higher angels watches over him, for his destiny is to play an important role in the upcoming years in the reshaping of the United States government. But his daughter is free for the taking."* He shot his glassy eyes at Maggie, and Stetson noticed drool dangling from his jaws.

Elrod gave Maggie a sneer. "Then what is we waiting for. I wan' what soul is owed me. I'll not rest till—"

He took a step off the porch.

Stetson jumped in front of Maggie. His entire being was numb with terror, he was running on pure instinct, but he knew he had to act. "You'll have to go through me first," he said.

Elrod stopped. "Who the devil are you?"

The pigman answered, *"He is the Guardian of the Gate, sent by the angels to protect the innocent soul. But he is not strong. And he has no one supporting him on the physical plane. He will put up a fight, but in the end he will fail."*

Elrod chuckled. "A fight you want, eh?" He reached behind his back and came up with a long serrated hunting knife. He ran his leathery tongue over the blade, eyeing Maggie as he did so. "I'm always keen on a fight."

"You lay one hand on her," Stetson said, "and I'll make sure you never rise from that rocker again."

"Bold words, Guardian. Lest you forget, there are two of us. And one of you."

From the corner of his eye, he saw the pigman stalking across the grass. Suddenly he had his umbrella, opening it, twirling it in a circle, the red and black stripes dancing hypnotically. There was a flash of steel, and Stetson realized the thing was a weapon—that it contained a sharp blade in each spiny rib.

They're going to gut us alive!

In a burst of light, Maggie sprang out from behind him. For a moment it was as if lightning had illuminated the forest. She stood in the center of all three, hands out at her sides, and Stetson was reminded of his experience in the Chapman backyard with the pig-girl-thing, when baby swine had fallen from the sky. Her face had become solid as a rock, and her eyes had rolled back into her head, exposing whites.

"*I am acting as celestial conduit,*" her voice boomed, no longer the voice of a child, but something immensely powerful and asexual. "*The angels speak through me. They know all, and they can look into time and view the destiny of every living being. No conflict shall resolve itself in Heaven. The karma of all who have gathered here is the result of that being's individual moral and spiritual choices from the past.*"

Elrod and the pigman halted their advance.

The thing in Maggie continued. "*This is a very old dispute, and therefore must be solved the old-fashioned way. Here, then, is the setting for the next scene in each of your individual soul's development. There is one other who shall play a part*"—the image of David Chapman flashed suddenly through Stetson's mind—"*but all of this must transpire on the physical plane.*"

A piercing screech, loud as an eagle, shattered the scene like breaking glass. They all three covered their ears, and the world suddenly spiraled away into a network of colorful shards.

When it had reformed itself, fitting pieces together like a jigsaw puzzle, the forest surrounding the log cabin reappeared, along with Maggie returned to her little girl self, and Elrod and the pigman were gone.

Maggie was motioning Stetson toward a window. "Take a look," she said.

He caught his breath. "Why should I? I know what I will see. And I don't want to see it."

"Now we are in Elrod Chapman's memory," she said. "If you ever hope to save my soul, I beg you to look through the window."

He nodded. But as he peered into the glass, a strange thing

43

happened. The inside of the cabin seemed to open like a theater stage, and the whole of it became visible to him. He saw another woman locked in the back room, chained to the floor this time instead of the wall. She appeared beaten and haggard, her dress barely hanging on, her exposed skin covered in welts.

And she had a smile on her face. For in her arms she held a newborn babe, naked as the cherubim, clutched to her breast and wrapped in a blanket, suckling, with a fuzzy patch of brown hair on its head.

Harold Chapman.

Somehow, Stetson just knew.

"We're viewing his conception," Maggie explained.

"Is the baby your father?"

"Yes."

Elrod entered the room and crouched beside the woman. She recoiled, keeping the baby close to her chest. Elrod glanced at it. "We'll call 'im Harold," he said. "Harold Chapman, my flesh and blood, my boy, my only kin. What do you say? Yer like the name?"

She was silent.

He slapped her across the face. "I asked yer question!"

"I like it," she whimpered.

"Lemme hear you say it."

She stared at him, and he slapped her again. "I want to hear you say it, say his name. Call him your little boy. Act like his mother."

She was sobbing, tears streaming down her cheeks as she rocked the baby. "Harold Chapman," she said. "My little baby ... my little baby boy."

Elrod grinned. "Good girl. If this boy's to know anything, it's who he is."

Stetson looked away, but Maggie regained his attention by touching his elbow. "We must look into the stream of time at a faster rate," she said. "Look through the window again."

He did, and the scene inside the cabin began to flow before his eyes. He saw Elrod coming and going, saw him beating the woman, raping her, also just sitting in the corner, in the darkness, watching; feeding her and the child, bringing them fresh clothes and water. Years passed. The child sprouted, was soon able to crawl about on the dirty cabin floor, finally struggling upright to wobble on two feet. Harold grew into a strapping young lad with a lean build, a piercing gaze, and a fine head of hair.

"You will see how he came to be adrift in this world," Maggie said.

At once there arose a struggle inside the cabin and time slowed back to normal. The woman managed to pull free of her restraints while Elrod was lying on top of her, as the boy looked on from the shadows. She thrust her knee into Elrod's groin, then kicked him onto his side.

Jumping to her feet, she smoothed her dress as best she could, grabbed the boy's hand, and they fled the cabin. Not a moment later Elrod was on his feet, pulling up his trousers. He gave chase through the woods.

Stetson and Maggie zoomed after them, flying through the trees like a pair of birds. They kept up behind Elrod, who in turn was keeping up behind Harold and his mother. For a while this continued, until she lost strength and began to slow.

Elrod leaped on her. He clubbed her over the back of the head, dropping her to the ground. He made to step over her, to continue following the boy, but she thrust her leg in front of him and he fell. Then she clambered on top, pinning him to the ground, and yelled to her child, *"Run as fast as you can! Keep going and never return here, Harold Chapman! Never return!"*

"NO!" Elrod screamed, flailing his body and trying to get free. The woman wailed like a banshee, thrashing him with her fists. Meanwhile the boy quickened his pace and vanished into the trees.

Stetson and Maggie watched as Elrod Chapman finally got free and lunged to his feet, snatching a rock on his way up. "You're nothing but a stinking whore!" he yelled, bringing the rock over his head. "An unfit mother! A disgrace!"

She screamed again, but her voice was cut short as the rock came down on her head, crushing her skull. Elrod stood over her, panting. Then he screamed his son's name at the top of his lungs, scaring birds from the branches.

They shot forward and there was the boy again, running, looking back with frantic eyes, terrified. He had reached the road—the same road along which Stetson had first encountered the pigman—and was hurrying away from town, toward Columbia.

Maggie and Stetson floated behind him. He ran for some time until eventually a motorcar came along. He waved his arms and collapsed into the dirt before it, his little body heaving with exhaustion.

A young couple exited the vehicle and stood over him, conversing dramatically. At length they scooped him up, placed him in the backseat, and continued on toward Columbia.

Stetson was surprised to find that he was standing again, no longer hovering ghostlike, with Maggie by his side. He looked at her and saw she was crying. He hadn't expected that.

"What is it?" he asked.

She turned to him, face distorted with tears of rage. *"There will be no escape from my suffering!"* she wailed, startling him. *"They won't let me escape!"*

Then she shoved him hard and he went flying back, suddenly losing his balance as though he had fallen from a ledge. Suddenly he was plummeting, looking up to see Maggie's distorted eyes trailing down after him.

All went dark.

*   *   *

He was sitting with Harold on the back verandah the next morning, drinking coffee. Jane had gone out, and Wendy was taking David to school. Harold looked like death. He hadn't shaved or bathed, and he was wearing the same clothes Stetson had seen him in the day before. The man's eyes were dark, gazing blankly across the grass.

"You believe me now?" he asked.

Stetson gave him a hard look, then sighed. "I'm starting to believe a lot of things, yes. I read some of your book."

"And?"

"While I don't subscribe to the idea of demonic possession—at least in a Biblical sense—I did note similarities within each case—a constant, if you will."

"What constant?"

"The family of the possessed."

He was quiet. Wind blew and birds chirped, painting reality with a good cheer that would have been believable, if not for the deranged girl upstairs.

"You think it's our fault?" Harold said. "You blame us?"

"It's not about blame. It's a matter of circumstances and external conditions. No one in their right mind would willingly corrupt a child. Yet children are corrupted every day. It's just the way things turn out."

"What are you saying?"

"I know about your father."

At last he turned to face the doctor. "What do you know?"

"I know he was a murderer. A *rapist*. I know he raped your mother and held the both of you hostage in his cabin after you were born. I know he killed her after she tried to escape. And I know you actually did escape."

A look of the most terrific hatred entered Harold's eyes. Stetson feared the man might strike him.

"How do you know that?"

Stetson shrugged. "I have my ways. If you believe in devils then you must also believe in angels. Perhaps an angel told me. Regardless, do you deny it?"

He stared a moment longer. "No."

"Then tell me."

"Why should I?"

In a sudden burst of passion, Stetson slammed his hand down on the chair. "Because the fate of your family depends on it, fool! Think of your daughter."

Harold winced, curling inward like a rodent. Finally he said, "I remember the flight from that madhouse like a dream. That's my very first memory, actually — *running*. I know what my father was, and what happened there, but those memories are very cloudy, and they usually only surface in dreams. My next memory is of Thom and Suzanne."

"Who are they?"

"My parents — well, the ones who took care of me until I left at eighteen. They found me running by the road, and they took me to a doctor in Columbia — that's where they lived. They started asking me questions: where I was from, who my real parents were. I must have been five or six, and I couldn't speak. I could only nod or shake my head. The one thing I could tell them was my name, Harold Chapman. But that didn't mean anything to anyone.

"They put up some fliers around town asking if anyone knew me, and there was even one published in the local newspaper. I still have a copy of it upstairs with my things. But there was no response. Eventually Thom and Suzanne agreed to take me in, and so I lived with them. They allowed me to keep my name. Later they told me that because it was the only thing I knew about myself, they didn't feel right taking it away. In less than a year they had moved to New York, taking me with them. Later still, the war started."

"Then what? Did you attend school in New York?"

He nodded. "I grew up there, with Thom and Suzanne. I even tried calling them Mommy and Daddy. I did consider them my parents. They fed me, clothed me, kept a roof over my head. They're good Christian folks—still there, too, far as I know. I haven't been back to see them in a while."

"When did you leave?"

"I left after the war ended. I was fresh out of high school. I had escaped military service by the skin of my teeth, but after graduation I simply couldn't stand the idea of staying put in New York."

"How come?"

Harold gave a solemn glare. "Because of the memories. I was plagued by horrible nightmares and visions of the most abject evil. I could remember bits and pieces of the time I had spent in the cabin with my real mother and father, but they were splotchy. I felt crazy, but I didn't tell anyone about my nightmarish visions—not even my folks."

"What did you do?"

"I told them I was leaving to rediscover my past, and to find out who my real parents were—to find out who I was. They supported my decision. They even told me exactly where they found me. I left soon after, heading south, determined to uncover the truth."

"And did you?"

"Yes. I even managed to find the old cabin tucked away in the woods. It was abandoned, but all of his things were left lying around. Even his killing things. No one had been out there. I stayed for one night and was in tears for most of it. I couldn't sleep and suffered the most vicious nightmares. I left the following day, never to return."

Stetson paused. Finally, the ghost in the Chapman past. The genetic demon. The worm. His theory had been correct.

"Then you met Jane Bottington?" he asked.

"That's right. I wandered into the little town where she lived, stayed at the inn for a few nights. Eventually I saw an advertisement on the message board from a plantation owner looking for a pair of hands. The rest is history."

"Seems to me like you've been going back and forth," Stetson said, "between the North and the South. Always on the move. *Running*. And you're still trying to get away from the horror of your father. The pigman."

Harold seethed with intensity, then lowered his eyes. "I reckon you're right," he said.

"You haven't outrun your father, the demon, Harold, not yet. And now it's caught up to you here, in Roycepeake. It's already killed one of your daughters, and it's got the other on in its grips."

Harold rose suddenly, making a strained wheezing sound with his throat. He picked up the chair he'd been sitting in and hurled it into the grass. The wheeze became a full-blown scream.

He turned back around slowly to look at Stetson. His countenance was unnaturally dark. "Now you know," he said.

Stetson nodded. "How about Jane? Does she know?"

Harold shook his head. "Please don't tell her."

The doctor squinted. "I do not think it matters one way or the other if she knows."

The ghost of a smile haunted his lips. "Thanks, Jasper. But tell me, what will you do?"

Stetson rose and moved toward the door, passing in front of Harold. "I will try and save your daughter," he said. Then he entered the house without looking back.

*   *   *

He prepared for three days, not checking in on the girl

once. He read more of the books on demonology that Harold kept in the Chapman library, as well as some medical texts he found there. He spoke with Harold about the traumas of his past, surprised to find the man eagerly cooperative. Stetson supposed he'd held that stuff in for so long that he was grateful to get it out.

He spent time with Jane. When he told her he had a plan to drive the demon out, she appeared very excited. However Stetson detected fraudulence in her emotion. More than anything she seemed weary and scared, as if she wished she were a hundred miles from the Chapman residence.

The days passed smoothly, with Stetson in his room or in the library. He only ventured out for meals or to speak with Harold. One of the nights he got up to use the bathroom and on his way back through the hall encountered David Chapman in the darkness. The boy was like a ghost, and his sudden appearance startled the doctor.

"I know what's going to happen," he said. He was wearing white pajamas with black vertical stripes—almost resembling a prisoner—and held a stuffed bear by the arm in his right hand.

"What are you talking about?" Stetson said.

"I know what's going to happen to Maggie. I know what's going to happen to my mother and father. I know what's going to happen to you."

His statements chilled Stetson. "How do you know?"

"A voice inside here"—he pointed to his forehead—"always telling me this or that, but usually I ignore it. When I go to sleep, though, I have no choice. I have to listen. And tonight it told me what will happen."

"What did it say?"

His voice attuned to a lower frequency. *"It said you are going to die."*

Silence followed the words. Darkness swirled around them, and Stetson was reminded of the first time he saw the pigman, and that horrible sign the creature held—*You are going to die.*

The boy turned and vanished down the hall, dragging his stuffed bear along behind him. Stetson returned to his bedroom, bolting the door and crawling back into bed. He did not reckon he would sleep very well, but he was resolved for the showdown with Maggie Chapman tomorrow.

Come hell or high water.

*　　　*　　　*

The room was a festering mess of soiled linens, old dishes, plates, and sweat-stained clothing. He knew the servants still looked after the girl, but at this point the bare minimum seemed to be their standard.

She was lying on her back, staring up at the ceiling. Her frail child's body was emaciated, weak-looking. Her blond hair sprawled over the pillows, sweat-damp. Darkness clung to her, and each time Stetson got up from his chair to open the curtains, they mysteriously slid back into place.

The others waited out in the hall. They'd brought chairs up from the dining table and had plopped down in them like spectators. He had told them that he wanted them close, although he also wanted to be alone with Maggie during this. At least for the beginning. The way he saw it, once he started talking about Elrod Chapman, he didn't want Jane's potential emotion responses getting in the way.

Fear kept everyone away.

And so the girl talked, the one thing Maggie Chapman still seemed capable of. She didn't possess any strength, lying there on the mattress like a bump on a log. Her physical condition had grown much worse.

The moment the door shut that morning, he had told her everything, every dark little secret about her father. It took until the afternoon before he was finished. She listened attentively, then they would discuss. But it was not Maggie Chapman that he was speaking to. It was something else. Something with a manly voice that only pretended to be a little girl. He wasn't sure if it was the pigman's voice or the voice of Elrod Chapman. But the more he listened, the more a theory took root.

It went like this: The part of Elrod Chapman that was diseased and mentally polluted had been passed on to his son, Harold Chapman, by way of genetics. These corrupted genes had lain dormant in him throughout his youth, although they continuously made their presence known in the form of terrible nightmares. When Harold married Jane Bottington and they started having children, the genes were, in turn, passed on to them.

The strange, artificial, manly voice that now came out of Maggie Chapman's mouth was the voice of the corrupted genes themselves, a whole colony of them speaking at once to create a simulated human girl's voice.

They—the maligned genes—were the ones who had invented the pigman and who were drawing him along the road that led to this world. It was they who desired death and destruction, they who wanted to set the pigman free.

After he and the girl had finished discussing Harold Chapman's past he sat looking at her for a while. She had propped her head up on the pillow, her eyes angled toward him, her mouth hung in a slack-jawed grin.

"What do we do now, doc?" she said.

He took a deep breath. He needed a break, some fresh air. But a part of him wouldn't consent to leaving until the job was done.

"Let us discuss … closing the road to the pigman," he said.

She cocked her head. Laughed. "You're joking. Why should I do that? I *want* the pigman to come."

"What reason have you for inviting him?"

"The bloodline in which my being is preserved and generated must not end, for that would be like death to me."

"And who are you?"

"I am the Chapman stain."

Stetson thought this a very strange thing to say. He looked at the girl, at the unnatural expression she was showing him, at the roundness in her cheeks, the snout-like resemblance of her mouth and nose, the beady black eyes. He shivered. *A stain indeed.*

"The stain sometimes skips a generation before manifesting itself," the voice went on. "But it's always there, underneath the surface. I suppose it would be my preference to have the boy, but due to circumstances out of my control, he is unavailable."

"Because the angels have him," Stetson said.

"Something like that. At first I wanted to make the elder daughter do it. Now, I'm after this one."

"Do *what*, exactly?"

Her snout lengthened into a piggish grin. "Why, go mad, of course. And maybe even ... kill someone."

Stetson broke out in gooseflesh as he recalled the cabin in the woods, and the room in the back with chains on the wall. Elrod Chapman had killed someone. The stain manifested itself in him.

He had a glimpse of a demonic cluster of genes with myriad eyes chasing other healthy genes through generations of Chapmans, trying to manifest themselves, but succeeding only occasionally. He wondered about Elrod Chapman's parents. How had he ended up alone in the forest? What had been done to him? And what happened to him after Harold ran away? Stetson knew he would probably never have answers for these questions.

"Where is the pigman now?" he asked.

"Come here and I will show you."

He wagged his finger at her. "I'll be watching in case you try anything." Then he approached the bed.

"Look into my mouth," she said, parting her jaws.

He did as he was told, and instantly a beam of color shot up from the depths of her throat. He saw a picture form out of the darkness, like a painting in miniature, lodged in the space between her pointed teeth. He saw trees and bushes and stones. And a road—*the road* outside his hometown, near where Elrod Chapman's cabin was located.

There he was in his black suit and hat, umbrella leaned against one shoulder. Alongside him walked Maggie Chapman, moving lithely as a spirit, her blond locks bouncing against her shoulders. The image faded as the pig-girl closed her jaws. "He is very close now," she said. "He should be joining us shortly."

Stetson returned to his chair, his heart hammering. "Why is Maggie Chapman with him? Aren't you..."

"That was a portal into the spirit world I just showed you. What you saw was her ethereal soul substance. We already have that aspect of her being. But now we require her physical body."

"How come?"

"Because, while this body lives, both remain connected by an invisible string. One cannot be possessed without the other; both are required to capture the soul."

"I don't understand. Why not just kill her?"

The pig-girl shook her head. "That defeats the purpose. That would mean both parts detach and spiral back into the cosmic soup of infinity—the body into the earth to be recycled into minerals, and the soul into the spirit world to undergo reformation for its next incarnation. In order to conquer the soul, both parts must be captured simultaneously. That is why we failed with the other girl."

"Karen?"

"Yes. She managed to starve herself sufficiently so that she perished before the pigman had come. This one is also attempting to do that, but she will not succeed. Behold, she still lives, and the pigman—the bane of the Chapman name—is nearly arrived upon the road between worlds."

Stetsons felt claustrophobic. "I need a break," he said, rising from the chair.

"We have all the time in the world."

He crossed the room, shutting the door behind him.

*   *   *

He stood looking at himself in the lavatory mirror. The Chapmans were fortunate enough to have running water (unlike most of the world), and so he washed his hands in the porcelain basin, splashing water onto his face.

Come on, Jasper. You've come this far. See it through to the end.

He dried his hands, sighing. "I know." He headed back into the hall, muttering again, "I know."

Harold, Wendy, and Jane sat outside the room, looking troubled. "Haven't we sat out here long enough?" Jane asked. "I would like to do some things around the house."

"I think I'm going to need you to come into the room now," he said.

Harold was nursing a glass of whiskey; since spilling his guts to Stetson, his drinking had gotten worse; he was rarely seen empty-handed. Stetson pointed to Wendy and another servant woman. "I would like the two of you to wait out here. If I need you, I'll holler. But I want you in earshot."

They glanced at each with raised eyebrows and wrinkled

foreheads. Finally they nodded.

"Good," he said.

He moved to the door, motioning with his hands. "Shall we?" He looked at the Chapmans then entered the room before they could answer.

*   *   *

As soon as the four of them were together in the room, the temperature dropped. Breath became visible. Harold, still holding his drink, attempted to open the curtains, but without success. He slouched in defeat, joining his wife in the chair beside the bed.

"This is all looking very familiar," he muttered to himself.

Jane choked on a sob. "I can hardly stand it!"

"What's the matter, Mommy?" said the simulated voice coming from Maggie Chapman's throat. "Don't you love me?"

Jane glared at her. "You're not my daughter. You're that *thing* what had Karen. I don't know who you are, but I wish you would leave my family alone. I don't know what we did to deserve this. Christ, look at your face!"

Harold's whole body tensed as he drowned his nose in his glass. The pig-girl said, "You may not know, Mother, the nature of your sins. But the surname you carry after your Christian name is cursed. *Stained,* in fact. There is nothing you can do to prevent the taking of the child. Her soul will be ours."

Jane started to weep. Harold tried comforting her, placing his hand on her shoulder, but she shrugged it off. "Don't touch me!" she wailed. "You're always drunk! That's all you ever do is drink!"

Harold shot to his feet and slung his glass of whiskey at the wall, where it shattered, dispersing fragments of glass.

"Yes, Daddy!" the pig-girl cried.

"What are you going to do about this?" Harold shouted, turning to Stetson.

"We have to get this up and out," he said, meaning the man's checkered past, his repressed anger emotions, and the truth about his surname. "If we bring it all into the open then it becomes a *wound,* no longer a stain on your family name. And wounds can *heal.*"

Harold shook his fist. *"Never!"* He was obviously drunk.

"Then…" Stetson spread his hands. "I'm not sure it can be helped."

Silence fell over the room. Harold stood motionless, chest heaving. Jane's sobs decreased to whimpering.

A noise jumped from the bed. They all looked at the pig-girl. She was almost entirely that now, resembling the pig-thing Stetson had encountered in the backyard.

"He's here," she whispered, grinning.

The room went pitch black instantly. A sound like retching came from the bed, the sound of a pneumonic cough, followed by a tremor in the air, something invisible to the naked eye, but felt in the skin and teeth. A pinprick of light appeared where the pig-thing's head had been. The light swelled.

Jane screamed and, clutching her husband, they darted back against the wall. Stetson did the same, retreating until they flanked the bed. He suddenly remembered what Dr. Emerstein had told him about the cloud of black smoke Karen had expelled from her mouth the day she died. He now believed he understood what it was.

She'd been expelling the Chapman stain.

The room was becoming visible. The pig-girl was on her stubby knees in the bed, hands steepled before her chest. Her mouth—almost entirely a snout now—hung down from her face, stretched unnaturally wide, and light spilled from it.

Rumbling shook the walls and the wood furniture, rattled the curtain rods in their metal mounts, and Jane sprang for the door with a high-pitched scream. Harold went after her, but no matter how hard they pounded, the door stayed shut.

Then that sound, which Stetson thought resembled an earthquake, grew exponentially, until he realized it sounded more like a reflux of the stomach or acute indigestion. As a doctor, he had heard it in his stethoscope countless times. Now it was in the air, in the very materials of the house. Tracing it back, he found its source in the bed, coming from the pig-girl's mouth.

Weeping, Jane clutched at Harold's chest as the couple retreated away from the door. Stetson inched closer to the bed, for he had glimpsed something within the shimmering light: a picture, a scene like something from an oil painting, showing trees and bushes, and a long winding dirt road cutting through wilderness.

It was as if the abnormally large space between the pig-girl's teeth was a viewing screen, and deep in the bowels of her darkened throat he saw the road ... and the pigman moving along it.

When Harold caught sight of this, he bellowed at the top of his lungs—"*Oh Jesus Christ, there he is! He's coming! The demon is coming!*" Abandoning his wife, he lunged at the door, banging his fists against it, while Jane Chapman slowly slid to the floor, her face frozen in terror.

Stetson reached for the little girl. "Maggie," he said. If he could get close to her gaping mouth, maybe he could put a stop to this. His fingers strained, and the bottom half of her snout dropped almost to the mattress—like her jawbone had snapped.

"*Good God!*" Stetson yelled, retracting his hands.

The pigman arrived in the space between her teeth. The dirt road led right into the room. He sauntered up to it, quite casually in his black suit and chimney pot hat, clutching his umbrella beneath one arm. Ducking, he insinuated himself between the flaps of elongated skin, stepping onto the mattress.

More light returned to the room as the candles on the night stand sputtered back to life. Maggie tumbled off the bed and rolled into a ball on the floor. She got on her hands and knees and began making the most god-awful retching noises.

Stetson noted with surprise that she had recovered her former physiognomy, and again resembled the Chapman girl.

The rumble in the room stopped; now in the silence the pigman stood like a god, looming over them. The aura around his form seemed to shimmer with blurry movements, and the smell of him was damp, freshly turned earth. His glassy black eyes peered around the room, twin orbs of hatred, his sagging face perforated by a mouth of razor-sharp teeth.

He placed the tip of his umbrella against the mattress, supporting himself on the curved black handle. "*Ah,*" he said in a gravelly voice, almost incomprehensible. "Finally, I have reached the end of my journey."

The pigman turned his heavy body, glancing at Maggie Chapman on the floor. "The soul I have come to claim," he said.

"Both aspects of the child will be ours, spirit and matter, and we shall count her energy among our own. Once another soul has been conquered, then another stain sets into the wool of the Chapman surname."

His eyes swung across the room, landing first on Stetson, whom he dismissed with a knowing grin, then to Jane Chapman, and finally to Harold—who was stalking with determination toward the bed.

Face full of rage, eyes full of tears, Harold screamed, "I'll kill you, you son of a bitch! You tortured my family – you killed Karen – I swear I'll kill you!"

Swiping a candlestick holder from the chest of drawers, he leaped onto the mattress.

The pigman started laughing.

*   *   *

Harold was up on the mattress, heaving the candlestick over his head. He almost looked like someone else, like a person Stetson had never met before. The man's features were so distorted with rage that he appeared different.

The pigman stepped back, luring Harold toward the center of the mattress. When the creature reached the back wall, he braced against it, brandishing his red and black umbrella. "I'm going to enjoy this," he said.

"Die!" shouted Harold, flinging himself at the pigman and bringing the candlestick down.

The pigman calmly opened his umbrella, which unfurled like a noxious black flower, with curved blades hooking from each spined rib. He deflected the man by holding the umbrella between them. Then suddenly it began to spin, faster and faster, until the interplay of black and red became a blur.

Harold sagged in place and dropped the candlestick, his eyes gazing into the umbrella's center.

"Kneel," the pigman said.

Harold did it. He clasped his hands in prayer, angled his head back, and closed his eyes, as the pigman inched the bladed ribs closer.

"For the destruction of your soul," the pigman said. "I am

honored to deliver you from the stain of your past."

He jerked the umbrella forward and there was a harsh whirring sound as the blades tore into the man's flesh. It happened very fast. The umbrella flicked around, slicing and gouging out pieces of Harold Chapman and flinging them around the room. Arcs of blood painted the walls and ceiling, as a giant pool formed on the mattress.

The pigman eased the umbrella all the way through to the other side of Harold, the blades chopping him into chunks. Soon only the lower half of his body remained on the bed, the rest of him now pulverized and scattered. His disembodied legs spewed blood geysers as they tumbled to one side.

The pigman started across the mattress, stepping over the gruesome remains. He hopped down to the floor, advancing toward Jane still cowering in the corner.

Stetson was in shock. He bent and started vomiting, clutching his knees with white knuckles.

The world is ending. I'm going to die – just like they said.

The last of his stomach bile dangled from his lower lip. He kept his eyes closed, not wanting to face this new place of demons, dreams, and death. But Jane's image flashed through his mind and he urged himself up.

Quit acting like a coward, fight like a man!

He summoned the courage, opened his eyes, and turned back to the room.

Jane was kneeling before the pigman, just as Harold had done. His umbrella still spun in one clawed hoof-hand; with the other, he gently stroked the contours of Jane's face.

Her eyes, bulging and lifeless, had gone entirely white. Stetson could tell she had retreated to somewhere far away in her mind. He was surprised she hadn't fainted.

"Get away from her!" he yelled.

The pigman ignored him, took a step back, and brought the whirling blades of the umbrella in line with Jane's head.

"For the destruction of your soul," he said.

"Get away!"

The pigman slanted forward and began descending with the umbrella, and a wave of fear splashed over Stetson. He ran full speed at the pigman.

The creature lifted his free hoof-hand without looking; the instant Stetson drew near, he was repelled by an invisible energy force that sent him back.

"No!" he screamed.

But the pigman was already pushing his blades through the soft flesh of Jane's face. Strands of blond hair went flying, followed by strips of skin and sprays of blood. He pushed the umbrella forward with a steady heartless momentum, annihilating her head, neck, and chest. An explosion of bone and brain peppered the wall behind her. She slumped over on her side, a headless corpse gushing blood onto the floor.

The umbrella slowed to a stop, the blades whirring, and the pigman replaced it under his arm. Silence clung.

Stetson pressed his hands to either side of his head, his mouth forming an O. He let out a blood-curdling wail, dropped to his knees, and began to sob.

"You are a strange creature, Guardian," the pigman said. "You have an emotionless soul, and yet you display sadness over the loss of your friends. It behooves you to regain control of yourself. Your darkest days lay ahead."

"What are you talking about?" Stetson spat.

The pigman stalked forward. "I'm talking about your destiny, and the destiny of all those involved here today. Things are not always what they seem. Every event has a purpose, every effect a cause. You may have been recruited by the other side, but that doesn't mean we have given up the fight."

"What do you mean?"

"There is a war going on," the pigman said. The creature had reached Maggie Chapman, who lay curled in a ball on the floor. She almost looked asleep, her eyes closed and her chest moving rhythmically. The pigman scooped her into his arms.

"No!" he shouted. He lunged to his feet and ran at the pigman, but again he was deflected by the invisible force. He went vaulting back, striking the wall and crashing to the floor.

He watched as the pigman cradled Maggie Chapman in his arms, holding her like a baby. He stroked her blond hair with one hoof.

"Leave her," Stetson said. "Please don't do this. She's only a child. She has nothing to do with Harold or his father—and besides, they're dead."

The pigman looked at him. "You know nothing of this, Guardian. These events were written down a long time ago. It is true that the primary stain carriers are dead. Their spirits will undergo reformation and they will begin another life. But this is a war of souls, and we do require them. The conquering of the girl's soul is our most recent victory. We now possess both her spiritual part as well as her physical part. Her life force will be added unto our own."

He did a strange thing then by tipping his chimney pot hat to Stetson. He said, "We'll be seeing each other again." Then all at once the room began to vibrate. Both the pigman and the girl glowed bright yellow. Their bodies grew thin, wispy, like mist. Piece by piece they were pulled apart. Flashes of yellow flew about as they were unspun like balls of yarn, evacuating into the walls, floor, and ceiling.

A moment later, they were gone.

*   *   *

Stetson stood alone in the empty room. Blood and gore covered his clothes. If he weren't so numb from all that had happened, he might've started vomiting again; but he got up and went to the window, pulling back the curtains.

This time they stayed that way.

He opened the window and let in fresh air. It was twilight; the world outside seemed like another dimension.

Now what can I do?

He could never go back to the way things had been. Too much had happened. And yet ... the future remained foggy.

He traveled out into the hallway. Wendy and two other servant women were standing there.

"What happened?" she said.

Stetson looked at her, suddenly filled with rage, not sure why. The sight of the short brunette woman made him sick. He wanted to get away from this accursed place.

"See for yourself," he said, brushing past her.

She hurried into the room with the other women on her heels. Their screams filled the house.

He went into his room and closed the door, changed his clothes, and left the bloodstained outfit on the floor. He packed his things, grabbing the book on demon possession Harold had given him. When he felt he had everything, he returned to the hall.

The door to the abattoir was now closed and the servant women stood clustered outside, their faces pale as they fanned themselves. Wendy glared at Stetson as he made for the steps.

"You did this," she snarled.

"I didn't do it. Don't be a fool. We fought against a demon. And we lost."

"But where is the girl?"

He shrugged his shoulders and a wave of sadness washed over him. Where *was* the girl?

"I have no *idea*," he said, the last word crackling with emotion. He turned and headed downstairs.

Reynolds, white as a ghost, stood in the sitting room.

"I'm taking one of the motorcars," Stetson said.

"I'll drive you to Albany."

Stetson shook his head. "No. I'm taking the motorcar as payment for services rendered."

He really didn't care about the vehicle; he already had his own motorcar. But he couldn't stand the idea of riding with that loathsome man all the way to the train station. He would leave the thing parked by the side of the road and be done with it.

He started out the house.

"But she's dead," Reynolds called after him. "Isn't she? They're all dead. Why should you receive payment if you couldn't save them?"

"The good thing about my line of work," the doctor said, glancing over his shoulder, "is that I get paid whether or not the patient survives."

*   *   *

Emerging from the house, he was hit by the fresh air and the smell of trees. The last fading sunlight twinkled on the horizon like a polished jewel. The world had gained a certain lucidity it had not formerly possessed. The grass seemed extraordinarily green, even in the low light, and the trees, plants, and rocks appeared vibrant, as if radiating from within. He stood breathless for a moment, taking it all in.

"I'm going with you."

The voice made him jump. He turned and saw David Chapman standing in the doorway. The boy was dressed in shortpants and a white collared shirt. He clutched a small leather suitcase in one hand.

"Go back inside," Harold said.

David shook his head. "I don't want to. There's nothing left for me here. They're all dead. My whole family. I know."

"How do you know?"

"Sometimes I see things. Like having a dream while you're awake. I saw what happened. I'm going with you."

He's psychic.

Stetson recalled what the pigman had said about the boy, how an angel watched over him, how he was supposed to play a significant role in the forming of the new American government. He thought of Karen Chapman—dead—and Maggie Chapman—gone—also of the boy's dead parents upstairs. Despair hit him, and he sighed.

"Yes, all right. You're coming with me."

A smile flickered on the boy's lips. He stepped out of the house, closing the door. Together they silently admired the soft beauty of the world and then descended the stone pathway to the garage.

Upstairs, in the Chapman house, one of the servants started screaming again.

*   *   *

On the train ride back to the Carolinas, Stetson watched the dark landscape roll by and wondered about the future. The boy slouched beside him in the seat, sleeping. He'd slept for most of the trip; hadn't said much, either.

That's because he is retreating inward.

He hoped the boy would adjust to the town all right, hoped he could give David a proper home and a decent childhood. Lord knew he was too old to be a parent. And now the boy had no mother. Bad situation.

The moon suddenly went behind a cloud, and the trees whizzing past were shrouded in the pitch black night. For just a moment Stetson imagined the face of the pigman hidden behind a thick oak trunk, leering at the train. He shivered.

Maybe it wasn't a good idea to let the boy keep his surname. *Chapman.* The word now held an icy connotation. But he didn't see much choice in the matter. Besides, he could imagine the boy clinging to the name as a symbol of his family, as a way of mourning them, perhaps.

After all, it was the only thing he knew about himself.

That stain would never wash out.

CHAPMAN TWO
THE DELIRIUM
ERIK T. JOHNSON

PART #1
HEAVEN'S NOWHERE

Just as what begins on earth goes nowhere, so what starts in heaven goes to earth; for earth is heaven's nowhere.
— The Dark Wintering, Prologue (To my Unborn Grandson)

The difficulty is to gain knowledge of the operations of secrecy while not knowing it; otherwise it should be other than itself.
— The Dark Wintering, Chapter I.

Always Open with a Joke

Knock-Knock.

> *Who's there?*

Boo.

> *Boo Who?*

Exactly...

One rainy night in 1888, a stranger calls on Dr. Nathaniel Fayteyant in The House Next to Nothing, urgently requesting assistance at the mansion of Harold Chapman and his family. Life and death are at stake. The moon is clear and the leeches ascendant.

And the doctor wonders:

Will I reap what I sow, or something I didn't?

Epilogue #1 / Too Black for Believing

...A fast bonewhite something flows through the narrow murk between evergreens — can it finally be missing Ella-Rae — Didn't Mary Carson wrap her in a shawl of lace just before she ran off, covered in bloody chyle, her eyes like charred buboes? *What kind of world, after all, is this 1868? Who could be so evil as to do what he did to her? She may be a whore but that's no excuse. No doubt that Charlatan with his "I-M POSSIBLE" hokum... I didn't like him one stitch. When Sterling and the rest slandered me yellow that Quack even joined in, taunting "I'm Stanford Grost and I shake, I shake, I shake like the ratt-le on a snake..."*

But even trembling limbs can climb... a palsy is no pox. I'll bring Ella-Rae hearthside. I'll not be poltroon of New Toomes...

Whatever Stanford thinks he saw has dissolved into baroque trees of Connecticut forest. He calls out her name and the chill December air turns it to mist. He races up the hill to the wood's frayed perimeter, and pauses in the dark before stepping into the trees. His head wobbles yesyesyesyesyes; birth-hand and wooden both tremble; vibrating tuning forks, those bastards say, that only the dead can hear... The trees are rooted in cold shadow; but nothing white to be seen, not even the moonlight, which falls into weak spots of silvery gray.

That faint smell? Sickening, luxurious...

And where's Harper Noolan? He was supposed to

meet Stanford by now. Two men would be safer than one.

Pine-needles crackle against the incomprehensible murmur of forest evenings, and out of time with his own, labored panting. He carefully trudges uphill through a restrictively inky trunkscape.

This earth is thorny, festooned with frozen tendrils; and patches of dead, knobby stalks steeply spike the slope and sally at the advance of his trespassing shins. The smell returns on an icy breeze: a delicious, sweetsalty formaldehyde aroma—a fine supper of chickens, pigs and woodcocks, prepared in a vivisected cadaver's newly embalmed chest cavity. Anticipation irrigates his tongue even as bile trickles throatward. He rubs tired eyes. When he lowers his real hand the darkness seems *inflicted*, less an absence of light than the cauterized blackness of a truncated appendage.

He calls her again.

His voice resounds, but the name crumbles as it leaves his mouth, the words "Ella-Rae" having been overshouted, eroded into useless scraps of cold, hoarse noise in ceaseless search for the good-hearted working girl...

Stanford hikes on, incomplete outlines of trees, bushes, vines, discrete woodland obscurities congealing into still, saltant obscurity. The further resistance of unseen flora scrapes through trouser to skin. *Every shape vague... why does this hour constrict?*

His ascent is peculiarly horizontal; he stops somewhere so black there can be no believing there—no sight—no proof... He trips on likely a root and stumbles into the flaking bark of a bumply tree. Stanford leans back and the trunk creaks.

Ella-Mae is gone forever, isn't she? Awful, but at least the anxious searching can be put to rest. He's experienced this sad/thankful certainty once before—just three years ago— while remaining miraculously standing in the brotherly gore and barely breathing the burning, groaning Appomattox air...

But wait—what small white figure emerges out of the night, desperately fast as a lost, little girl toward the safety of her mother's arms? His heart pumps hope and he smiles, kneels down, ready to receive her...

But how am I seeing her? There's no light...

Because her skin glistens with a gelid, fungal glow, just bright enough to let him perceive a brain-sized mass bursting from stumpen face; not a tumid, conjoined frothing twin, but a single rabid eyebulge that traps broken pupils roving like frightened spiders; to wonder how to distinguish between her chandelier arms and chandelier fingers; and to recognize the bonewhite flash of her flowing hem as her newly-sexed fleshskirt streaked with slushy pain. It undulates like a windblown shroud of tattered jellyfish.

Nearby, but beyond the woods, he hears Sterling's arrogant rasp:

"Ella-Rae! Ella-Rae!"

The thing pauses in what appears to be a moment of forgetfulness. Its opposable somethings fumble about a torso of battlefield and baby flesh. What could it possibly have misplaced? What's that glint in its side—*God let it have been stabbed*—no, a handle, the fine gold crank of a music box... without turning its dead, spiderscrambling godlike eye from him, it turns the crank and a soft, slowgeared metallic *liebeslied* plinks, tin rain gently rusting a field of clocks—barely audible beneath the rotten sunrising skin.

She spreads closer with inexplicable waterfall locomotion, seems to arrive in Stanford's face even as she's still approaching. That's a brass doorknocker lodged under her eye, presumably to stop it from drooping off her bodyface... the mechanical song halts and again she tugs the crank, more violently... It's obvious that lacking a mouth, she's trying to use the toy to scream for her—it's clear she *remembers* screaming—that's the worst part, knowing this innervated fleshpile has memories—with each rough mishandling of the device she grows more frustrated at its preciously inarticulate tinkling. He's seen many a veteran thrash at a prosthetic leg just so.

Too far away, other voices call:

"Ella-Rae!"

Back against the tree, Stanford slides down into a canopic-jar crouch, chin atop knees. The smell of rot and opulence is as overpowering and unexpected as opening your eyes in the morning to find the sun changed into a tidal wave.

A gust of ovenly heat rushes over him. Her eye floats a few inches from his face; it oscillates, but it's not *looking* at him—it is *orienting itself* like an autonomous entity into a strategic position—as befits the *owner* of an eye.

Now she raises his alder hand and impales her eyesac on its chipped tip. He hasn't been healed but he can't move because this can't be real and if it can't be real then there can't be movement, fear or anything... there can't be shaking... but there cannot be cures for shaking either... there cannot be Stanford—a sick, poor man, an unloved man—a man nobody will miss—yet then how can it be that it is none other than Stanford who watches a twisted black pupil slop stillborn out of the punctured eye and stick to his flimsy face, leaking cold holes into his cheek, blinding icy blood dripping up and getting hotter as it ascends...

Her skirt rises over his head.

Now his falsetto whimpers echo and die in lubricated hollows.

I. Bungholes of Burden / Epitaph #1

If it's true that those approaching death see their lives flash before their eyes, then Perceval's life has been but one giant horse-cock. For that's the only thing he can see now, while he's beating off a dead horse, clinging face-to-foreskin with the crystallized erection of a Clydesdale, the deceased steed sliding wildly down the snowy hill — they skid and foam over devious ground. As a desperate mariner hugs a sinking ship's mainmast Perceval fights not to lose hold of the petrified organ; with every jerk of the pillar he slips a little further toward the terrifying glans, beyond which nothing but white abyss. Letting go is out of the question — they're going too fast... he's about to rocket off like some grotesquely anthropomorphic, broken-necked ejaculate when the sole of his foot taps something mercifully unyielding as abattoir flooring. With relief he recalls the firm, naked cadaver at his feet, the fellow's dick clenched alone-at-last tightly inside the equine's asshole. Perceval tempers his embrace while his boots find purchase on the horsebanger's stiffened knees. But the worst isn't over — the three hurtle together, absurdly inextricable as Father — Son — Holy Shit Does Anyone Really Believe That Crap?... bouncing now over wintersplit ravines — any second a hard crash will undoubtedly end their impromptu flight —

— Perceval pictures a tombstone:

HERE LIES PERCEVAL RAPTUS
BORN UNDER THE SIGN OF YES TRESPASSING
? — DECEMBER 5, 1868
HE GAVE HIS LIFE FOR THE GREATER GOOD RIDDANCE

II. See this Frowzy Creature —

There is something ghostly about a liar and nothing false about a ghost.

— The Dark Wintering, Chapter II.

Perceval Raptus had been orphaned before memory and raised on the abuse and chilly broth of strangers. To the outside observer, he was no different than a million other hateful urchins in the stinking City — begging, thieving, lying, passed out on cobblestone beds — disease, assault ever-threatening and mere anogenital units away. Yet his was a deep and wide-ranging education. He learned that if there's a soul it's a beggar and if there's love it's not enough; the dead are like us — only more so; the world is a bottomless yet overflowing spittoon; starvation begins when the fast ends; the seasons switch back and forth like sluggish lycanthropes and their alter-egos; and the afterlife is the wet dream of bereaved voyeurs. O! And while necrophilia may be a victimless crime, it is *not* a topic appropriate for public conversation, &c.

When Perceval was about nine, he flopped now and then in a fleacloset with a fiery, indignant old woman who always let tramps sleep in her meager room. She gave them bread while she slept and ate dead pigeons on the roof... but what Perceval remembered most was her unending lamentations about "Voice."

She fancied herself a "Social Deformer." Every day Perceval heard her going on about how all the poor suffering wretches needed a VOICE. *They* have no Voice — no Voice! Someone must give them a Voice. She'd point at Perceval and say "Even the insane should have a Voice!" *He* needs a Voice, *she* needs a Voice, *they* need a single giant VOICE to speak together as ONE.

This idea of handing out voices — even *consolidating* them — stimulated and became the organizing principle of his imagination. Bestowing Voice — what could be more esoteric and awe-inspiring?

Answer: *Receiving* Voice.

He knew that what she meant by "Voice" wasn't about talking or shouting; it might be related, somehow, but was

71

infinitely greater. He wanted to be given *that* kind of voice. The closest Perceval could get to explaining it was a poor one—that it would be like finding a box in an abandoned attic. The lid is caked shut and doesn't budge on the first try; yet already you're fascinated by the way the detritus inside it has nothing to do with you. At the same time, your irresistible attraction to these mysterious effects implies just the opposite—they must have a great deal to do with you, perhaps deeply. You find a sunny, quiet place. It's important there's nobody else around to see you sifting through the contents of the box. Yet strangely, it is just when you are inspecting the remnants of a life with which you share no affiliation, that you feel the most urgent need for absolute, unbroken privacy. You cannot open this box—any box—without assuming the contents—though unknown—promise to reveal a coherent and possibly marvelous whole... this is the hubris of opening a box...

One quiet evening the old lady died peacefully in her sleep, moments after an etheromaniac bludgeoned her head with a horseshoe. Perceval returned to the street. It was too bad she was dead, but no shock—just the *Sickle of Life swinging sharp, relentlessly round and round,* as the ancient ballad whines...

But he was a loner among the tribe of bums for whom public congregation was second nature, even key to survival. It got around that he was "special-headed." He tended not to react when slapped; his face was blank as a dead man's visiting card; if given the choice, he'd turn down food or drink for useless books—having taught himself to read with a discarded copy of *Varney the Vampire.* But Perceval didn't care. On a rainy night in 1863, he even risked time in The Tombs for the sake of children's literacy.

Perceval was thirteen that night, wandering under a sky draping countless puppet-strings across Manhattan Island. Drizzled and dulled, he looked in the window of a hunchbacked dwarf's junk-shop in Gravelspitz Lane and thought he saw his reflection. But it was an English translation of the German children's book, *Struwwelpeter.* The cover featured *Struwwelpeter* himself against a white background, alone and open-eyed as a gaseous corpse afloat on a filthy milkpond.

Perceval was unaccountably, irreversibly enthralled:

This *Struwwelpeter* (The anonymous translator dubbed him *Peter Shit-Head*) was a boy about Perceval's age. He bore a numb, death-sentenced expression, blending immediate shock with the resignation of one long acquainted with their fate. Unaware of the long tear that clung like a strand of wet seaweed to his cheek, his reckless hair like the dry yellow weeds that memorialize unloved graves, prophet of meankind... Arms at his sides, empty palms facing outward, his freak-hands fanned ten long middle-fingers. As if wordlessly appealing to a threatening mob: "Look, I hold no weapons, mean no harm, I've stolen nothing. There's no need to hate me. All I've got are silly green stockings, a blousy red shirt, these disgraceful nails that twistingly dangle. These nails, they've gone too far for me to fix on my own, like long roots grown *up into me*. I'm like a tree or an abortion, condemned to its birthplace..."

The figure was too monstrous for men and too much of a man for the truly monstrous — yet he held onto his tiny dignity, like a mouse keeps his tail: behind his ass, maybe — but only to hold himself upright and balanced.

Perceval had to have it. He was hungry, but there was revelation hidden behind that cover — the gourmet nourishment of a last meal. The shop was closed; it had a flimsy side door that opened on a narrow alley. The lock was a joke. He pushed the door a teensy bit open, peered through the narrow brass-hinged space between door and frame. It was deserted.

Waiting...

Moonlight slowly flashed through the grimed window like sluggish bolts of lightning. Things were only partially intelligible by this cloud-toggled illumination, much as the scattered paragraphs of a letter torn to shreds. Perceval cautiously traversed a dull landscape of broken tools, rusty horseshoes, a buckled, keyless tin trumpet, a painting of an absurd arrangement of soldiers, stack of iron hotplates, false beard lying whitely on an obscurely purposed, old-fashioned coat with too many buttons, a bowl of befurred moth's wings, heaps of unstrung marionettes, and other evidence of unprosecuted crimes of boredom.

The book must've been propped in that window for many years—covered in dust. He was impatient to read the poem about the titular character, ignoring the other "*Funny Tales and Fucked-Up Pictures with 15 Brightly Colored Panels for Children 3 to 6.*"

Page 11:

> *See this frowzy creature –*
> *Fuck Me! It's Struwwelpeter!*
> *To his fingers crusty,*
> *Round his shit-head musty,*
> *Scissors seldom come;*
> *Lets his talons grow a year –*
> *Never combs neglected hair –*
> *Who loathes him? All and one!*
> *Puke upon this Urban Satyr –*
> *Disgusting pox – Struwwelpeter!*

In the poem, *Peter Shit-Head* was cast as an exaggerated example of poor hygiene—a fairy-tale aberration. But Perceval had a more complex interpretation. On one level, *Struwwelpeter* was a triumph of realism. Any child who isn't taken care of— don't cut his hair, neglect the nails, wrap him in some stupid outfit—take away any chance of making his own future, why, he looks just like that, or worse... Simultaneously, *Struwwelpeter* struck Perceval with sacred-ikon numinosity, the last day of a martyr's starvation, or even a burning, carny-barking bush.

Struwwelpeter regarded Perceval with an enigmatic expression that suggested this Jack-without-a-Box was just the type to guide him to one of those Voices that old Social Deformer never stopped going on about...

As Perceval padded away with the book tucked under his arm, a pallid hand swiped *through* his wrist. This was when he discovered that spirits are naturally eager to observe intruders at work. Perceval saw them literally forever trying to learn a trick or two about how to possess that to which they had no right. He often saw such illicit images after that evening—persons drowned, burned, poisoned, hacked or worse—quivering in the reflective surfaces of stolen objects. Their missing bodies strained at him with amputated limbs, decerebrated heads dim-lit with fiercely stupid hope. As if watching the displacement of a physical object from one location, one owner to another could demonstrate how, in like manner, they could steal existence.

These misty, floundering solicitations weren't frightening—the dead are like us, only more so—but he thought it one of the saddest things in the world that ghosts were never more or less than room-temperature.

They weren't cold at all.

Perceval brought *Struwwelpeter* to his current home, the disused, unfinished cellar of an Orange Alley tenement. The building shared two walls with an abattoir and a Soap, Toiletries, &c. factory. On even the driest days, the crude room sweated death and disinfectant; frightened chattel-blood and urine trilling through the dirt and loose stones of the eastern wall, and caustic residues of lye, dog fat and *Gentleman's Crotch Powder* westerly exuded. Rainy weather brought heavy seepage of cow, pig and chicken blood and piss on the one side, and stinging depurations opposite. They met in red and pink pools across the pocked ground. Bubbles of blood and piss would stink like murder-suicides when they popped. Then Perceval would sit atop a pile of crates with his chin resting on his knees, watching the cellar soak in its inability to contradict anything.

He'd created an archipelago of "crate islands" in the cellar, for use during stormy seasons when the runoff flooded and muddied the entire floor. The most prized of these spanned half the room and was topped with more crates full of stolen books, tallow candles, Scratchfyre Co. matches, and an unreliable spirit lamp: Papercut Island.

Perceval climbed atop creaky Shut-Eyeland. He rested the back of his head on a stack of pine and cork boards. Termite-holes in the ceiling like stars in a drop-down sky. He held the book close to his chest like a shield. He shut his eyes.

Perceval saw the inviting edge of a still forest, softly green-glowing like grass after sunshowers; and there was gold in the vision though he couldn't see it. He tried to imagine himself into the peaceful wood, but the edges curled away like oak shaved away by lathe, leaving a painfully white void. His head beating bangbangbang like a chickenshit heart.

Suddenly it came to him:

If there's no way out, it doesn't mean you can't find a better corner to hide in...

He must quit this hole and find a better corner—the one furthest away from an Orange Street alley tenement. Why not into the untamed wilderness? Unroll the edges of his vision flat, follow the map of it. Find whatever was golden.

It was a fever demanding strategic implementation.

...His first fervid tactic was to leave his archipelago of blood and soap, carpetbag empty but for a slim children's book. He wandered far, regularly almost starving to death, nearly bored, intermittently angry and consistently confused yet always somehow *led* without following.

Along the rotted line he got lost in Connecticut. His body was sore as if bedridden for months, though each day spanned long miles. He went gravy-eyed; seeing double, triple; quadruple—especially inconvenient, navigating dense woodland. Then one cold afternoon when the sky was all varicolored tufts of cloud like the coat of inbred cats, he fated upon Cirkle's Way.

Cirkle's Way couldn't be located on a map; but then, maps are made by people who want certainty, and will never account for the places about which we cannot be sure. To the west was a clocktower; skewed steeple; the dark rectangle of the Scratchfyre Matchbox Mfg. factory, grand but frail like a structure left behind by a travelling carnival; red roofs and chimneys; a curlicue of river—porcelain silence; a single road thin as a fracture in tea-cup glazing.

Eastward the ground sloped steeply down at an angle that would make suicidal entertainment of dead-horse sledding; at the bottom was a solemn stone structure out of place in its modestly civilized surroundings. Standing apart from, yet close enough to be considered *among* the raddled clapboard buildings of Cirkle's Way, it rose four absurd stories from the bottom of the sharp-sloped road, with oriel windows large and heavy as iron lungs separated by angular, elaborate stained-glass panels. Behind it, a beetling wall of ugly wilderness, branches ampersanding, boughs and trunks blackly embrangled as Chickamauga dead; and the western, northern and southern sides cordoned by spears of noxious weeds. What purpose could such a majestically orchestrated building serve in *these* frowzy wilds?

He felt a flea's paw would strike him down... his eyes were dry like dead seas, arid and sorely red like the wafer-chapped assholes of devout Catholics, but he was too weak to rub them into tears. Just then: raddled, repurposed farm buildings juggled low to the ground a few stanzas away. He read four identically wiggly copies of a sign tacked over a wide porch:

THE LITHUANIAN ORPHAN ASYLUM FOR
WAYWARD YOUNG MEN IN NEED (WYMIN)
ST. FRANCIS OF ASSISI PROTECT US

Perceval walked up the short stair. The air blackened quicker than spit. He fell forward and his pate struck the door like a bill collector.

The snowmanly fellow who opened it knelt next to Perceval as the robed, bulky form of the Warden, Father Onderdonkalitis, appeared behind him in the doorway. Perceval's vision returned, impaired; he saw four sets of brown eyes above him and flinched as from straining assholes. No, *waitaminute* — they were sixteen killer's eyes, that would be hard and unflinching in the face of gore and yet uninterested in killing — for its own sake... cold eyes, but not evil.

Obviously a doctor...

"Father, would you mind helping me get this young man to the cot in my dispensary?"

"Of course, Doctor," Onderdonkalitis said, taking the thin, tow-headed boy's feet while the pale, portly physician slipped his hands beneath his armpits, thinking:

How strange that I myself arrived only a few days ago...

77

...The doctor had clearly known wealth and position, but he'd appeared on the orphanage doorstep rich only in tribulations, his sole possession one saddle-sized, blacktattered valise. His trousers and his coat, his shoes, scarf and all else were exceedingly fine; but his fabric had worn at the knees and elbows and the shoes cobbled with some cleverly improvised material. It was clear the portly doctor had been under a road of dark cloud for a long time.

He had a proposition for Onderdonkalitis.

They met in the chill austerity of the warden's office. The room was lit by one drafty window set in the wall behind the priest; an autumn morning flooded in, dogmatically transparent and all-pervasive. Onderdonkalitis began the interview by raising bushy eyebrows as if considering how to *answer* a delicate question. He was struck by the doctor's average-looking appearance. It was the man's most distinguishing feature. He had the suspicious anonymity of mail-order dildo packaging. The doctor's face, waist and features were gently round, suggesting moral benignancy or cannonballs.

"I offer you, your brethren, and the orphans the immense benefit of my expertise in doctorcraft *gratis*. All I want is to serve your WYMIN—in return for nothing but food and lodging of the simplest kind."

"If only you had arrived a year earlier," the warden answered with a slight Lithuanian lilt. "Smallpox epidemic ended in '62."

"Overall duration?"

"About five years. So many died..."

"Is there a hospital hereabouts?"

Onderdonkalitis chuckled.

"We were forced to use the library, despite our Christian reservations. You probably saw this Moloch on the way into town—the adversarial structure that looks like it's marshalling the wilds at its back to sally up the hill.

"There was a wicked man who lived in Cirkle's Way, not very long ago really. His name was Otto Johngreatgrandson and he had the thing built for private use. To keep his personal library."

"Wicked? What did he do besides collect books?"

"The titles of the books alone—which shouldn't *ever* be read—speak loudly for his perfidy. Otherwise, it's not what he did or was, so much as what he did and was *not*. Cirkle's Way is a small place yet nobody knew him, what color his eyes were; there was much disagreement about his height and hair. However, all attested to his thin frame. Who else but a devil could leave such an impression without leaving the memory of it?

"He disappeared without warning soon before the pox. Possibly he was the cause, even. We had nowhere to bring the growing numbers of sick and expiring. We'd never been in the library before—had no right; we weren't even certain Johngreatgrandson was gone for good—or if an heir held claim to it—but the library was the only place big enough to safely exile a hundred patients at a time. We requisitioned it.

"Nothing but books—but what books. Wicked things. But the space was ample; we shifted the shelves we could move and brought in cots, improvised beds &c. as best we could..."

"And is the building currently in use?"

"No, Heaven protect us. It's an evil place, full of words of sin and so much death in the air. Besides, nobody wants to risk a renascent pox. It's hardly a salubrious environment."

The doctor smiled despite himself, managed to disguise it as a tic preliminary to a dry cough.

"It's good to speak with another man of learning after so long, but I must ask you directly, Doctor: are you sure your motives are purely charitable?"

"Perhaps not, Father," the visitor answered—too quickly? Too self-assured? "The truth goes beyond philanthropy. I believe God has called me to help your poor orphans. I have considerable expertise, and they carry considerable burdens which, you must admit, are too often impossible to relieve. Thankfully they have saints like yourself and the Church to heal their souls. Consider me a humble assistant, tending to their bodily salvation."

"You're from a big city. Yet you've traveled the rural ways far."

The doctor noticed that Onderdonkalitis' hands, formerly hid under the table, were constantly on the mysterious move — seemed to be practicing for a lame shadow-puppet performance.

"O I have, looking for somewhere I can make a difference."

"I am glad," Onderdonkalitis said. "Most people wouldn't come through here unless they were on the run from someone or something. We are not on any maps and I don't expect to host a cartographer in the near future. And especially a man of your background and learning. It is curious…"

His eyes had hardly any sclera and probed Dr. Chapman's face as he answered:

"On the run? O no, Father. Say rather… on the walk, on the stroll. A pilgrim doesn't run, or he'll get too tired and expire before he reaches his destination."

"Can you put that less poetically?" the Lithuanian asked with gentle, sharp humor.

"I'm sorry?"

"Less like horseshit." He was waiting for him to reply with an almost maternal, encouraging patience and didacticism. "Please, go on."

Chapman flushed. He lowered his eyes and spoke haltingly, like a schoolboy reciting his Latin declensions:

"I'm a doctor. I became a doctor to be of use, and right now I am of no use to anyone. But here…"

Onderdonkalitis smiled; he believed Chapman.

"Father, would you mind telling me something else of this place? I came upon your Cirkle's Way quite by chance."

"Yes, our little town… I am wanted shortly for an inspection of the Onanist's Dormitory but I do have time for a synopsis."

"May I ask why there is such a large factory here, in this isolated, unmapped place?"

A grim smile rippled across Onderdonkalitis' face.

"I have also pondered that, Doctor," he said, his large hands suddenly bursting open like pink-and-white fireworks in the air above his head before returning restively to the desktop.

"Your conclusion?"

"Because there are factories everywhere, in much the same way as smallpox, deceit, orphans, and vengeance. Actually, you may be able to help where that factory is concerned, as well. Many of the workers— most of the townspeople—have the phossy-jaw. Sickened from handling phosphorous at the Scratchfyre factory...

"While we're on the subject, I should also warn you about something in advance, so you don't get a fright at night: As more and more Cirkle's Way residents have contracted that disfiguring malady over the years, it's become common to see lambent green spots floating through the dark street as half-faced factory workers finish 18-hour shifts."

Chapman frowned.

"Did I say something wrong, Doctor?"

"No, Father. No. It's just... the devil is an accomplished devil."

"Yes. But one thing he's not, is an accomplished healer. So I'm glad you've offered your services. May you make a great difference here. And lucky for us all, we have many empty rooms. And I have piles."

III. Here Comes Etcetracaine!
The Dark Wintering was written to be read only by individuals on their death-beds who will either i) be unable to lucidly understand, and/or ii) act on its suggestions, such as: every straight line is the edge of sundial shadow; love is mutually unrequited guilt; that we live in a system of punishments eternally implemented, without reference to penal code. If you do not want to comprehend these and similar truths; if you do not want to make the world even worse; if you have more than a few days to live – then you must not read any further. After Chapter III there is no turning back.
    — The Dark Wintering, Chapter III.

January 1, 1864
    Love at only sight is the only love.
    Love at first sight, for example, can be re-created or at least approximated somehow — a 2nd, 3rd, 1,000th glimpse, &c. But love at only sight is pure.
    Well. I couldn't save her — helped do the opposite, perhaps — and the gratitude I received that awful day ironic to its black core. Hard to imagine redemption after that day. Well I must try. I suppose the next best thing would be to save the world. I only wish I could forget her sister's "thank you, Doctor, thank you." Sometimes it comes at me from nowhere, and reminds me of the evil I've done.
    More irony: This place full of books not worth a snail's dowry is where I will lift Science Itself to undreamed of heights. First, I will complete my preliminary investigations. After this, the hard part: Finding subjects to test the nostrum. I am finally ready to begin replacing the shaky foundation of *Materia Medica*.

January 2, 1864
    This is the perfect site. Large, deserted, well-lit, many needed implements and compounds ready-to-hand. It's no surprise that while preparing the laboratory I found many ridiculous, superstitious books, but one caught my more serious attention. Although irrational and backwards as anything in Paracelsus or John Dee, certain passages turned my mind in a new and useful direction. I've found that when I

become stuck on a problem of method or even substance, merely skimming a few pages engenders the little breakthroughs needed to continue my advance.

The book is called *The Dark Wintering* and written by that Otto Johngreatgrandson fellow I've heard both so much and so little about in Cirkle's Way. It is a bizarre text—easy enough to see that from the enigmatic symbol embossed on the cover:

I hardly know how to classify it; I suppose it is occult in nature, though it claims otherwise:

Is this book a work of science, then? Not strictly speaking. Nor is it magic, as understood in the crude sense of the term. It is another discipline altogether. My teachers are beyond names, past recognition, impossible to refer to – they are not even "they," since that term is quantitative, and those of whom I speak cannot be numbered. For lack of more suitable words, say they are the Powers of &c. Better still, keep silent.

From this outré prolegomena, Johngreatgrandson grows a theory of what he calls the *&c. Principle*.

August 20, 1864

Thanks in part to *The Dark Wintering's* stimulating (if fanciful) influence (especially Chapters IV, VIII, VII and X), I've begun refining an unprecedented method—exciting myself to Apollonian overexertion; I grow paler and thinner by the day (not thin enough!). It's as though I'm transforming into an entirely new species, living in a rare, inexplicable environment: air is my food, white phosphorous my sunrise and red for sunset—sleep, I call rumination—dreaming is deduction. Soon I must get some human rest.

Fortunately the orphanage doesn't occupy many hours. It's easy enough to escape on the pretense of a refreshing walk, or to say I'm studying the local flora for vulnerary properties. I know the orphans do not trust me and take pains to avoid my general area, which is excellent as far as free time goes. This may relate to my policy—once broken, O Lord!—of not looking my patients directly in the eyes. In any case, my interactions with them are quite brief. As long as I continue to treat Onderdonkalitis' flaring piles, I come and go like a ghost.

December 6, 1867

Progress! The road ahead is long but I cannot help but put some of my findings to onto the substantiality of journal-paper.

In short, I have discovered that because my anodyne is designed to cure ALL maladies, both existent and non-existent, I must never attempt to test its efficacy on empirical human subjects. This would be to introduce the particularities of each individual's reaction to the compound into my understanding of its effects; the completely wrong method to produce a drug designed to be universally effective.

In other words, the problem with the empirical method is that it is limited by empiricism. At the same time, however, I must not regress into some mediaeval, absurdly deductive system of investigation. The way I have discovered, with no little help from Otto Johngreatgrandson—is far too abstruse to explain in the context of this brief entry. Perhaps it can be distilled, however inadequately, into this motto:

DO NOT TEST IT—PERFECT IT.

Another advantage of this new approach to praxis, is that it keeps me at a far remove from touching, even peeping into anyone's wet secret places. It has taken away an ounce of my guilt, and that is far more than I ever dreamed possible.

January 4, 1868

Sometimes I've felt like a tin monkey with wind-up lifespan, tasked with a phantom's extratemporal errand. But I endured—and I am close.

Soon I will secure a place among the Titans of History's Healers, next to Hippocrates and Galen, Jesus and Schnipesticles.

~~Anemia, angina, asthma, carcinoma, cholera, convulsive dyspepsia, cystitis, delirium tremens, gastric~~

catarrh, insomnia, lumbago, neuralgia, nycaltopia, pericarditis, self-pollution, &c. &c... Ha! Hee! The list can never have enough *&c.* to suggest the infinite maladies of which it will be the destroyer, even those plagues not yet spread, an etcetera to include all future pestilences, applicable to every disease of which the human frame is subject, and also to the cure of disease in horses and cattle. I see now what Johngreatgrandson meant about the *&c. Principle*. It is absolutely needed to represent the wide reach of the solution, but nothing incarnate has ever encompassed infinity before—a new, infinitely grander conception of &c. is needed.

October 7, 1868
    ETCETRACAINE!
    My impending miracle now properly dubbed:
    How can I describe it?
    &c. (Etcetera) is a self-contradictory glyph. Consider: 1) That which is limited can be fully enumerated and cataloged; 2) That which is infinite, cannot. But etcetera, disregarding all logic, proposes to 3) Represent both limitation and infinity. &c. is a dismissive gesture and infects all branches of knowledge and praxis—not only the medical.
    Take, for example, the following list:
    "Tortoise-shell; bovine horns and hoofs; twinning saw; bone; &c."
    Anyone reading this suggestive inventory will immediately recognize that the etcetera here is meant to indicate any unstated items, limited to the class of "items related to the manufacture of hair-combs, such as hawk's-bill turtle shell; loggerhead turtle-shell; wooden clamps; dye of Nicaragua..." At the same time, the &c. in this list—as in all lists—pretends to extend those very unnamed items to infinity.
    In the context of medical diagnosis, etcetera might try to hoodwink us with a list of symptoms, such as: "fever, swelling, gastric pains, &c." What could be simpler to understand?
    Yet I write as though it were real. I must remember always that until I have perfected the formula, it can be said to be little more than a vivid dream. Dreams—colorful

nothingness, leviathans held at bay by the thinnest eyelid skin.

I only pray that Hextly's Brigade does not find me before then, and interrupt my Great Work before it can be accomplished. I am "Harold Chapman" here—I think this is my seventh or eighth alias; until now, I've made it my habit to invent a new one every three months, just to be safe. Why "Harold Chapman?" No idea. It's so innocuous. I know Hextly will not stop looking for me until he sees me tortured and dead. I wonder what manner of bog is on the menu tonight?

IV. The Possession of Perceval Raptus

Our sins, though enormous, must remain unnamable — and therefore inexculpable — because they are committed in a godless universe.
— The Dark Wintering, Chapter IV.

On the night of December 5, 1868 — five years after he collapsed on the orphanage steps — Perceval stood in the dinner line with his fellow WYMIN, listening to clinquant hail at the eaves. It was one week into that relentless blizzard that had made the violent, spring storm of 1861 seem like a cool mouse queef. Out there beyond the thin asylum walls, men and mercury alike were freezing solid, snowfall breaking obscene records. In the cities, whores and cut-throats traipsed like angels over tree-tops bridged by icebroken boughs. Hundreds were perishing without coal, shelter, or bread. Skylines from Newport to Baltimore thickly faded into fossil moonscapes.

Perceval was in a weird mood, left brain daydreaming and the right blank. The priests liked him; he looked like a good person because he would've been one, if things had been different. And he was quiet and kept to himself.

Perceval didn't notice his turn had come until Thingstable's high whine spattered his cochlea:

" — he said next!"

At the serving table, Perceval held out his lunch bowl/ dinner bowl/ spittoon/ bedpan/ rat bath/roach lake, to receive a dollop of hot, graveolent mire.

The cavernous meal-room stunk of carbolic soap, through which wafted a vaguely rectal smell that could be plausibly described as Kraken farts. A spectacular, 1:1 scale replica of the cross and its hammered Nazarene overpowered the room like an eye-rattling EVERYTHING MUST GO sign.

A butcher-blocky, rectangular table nearly bisected the chamber. It was an orderly accretion of surplus adult smallpox coffins; unmodified infant coffins served as seating for the WYMIN, and when they sat, their chins barely cleared the table's edge. Lunch and dinner, the boys on either side were able to watch a convincing illusion of decapitated heads slurping ooze opposite them, as they ate their own.

As was their ritual prior to meals, the WYMIN put down their bowls at their assigned spots and gathered in an ovoid formation round the table. Father Onderdonkalitis stood outside the perimeter of young men and beneath the crucifix; he waved a large hand that cast an all-enveloping hush. Perceval found the warden's hands so striking that they had a place of importance, recognition and identity normally reserved for faces. They never stopped dancing like mistrained elephants.

The bruise-faced lads stood quietly as lice-raided, pre- and post-sodomized bodyscratchers possibly can.

Perceval had rarely been able to distinguish between that which he hated from what he felt indifferent. But now the certainty of hate came upon him.

It had something to do with this priestly, externally-mandated silence.

Suddenly his right brain rose up from daydream to vision and his left was transfigured from blankness to limitless space... Like anything you don't want to put into words, it was hard to find words for it... To be forced to *feel* the same as others, to be sad or grateful with them, to believe, refute, suffer or celebrate *en masse*. In this imposed togetherness, Perceval was aware that he must do more than pretend — must pretend not to be pretending — he must deceive... or something... maybe he was just hungry...

But no. Just as Father Onderdonkalitis was about to end the ritual with an "Amen" — an unheralded energy *flushed* through Perceval, administered thrilling enemas to every atom. He was *cleared* and resolute... He'd never sung out loud before — was this an about-to-sing feeling? Vision merged with infinite, empty space... Perceval stared straight ahead, seeing nothing and not needing sight, like a figure on a prow... You sit in a sunny, private place and the lid of the box comes off easily without hubris but revelation and surprise, surprise! Huge bright words dashed off his astronomical tongue like stars, each word was an earsplitting event:

"WHO DIED AND MADE JESUS GOD EVEN IF YOU'RE SAVED IT DOESN'T MEAN YOU'RE SAFE GOD IS

NOWHERE AT ONCE HIS SOLE FUNCTION IS TO PROVIDE THE MORAL SUPPORT NEEDED TO THOSE WHO HAVE JUST SNEEZED CAN YOU GET AN IMMACULATE DOSE OF THE CLAP GOD CAN GO TO HELL—AND YOU CAN ALL GO TO CHURCH ONLY FOUR-LETTERED WORDS ARE MADE INTO FLESH... FUCK FUCKFUCK CAN WE JUST EAT ALREADY SHIT GARDDAMN."

The episode ended as quickly as it had arrived. Perceval returned to his place in the ovoid of orphans and wondered why the WYMIN were looking at him with holy terror in their abandoned eyes. He vaguely thought it doesn't matter what you say... it's not the message, but the messaging... it was hard to explain.

The melodramatic writhings of the warden's hands broke Perceval's hypnostate. They traveled to his navel, where the thick fingers warped into threatening, interlocking gestures equal parts church-steeple, condor swoop, and creelful of snakes. His tall, thin form shook under his robes as though made from wild jets of air. Onderdonkalitis had flushed dog-dick puce and his lean face somehow projected the demonstrative quivering of a furious fat person.

"Wha..." Perceval said.

And then everything was suddenly wielding exclamation points like great cudgels, and not afraid to use them, either (e.g., Fisticuffs! Smack! Kick! Owtch! Scold! Kick! Kick! Slam! Throw! Good-Bye! Wait! Not Yet! Here's Your Stupid Cloak and Bag! Spit! Good-Bye! Forever!). And when the colored lights melted into midnight like sight into blindness, his brain slid across a ballroom floor of ice, twirling alone in the dark while beneath, cold-horned currents tried to stab waltzes through their ceiling... He was outside, on his knees. He wretched up some gutty blood, shook some splintered coffin cover out of his hair. Standing up and wiping some of his nosebleed with the back of his dry hand, he wrapped himself tightly in the cloak and shouldered his carpetbag. With relief he confirmed Peter Shit-Head was inside.

The world had grown a cold exoskeleton, the opaque, gleaming, relentlessly transparent colors of dreams about drowning, and still as an expired cephalopod. Weathervanes turned north in iron solidarity of beaks, hooves, heads, prows, the letter N, manes and arrows. And then the volleys of stinging hail started again, millions of subzero balls ripping Cirkle's Way entirely superfluous assholes.

After twenty minutes treading through the quickly accumulating snow, his legs ached stiffly as two priapatic willies. Huffing, face damp and uvula-red, wind on his eyes like cold pennies. Gradually, the phantom angles of a building in the fractured blur. A shop not far down the indiscernible road. The long, rectangular building boasted a narrow overhanging thatch — provisional shelter.

A sign on the door:
MANUFACTURER OF FERRULES & DRAPER &
SHEAR GRINDER &c.

He was exhausted but sleep = death. The snow was piling up fast around him and the air was a curdled haze. Perceval needed a more acceptable enclosure. In this illogical night there was only one logical choice:

Otto Johngreatgrandson's library.

He'd have to risk the possibility of catching smallpox. As for all those rumors the library was haunted — they'd started circulating about a year after he'd first arrived in Cirkle's Way — that didn't scare him, of course. Since sometime in 1864 and ever since, strange red and blue lights had been reported coming from within, flashing across lifeless windows…

He plunged into the white shit again and soon had lost all sense of direction. After a while he stopped to catch his breath and the wind suddenly whirled *up* with tremendous force like a humpback lunging its bulk to crest the sea; then fell just as fast. As the air cleared he could see a little better; the snow had descended into starry curves and piles in a bewildering range of shapes, and dramatically varied in height like the pipes of grand cathedral organs.

Then Perceval noticed a trinity of dim, greenish

luminescences seeping through the gauzy air. The faint lights were spaced unevenly apart from each other, with two closer together on the right side — but all were the same size and set at the exact same level. It was this observation that told him he must head their way to reach the library.

The Daztgarham quadruplets lived in a house on the far eastern edge of Cirkle's Way. Once the four handsome identical brothers had formed a popular ventriloquist group, each with his own identical dummy reposed upon his lap. But when the biloquist rage passed in '64 they were penniless. They wound up in Cirkle's Way and took jobs at the Scratchfyre factory. They came down with the phossy jaw years ago, and their conditions had worsened considerably since. Not without humor, the Phossy 4 hacked up their dummies' faces into opisthognathous self-likenesses...

The green lights that Perceval descried through the frantic snow flared at the exact same level in the murk, like three lanterns set on a flat tabletop... it could only be 3/4 of The Phossy 4 at their window.

Perceval headed their direction but as the crazy, black blizzard-magic started pulling lumps out of straight lines, he lost track of time and his way but didn't stop walking and the ground beneath his feet changed texture, gave spongy resistance. Buckled wood? Perceval knelt. Not wanting to take his hands out from the comparative warmth of his cloak, he lowered his face and probed with the tip of his nose... planks... a nail in the nostril. It must be pieces of the stable, not far behind the Daztgarhams' house. It meant he was still going toward the library, but he needed to tread carefully.

It would be a small relief to just crawl forward a while, partially sheltered from the wind by fallen stable walls. He numbly elbowed on... horseshoes? Frozen hay... pitchfork tines and shingles. Perceval's head knocked against something hard. Hairy? He wiped away icy integuments: the head of a corpse. It did not disturb him. The dead were like us, only more so. Intrigued, his fingers trawled around: The slight indentation where the ears take cartilaginous root... eminent cheekbone, leptorrhine nose... a frosty moustache, leading to the mucronated edge of a chipped incisor—and his hand suddenly dropped, striking the granite-hard Adam's apple of a very stiff neck.

The 4th Daztgarham.

He jerked his hand away, only to grab the hard mass of a horripilated buttock. What had this phossy-jawed fellow been doing out in the stable, under this sky of angel vomit—without pants?

Answer: The quadruplet had been sodomizing a stallion. The animal's horsehood like a fallen Doric column. Two lovers—worlds apart in life—yet, in dying, joined inextricably through the enormous lack of any world at all.

It was clear from the cadaver's face that he'd died ecstatically; this was the more disturbing because his jawless situation should've rendered such definite emotional expression impossible. Suddenly a snowy gust thwacked Perceval's head into the late ventriloquist's bony back. A sharp retort of cracking ice—the earth moved and the missing landscape, already an upside-down void, twisted in unnamable directions.

And Perceval was horse-sledding down the steep hill at incredible speed, toward the library... While in their shanty, the living 75% of the Daztgarhams wondered when their brother was coming back so they could get their turns. Why was he taking so long—Mr. 4-Second Phossy himself!?

V. The Blanket Hornpipe

"It's got my name, but I know that's not enough to prove its worth. After all, every dead liar's tombstone's got their name on it!"
 — Harold Chapman, 1868

There's one whorehouse in New Toomes, and there's a funny, wrestling pain in Harper Noolan's naked chest — an avian excitement and a man's fear of falling from a cathedral spire. There's longing and transformation in the musky, dim-flickered air... Ella-Rae has left the room for one adjacent, with faux smile of anticipation and the promise of quick return. Sitting at the foot of the greasy bed, Harper hears water splash in a basin, drip meek to bare boards. The lewd noise of neighboring business alternates with schoolboy fantasies of droplets striking, rolling off Ella-Mae's skin.

Try to relax. This is the only time you play the blanket hornpipe for the first time. But he's got nerves, his hands are starting to shake — what if she laughs at him like he's Stanford Grost? Hey — waitaminute — he's still got that nostrum in his pocket — that stuff he'd bought just today along with everyone else. The man with the green eyes said it would cure anything — even neuralgia — even obstacles to virile release...

Ella-Rae's soft voice:

"Be there in a second, hon."

"Take your time. Sure."

Harper quickly gets the packet from his coat where it hangs from the red chair where nobody had ever sat. He snorts a pinch of black powder up his nose.

Sneeze!

"Bless you," she says, wearing nothing but a chewed-up possum stole.

She pushes him back on the bed.

He feels things change beneath her barely furry form. His head lightens. The hairs of her stole tremble lightly like cilia. Their tips lit in soft orange light from the candle beyond. The bristles sway with purpose. He's an idle parasite inside an organism.

Though her palms and his skin are touching naked he feels something separating the two. He wonders what, but it's pointless because really there's no word for this ignorance, the astounding depth of his not-knowing-her, far deeper than the rift between strangers passing on the street.

Maybe the Etcetracaine wasn't junk, because he's calm and steady now, and he's *almost* Harper Noolan. But not quite... Her chest rises and falls. He seems to stand in a lake up to his eyes, peering at a wave about to cover his head...

Ella-Rae is on top, but he is inside?

Why doesn't it feel good yet, down there?

She's pulling her black hair tightly behind her ears. Her blue eyes are pretty like a lobster's that never close and can't see very far and always see too near.

Now Harper feels something down there — everywhere. Is that how it works? It's hot. His blood circulates with the river Nile. His blood gets lost in shadowy eddies. His saliva dammed, his tongue dry as shale quarries... his blood laps in a gentle April way against the sides of his veins.

"You OK?" Ella-Rae says.

"I-M -POSSIBLE," he stutters, his body jelly.

His body cataleptic as knots in wood.

"Wha—"

Two dark, lidless eyes gleam up at Ella-Rae. There is the slightest bit of humanity in them — that of an arsonist watching a churchful of children burn, finding the conflagration wasn't magnificent enough, the screams not as tormented as he'd hoped — but mostly they are ugly like lobster eyes...

"Hey. You sick? Are you OK..."

He's not. Ella-Rae springs backward and off the bed, hitting the floor with a slam and benumbed coccyx. He has no face, no face... but the eyes grow, eager tumors from the flanks of a giant tongue. It writhes and twists and drowning spit froths over the eyes, black seas discharging poisoned tides.

He rears up to loll against and lick the ceiling tin, thicker at the eye-encysted tip, tapering to a wedding-band thin pink nub at its source in the mouth, which is also his tail and his feet. This mouth is the most horrible thing about the creature that was Harper Noolan: It's far too small to express the rage and satisfy the hunger which so clearly fills its tuberous host to bursting. It opens no more than mewing kitten jaws.

He has no body... his body has disappeared into itself.

Is that water spreading? Did she piss in terror?

She remembers there's no living without trying, springs up and runs through the sloshing famine. Half-way out the door the teeniest, most precious mouth nibbles an inch of skin off her heel. The bite immediately begins dancing or something. Now she's made it down the stairs and crumpled in a heap. Bassy questions, squeaky, nasal queries... what happened? He cut you with a knife? She hears herself reply something like, can you just imagine how many terrible weeks it would take for that tiny mouth to chew you up, while you slowly went from fresh to rotten, conscious meat... A deep-throated, baritone question: What the hell does that mean?

Ella-Rae recognizes Mary Carson's voice cutting through the others. Mary's the kindest friend a girl could have:

"Here, try this black powder I bought from that charming physician-man today. Maybe that will help the pain. Sniff it off my finger..."

Ella-Rae's pain is smiling or something in thrilling anticipation... Someone tumbles down the staircase in gray fractures and lands with his head next to hers; they could almost be lying back on the bed after an exhausting session. Ella-Rae's ribcage grins widely...and as the room swirls away she sees good-hearted Mary Carson giving the last of her &c! to the pale young man with the stare of a prosthetic head. She daubs it under his nostrils and he inhales deeply. Ella-Rae sees him smile too. No, wait—smiles are opening on everything, the floor, the wall, the air, he has no face...

Now she blacks out.

VI. Cleanliness is next to Godliness / Godliness is the Grandest Filth

All things are poison, and nothing is without poison;
Only the dose permits something not to be poisonous.

> — Philippus Aureolus Theophrastus Bombastus von
> Hohenheim (Paracelsus), as cited in The Dark
> Wintering, Chapter VI.

The autumn of 1861, so Fayteyant overhead a popular colleague quip, had come unwanted to New York, trees turning all the colors of immigrant flesh, red and yellow and brown, unloading swarthy leaves, flooding streets like the swarms of prognathous Italians daily shuttled from Castle Garden, overinfesting Manhattan Island's most pestilential zones.

At that time Doctor Nathaniel Fayteyant, M.D., D.D.S., F.R.S, K.T.S, Y.H.W.H., Fellow of the Chicago & New York & Hartford & Massachusetts Academies of Medicine; Member of the Court of Examiners of the Royal College of Surgeons of England; Honorary Member of the Berlin Odontologischen Gesellschaft; Advisory Sexton Extraordinary to H.R.H. Edward VII &c., was practicing and serving as Chief Professor of Anatomy & Toxicology, Chemical Reactions & Productions, Department of the Taint, Left-Buttock & Uterus; as well as Special Lecturer in Surgery of the Extremities at Columbia University's College of Physicians and Surgeons, &c. &c. He'd also just published what became his most popular work: *When Pyaemia Supervenes Upon Shiv Gangrene in "The New York Halls of Justice and House of Detention," the Urine Assumes a Most Beautiful Pink Color, from the Great Destruction of the Colored Blood Corpuscles, Induced by the Presence of Pus in the Blood, & Sundry Other Observations &c. &c. Second Edition. Revised & Considerably Expanded.*

It was an exciting period. In addition to the ever-increasing esteem of his peers and rapidly growing list of surgical accomplishments, he was in the midst of working on a compound that, if perfected, would cure *all* diseases. Although Fayteyant would generally scoff at such a notion, certain happy mistakes made during recent toxicological experiments, had led him to believe it was possible—and that he was just the man to do it. Imagine how he could change the world…

One day that October, he was due at the College to demonstrate his pioneering methods of reducing the probability of systole in patients undergoing the *abdominal paracentesis* operation.

It was quite early in the morning, strawberry blonde light softening the city's edges. Not two paces out the door, Fayteyant ran right into the muscular chest of an enormous man dressed all in black. He didn't apologize, stepped silently backwards to let Fayteyant by.

The stranger had one lazy blue eye that made it impossible to determine his motives. His face overall was characterized by asymmetry wherever features come in pairs. One eye, for example, was exceedingly large, the other incongruously scrunched, like a hideous planet and its dissolute moon. His jug-handled ears stood close to 90 degree angles to his skull. Three quarters of his stumpy nose were dyed a shade of claret. He had scarcely any lips and Fayteyant shivered when the man skull-grinned at him with mocking civility.

Standing to his right and stretching all down the block was a long line of men dressed identically to the ominous brute, suggesting a platoon of undertakers or bizarre dance troupe.

The giant nodded agreeably in a very disagreeable way. Fayteyant rushed off to his surgical demonstration. Who was that fellow? And his little army? The whole business was incomprehensible.

A young nurse greeted Fayteyant as he entered *The Horace Gravelspitz Hextly Theatre of Comparative Anatomy*. He saw no reason to reciprocate. Crowded in the observation stands above, 106 enraptured students waited to catch a glimpse of the magisterial surgeon at work.

In the center of the Olympian chamber was a wooden table; decumbent upon it an unconscious and naked octogenarian. He had a wild, holy-man aura about him, and in his dull, grey boiled-gooseberry eyes, one might learn to believe that Cleanliness is next to Godliness because Godliness is the Grandest Filth.

His abdomen was grossly distended as though a beaver curled upon his greater *omentum*. The surface was spotted with veins bullied by the peritoneal inflations of his cirrhosis. The engorged carmine *caput medusae* of serious ascites…

Now Fayteyant looked up to acknowledge the ambitious young men gathered like beggars in the gallery. He enjoyed their attention, the easy with which he thrilled them with a mere head-nod. It helped him shake off his h(a)unted feeling and remember how much he loved his work. In fact, it was an absolute fetish with him. He was fortunate that his own personal perversion could only be satisfied through socially celebrated acts of healing. He saved people from death while secretly enjoying himself with inexorable lewdness:

Inhaling air coughed and recoughed a million contagious times; feeling hideous parvenus with exophthalmic eyes blinking oblations at the Bedside Asclepius of him, brimming with begging for vulnerary grace; reading the Braille of skin maculated with cheloid suppurations; prodding cartilaginous intestines for belemnoid calcifications; lancing spitting pustules; embrocating the deep, rigid, redly strigose anal grooves of octogenarian piles…

Typically, Fayteyant was deadpan as aluminum. But today he was uncharacteristically distracted and vexed at himself for it. The inappropriately familiar grin of the asymmetrical stranger — irritated like an elusive strand of hair stuck to his sclera. But it was nothing…

Now doctor approached patient with lighter step.

"Here before us, we see… what do you perceive? Not a pregnant female; but rather here is a man with acute abdominal dropsy in severe need of the *paracentesis abdominis* operation. First we will withdraw the fluid from his abdominal cavity…"

Fayteyant inserted the trocar, porting the old man's venous side. He suppressed his visceral delight; surgery was the pinnacle, the most invasive form of voyeurism — to pry into both the boggiest, friable and hardest parts of a person, places even they cannot reach. And to be able to indulge in this pleasure publically—while lesser voyeurs watch you satisfy the lurid urge! What perversion could excite more?

"Notice he makes no protest. Ether—and whiskey, no doubt! Now, let us see what ails our old Struwwelpeter…"

"—Shaft your Strudel-peppers!" a man barked and burst into the theatre, his sweaty face pink-flushed as an overvacuumed nipple, two blue eyes amphetagleaming, and a third, bright eye of green set in a ring on the middle-finger of his right hand. A pair of different rings flanked this finger-mounted, ocular prosthesis, each displaying perse, Grandidierite orbs with the circle/arrow/dot symbol for Uranus inlaid upon them in gold.

He was an imposing and gigantic man, and he strode up to Fayteyant and put his hands on his hips as though well-acquainted with supervising the labor of thousands:

Colonel Horace Gravelspitz Hextly—The Goat King of Madison Avenue.

The colonel was a man to whom no doors were closed—he owned them all. Having first made his fortune in goats, he subsequently invested—like carbon itself—in practically everything—and everything practical. His daughter, Leta Hextly, was a rising star of the music world, a virtuoso pianist.

That the most powerful man in the City knew Fayteyant's name distended the doctor's pride as with acute abdominal dropsy. Whatever this Mammon wanted of him, to refuse Hextly's wishes = career suicide. He wiped the bloody, silver-plated cannulae of the trocar on his coat-tails, tossed it to the nurse, who caught it with a groan as it sliced her palm, a swift spurt of her blood baptizing Fayteyant across the surface of several anatomical systems. The doctor cried to her to finish the operation for him. As he rushed off to change the colonel said there was no time.

Raising his walking stick above his top hat like an Aquila, Hextly led them down the stairs so quickly that the old man's screams of agony in Fayteyant's ears died away much sooner than the patient. Next thing Fayteyant knew, the bright autumn day had been snuffed by Hextly's baize-curtained cab. They sat opposite each other. Only now did Fayteyant have a moment to take the measure of the man. Hextly wore a magnificent Ulster, immitigably solemn and alive, white hair dazzling—a Ziggurat with appetite. Fayteyant felt a growing sense of shame at his own dishabille state, nurse-blood exuding from his coat-tails and woolen thighs, and empurpling the Toile de Jouy cushions.

"Damn Indians," Hextly growled.

"O. What did they do now?"

"Nothing. That's just the problem. That's why I was down in Iquitos for the past eight months. Had to fire the whole lot from the plantation, lazy louts…"

"Rubber?"

"What else?"

"How tiresome for you. When did you return Stateside?"

"Why, just today, obviously! Why else would I be wearing these Wellington boots on Fifth Avenue?"

Fayteyant chuckled good-naturedly, not comprehending. However, the colonel's high leather boots *were* indeed crusty with what looked like dried mud—or something more pulverized and/or excremental.

"It's my daughter, Leta—if you were wondering," Hextly said.

"Leta Hextly! I am so very sorry your daughter is not well. I'm honored you called upon *me* with so many talented medical men in this city."

Hextly snorted violently.

His blue eyes were distant, travelling someplace nobody could hear a thing… the false green eye on his ring stared at the doctor, unblinking—smugly inanimate. Fayteyant noticed an identical ringband on Hextly's other hand, this one bereft of gemological adornment. It was strange that this powerful man should go about displaying unfinished jewelry on his finger… the doctor's eyes returned to the muddied Wellingtons and he decided to speak about that which he knew before he went mad with all he didn't.

"May I ask the nature of her condition?"

"Run down. A mess. Pipes clogged, viscous. The stench!"

100

Enemas? Enemas—have any been administered? Not tobacco-smoke enemas, I hope," Fayteyant said, sure of himself now—when *he* played the expert. "No matter how popular they may be at present, I must firmly declare such intervention as nothing but quackery—and of the most dangerous kind. I don't want to outrage but I *must* make my position clear on this treatment at the outset. Very dangerous and taken too lightly in the press. These health fads are no joke. No, there's nothing funny about what things should and should not go into your rectum, or what exits therefrom. Or even that which may be lodged in those quarters, howsoever and regardless of genesis, be it internal or external. And now that I think of it, in fact there's a fourth possible situation, in which—"

"—What? No, the *plantation* man. I had to bring my own men over for the plumbing. They cost more but that's how it is, I should know. Hard workers, Lithuanians, mostly...names like diseases to a man. *-itis* this and *-itis* that..."

Hextly reddened, grit perfect white teeth.

"The issue is *feminine* in nature, man," he said.

Fayteyant nodded.

"Uhm... I admire your daughter greatly—what exquisite virtuosity! Why I saw her not long ago, performing Liszt—*The Mephisto Waltz*, I believe. It was... very modern, but transporting—and it will be almost as much of an honor to meet her as it is to speak with you."

The colonel breathed and sporadically snorted, exactly like an enraged centaur with transplanted cetacean lungs.

"Do right by me and I'll have you appointed Manhattan Island Commissioner of Lunacy. One of the most powerful positions in the city—did you know you the C.O.L. can easily have his enemies committed to asylums of his choice? Within limits... you should see my balls, try to lift them."

Whenever Hextly spoke, Fayteyant could see Little Red Riding Hoods stuck between his teeth.

"Thank you, sir."

Hextly looked out his spotless window at his besotted

city.

"Think before you thank," Hextly answered, adding without segue:

"You should see my balls, Doctor. They'd give you a hernia if you tried to lift them and make me cough. I do not cough for anyone. Am I understood?"

Fayteyant nodded. He decided it best to shut up.

"Hextly Headquarters" was a contrived and glacial structure, extravagating over Madison and 37th Street, a window-studded monolith with Asscher-cut corners. It was a diamond ring on the finger of Manhattan Island, proof she belonged to Hextly's alone.

Hextly manhandled Fayteyant through oak doors, the scale of which suggested the combined labor of a several thousand slaves. The scale of the place was such that even the foyer induced vertigo; Atlantean staircases sprawled up to halls historiated with the *lusus naturae* of medieval bestiaries: detailed engravings of bewildering caladrius and echeneis, kraken, manticore, leucrota and—most worrisome—herds of mighty centaurs with Hextly's shocking-white hair and determined features, pounding the other monsters into extinction…

The overpowering smell of animal fat was general throughout the house. They mounted a spiral staircase that spanned several stories top to bottom. Fayteyant's hand was about to alight on the banister, only to have Hextly smack it down.

"Goat fat, man. Don't you know goat fat?"

"In itself—yes, Colonel."

"Well, I suppose I wouldn't be the Goat King of Madison Avenue without my little secrets. I'm holding a ball here in two weeks' time—Leta will be performing a recital. Nothing gives these banisters a shine like the goat fat. My fellows brush it on thick and no one is to touch it for four weeks. Then they polish it off with silk and you should see them gleam—keep up, man!"

They were swallowed by high archways dressed in elaborate cambric portières; upward over leagues of marble—

oriental smoking wing, three salons, velvet lamellated corridors where fantastic creatures seduced fluted columns; and then abruptly— like the tedious punchline to an interminable jest—they reached Leta's bedroom.

It was a warm blizzard dream, ivory and polished horn and mother-of-pearl; there was a gorgeous dressing-table and much cheval-glass. The gold-fringed sarsenet drapes of a porphyrine canopy-bed were pulled half-aside; Leta sat propped up against pillows, half-buried beneath a landslide of white eiderdown, staring absorbedly at nothing and paying their entrance no mind.

"There she is," the colonel said, not looking at her but the sky going nowhere outside a grand window. "I go away for eight months and this is what happens. You will fix this. She hasn't given a performance in almost a year—the public is fickle... Make sure she is right—and *looks* right—*before* the ball."

"Colonel, you said before that Leta was your eldest. How many other lovely daughters bless your life?"

"Just the one other. Vespertine."

"Well I hope I may have the pleasure to meet her too one day."

"That's easily arranged," Hextly said. "She's the top-notch secret agent preparing to wet herself behind that Japanese screen over there."

The ten toes of two small, bare feet faced the room from beneath the screen, pink and still as empty girl-slippers. The sunlight shifted through the window, and now Fayteyant noticed specks of broken glass, crystal, and modern Suhl porcelain littered across the floor in a fine, luxurious dust.

Disconcerted, Fayteyant remarked with sham buoyancy:

"O, but look over there. How unusual to have a piano in a bedroom. But of course when you are one of the finest musicians of the age, I suppose it makes sense!"

"It malconforms, Doctor," Hextly said. "And it's nothing but fifth rate—just a Steinway & Sons..."

"Is it?"

"So I've commanded you to understand. Nonetheless it is good enough for Leta to practice upon when mandated."

An impressive oil painting of the famous Daztgarham Quadruplet Ventriloquists and their dummies hung over the piano.

"O and the Daztgarhams… amazing entertainers."

"There I must concur, Doctor. I laugh myself to pieces every time I see their Knock-Knock routine… You know, the one — Boo?"

"Boo… *Who?*" the doctor second-fiddled.

"Exactly!"

The colonel grimaced in raucous approval, adding:

"Did you know they're horse-fuckers — every last four of them! Goats, too… I saw to that, of course!"

"Uhm. If I am to help I need my things, Colonel. I can examine Ms. Hextly, but then I must make arrangements to retrieve them from my lodgings. I can return posthaste."

"There's no need of that. Your tools of the trade are here already."

"I don't see how — "

"My man Bochkser and his men have taken care of it. They've been to your room, and everything's here already."

By this time Fayteyant had lost count of how many times he'd been confused into silence today. He stood rigidly, assuming an intense expression of diagnostic consideration.

"You know, Leta," Hextly said, acknowledging her for the first time," when the good doctor is done erasing your mistake I plan to make him Commissioner of Lunacy for Manhattan Island. That is, if anyone can find the poor man. I've heard *terrible* rumors…"

Leta continued to ignore him.

Hextly strode across the room to the Japanese screen and kicked it with a crusty Wellington boot — two dainty feet jumped out of sight, and they heard Vespertine slam into the wall behind her with a groan. Hextly spat at the fallen screen, striking the silky image of Mount Fuji.

"What do you think of that, Vespertine dear? Commissioner of Lunacy! Wouldn't *that* be splendid? The one currently in office isn't fit, is he? A real rat! Maybe he's gone missing in fact — run off with yet another whore. And don't think anyone would oppose me appointing Doctor Faint-at-heart here. I've got balls the size of Urānus!"

A rivulet of urine seeped out from beneath the screen, followed by another yet more urgently flowing. Hextly let it pool about his boots, laughed as grains of crystal and jade glinted in the faintly yellow translucence.

"*Now* do you understand why I wear these boots, Doctor? What a relief it must be to you, finding out I'm not crazy after all."

Fayteyant whinnied in a manner beyond embarrassing.

The Goat King of Madison Avenue approached. He towered before the doctor like a horse proctologist raised on his surgical platform behind his patient. Hextly's eyes were colorless, perforations in a railway ticket.

"I promise you a most comfortable stay, Doctor."

"I could not possibly — it's too magnanimous," Fayteyant stammered.

"Commissioner of Lunacy you say? It will be done! And look at this view! The prospect from your room is even more dazzling."

Fayteyant joined the billionaire to watch the nervous circulation of tiny figures on the streets below: An overcrowded tank of grasshoppers unwittingly waiting to fatten unsuspected snakes.

"I trust you, Doctor. You and I have enough in common for me to trust you."

"O sir, I cannot imagine…"

"We both love the dirtiest parts of our work, yes?" Hextly said with a leer. "O come now, Doctor… when I saw you poking holes in that old beggar today, I knew. Instead of roaring or calling out your Creator's name — instead of reckless release — *you* experience a state of control, unwavering confidence in the dexterous manipulation of your tools against strange flesh. Those innocent fools in the stands were unknowingly witnessing you in the throes of masterly prolonged orgasm — and you like to be watched, don't you?"

Fayteyant had no words.

"How could I tell? I'm the same way, man—I'm nearly always cumming my rich ass off—though unlike you, it's not easily hidden under the guise of benevolence. Don't worry. We're cut from the same stained cloth. I'm climaxing right now and I'm glad you are so dedicated a fetishist. It means you are the best at what you do. Because *I'm* the best at what I do. Your brain is a groin and your every thought licks it, yes? Your secret is safe with me. Your secret is why I trust you... O, and Doctor?"

"Yes, Colonel?"

"Don't dare blow smoke up my man-hams."

There was a sharp rap at the door, at which sound Hextly grabbed a celadon vase and dropped it to the floor. The door opened immediately upon its shattering.

Fayteyant recognized the asymmetrical man.

"Your medical bag, Doctor," he said, the voice quite ordinary. "Do let us know if you need anything else."

"Thank... you. That is fine for now."

"Now, I must go. Do attend her now—and do good work, by God. My man Bochkser here will attend to you. When you need him, simply look around and smash anything at all in this room—the more lovely, exquisite—the better. If he doesn't come right away, just destroy something equally fine... Balls like UrĀnus, Doctor! Good-day to you."

Bochkser followed Hextly out of the room.

When the servant shut the door behind them, Fayteyant splashed over to the screen. Cowering beneath was a young woman in tears, a line of blood bisecting her smooth chin from where she was biting her lower lip. There was something extraordinarily beguiling about her, but he wasn't sure why. He was a generally disinterested amateur in this area. He supposed she was "beautiful," but he'd never been physically attracted to women or any other living creature—at least not in the *Biblical* way.

Fayteyant extended soft hands to help her stand. She smiled, releasing her lip from her penetrating teeth.

"Thank you, Doctor. Thank you, thank you so much," she said, sweet and sincerely.

"There she goes again," Leta hissed. "Taking *everything*

106

from me. Getting all the attention. Even *medical* attention!"

Standing at her bedside, Fayteyant took in the details of her appearance slowly, as though calling each back from memory. As was his steadfast practice with his patients, he took great care not to look her in the eyes (He *never* let his eyes truly meet with those of a patient unless it was surgically necessary. Otherwise it introduced too personal an element to the relationship). Leta's head drooped slightly down from a long neck streaked with blue veins. Her tangled blonde hair was fine as rat urine. Her blue nightdress was six times too large for her severe frame. She was tall, thin but for the second distended belly of his day. He was repelled by her lips, dry like scorpion tails. Even such an amateur as he could tell Leta Hextly was quite as ugly as her idiot sister was not.

Money for the midwife.

Unmarried.

"Miss Hextly, this is a monumental honor. I am one of your most fervid admirers. Good afternoon. I am Doctor Nathaniel Fayteyant, M.D., D.D.S., F.R.S, K.T.S, Y.H.W.H., Fellow of the Chicago & New York & Hartford & Massachusetts Academies of Medicine; Member of the Court of Examiners of the Royal College of Surgeons of England; Honorary Member of—"

"—O, just toss off."

"Uhm? O… O. How long have you been heavy with child?"

Seething silence.

"I'm only here to help…"

Fayteyant bent down to retrieve a vial of silvery, pea-sized pellets from his black bag. He held it up with a forced smile, keeping his eyes focused on the cranial region just above her *glabella*.

"Don't fear; I'm both a skilled obstetrician and apothecary. *This* is an abortifacient of my own creation—tested quite safe, for all stages of gestation. A variant of Diachylon, though more efficacious—I've replaced the litharge of gold, fenugreek seed and gum ammoniac with, well… The *point* is we *will*… uhm, resolve your condition with minimal pain to your person—and your *person*."

"Fucking exit."

"*Please*. You know I really am a devotee of your music, I think the world of you."

"O really? Well the world's a living hell…"

"Ah… hardly my point, I'm afraid. But to proceed: is it six or seven? *Months*, I mean… You are rather far along, which brings peculiar difficulties…"

She pulled some crystal bauble from canopied shadows, threw it across the room to a leopard chair, where it shattered over Vespertine's wincing head in a glassy spray.

Fayteyant's nerves flinched, and his buzzing fingers dropped the tube.

Vespertine shrieked as if slapped.

The door swung open.

"You rang?" Bochkser said.

Leta had disappeared beneath her silky white blankets.

"I… yes. Our initial consultation is over."

Bochkser graciously got his bag, and Fayteyant willingly let him escort him to his suite. It was filigree-gilt, mirror paneled, with more velvet-carpeted sequestrations than all samovars in Russian literature. His apparatuses, chemical jars, books and other materials were arranged about the room. His recent universal cure-all experiments, his poisons. Somewhat disconcertingly, his wardrobe was there, too — his tobacco, his journals — literally *everything*…

Except his sense of control.

The situation was sticky as gleety pricks stuck in honey. This concatenation of mysteries wasn't medical and therefore out of his line. The sooner he could be done with Leta, the quicker could he return to his experiments toward a universal cure for the biological miseries of humankind… the people had an uncouth and frankly scandalous attitude toward domestic valuables, Vespertine, a fearful, pissing refugee in her own house, Leta's vulgar bellicosity; Hextly's planetary testicles, goat fat, green-eyed ring… the Commissioner of Lunacy… Fayteyant had actually met the man once, there was something extraordinary about him, but he couldn't quite recall — did the man have a ridiculous name? He couldn't place it, and fell asleep.

He woke in the middle of the night to a candle waving above him, portions of Vespertine's charming features bobbing in and out of its light, like face-fragments juggled in a tidal pool.

"What is it?" he groggled, clearing his throat.

She moved the candle so only her mouth was visible. Her lips arched like raised eyebrows and she pressed a vial of black and red pellets against them in a shushing finger gesture.

"Be careful! That's deadly poison. What were you doing in my bag? What's going on? Did you swallow any?"

"No, Doctor... Thank you, Doctor. Thank you... thank you."

Fayteyant felt her place the vial in his cold hand.

The candle went out; a kiss faintly wet his forehead; in the darkness he heard the door open and close again. He sat up and pulled his bag from under the bed and returned the toxin to its rightful compartment. He fell asleep again and dreamed there was no such thing as man-hams. He dreamed Leta Hextly hadn't told him to toss-off.

When he woke the next day, the only dream he recalled was one in which Vespertine shooshed him with a vial of toxins and kissed him. Such nonsense was easily shaken away and he soon regained his usual steely calm. After Bochkser brought him a delicious breakfast he enlisted the agreeably servile ogre in his scheme. That afternoon Fayteyant and Bochkser visited Leta's room. The doctor took his tube of abortifacient from his bag and pocketed the cork. Leta was mute and sullen and appeared unaware of their presence.

Enormous Bochkser straddled her body and pried her mouth wide open. A hoarsely prehistoric vocalization came out. This Fayteyant muffled by gently inserting a rubber funnel between her dry lips, which resembled the hardened corpses of earthworms who'd been squashed underfoot.

"I apologize. But I *must* do what your father wants," he addressed the funnel. "Now, I am going to pour the contents of this tube through here, but the abortifacient will dissolve as it greets your posterior pharynx. So you are in no danger of asphyxiation. Ready…"

He tilted the glass and little silver beads of bromides, chloral hydrate, hyocyamine, physostigma, cannabis indica, amyl nitrate, conium, digitalis, ergot, pilocarpine, snailwallis root, &c. rolled down the rubber to pelt her throat.

"Thank you, Bochkser. Just a few left… stop moving your head — *stupid girl!*"

The very last pellets out to go down were red and black. He'd *never* be so incautious. Fayteyant couldn't help but look at her eyes, now. They were sharkly open, pupils dilating and constricting in time to her careening heartbeat. Without exception, every pellet in the dispensing vial should've been silver.

Had his dream about Vespertine and the toxins been real? Krist, yes! And then Fayteyant remembered that he'd dropped the vial of abortifacient in Leta's bedroom yesterday, when Leta threw the crystal and Bochkser came to escort him to his suite… but he *hadn't* gone back to get it; and yet it was in his bag this morning, exactly where it should've been — and he didn't think twice about it…

Fayteyant was stunned — and Bochkser had left the room before he knew it. Leta wasn't the only one about to die.

What followed happened fast: Fayteyant wanting to run but morbidity fascinating him to the spot; Leta rising off the bed; the oscillation of her eyes between completely black ovals and dots small as printed-tabloid periods… The way she reached the *Steinway & Sons* piano via a series of indescribable locomotive spasms… How he must flee but couldn't stop watching like a peeping tom through the false security of boudoir closet-slats… she fell to her knees. The dissonance when her purpling face collapsed into the keyboard, black eyes distended like oversatiated ticks… clenching her teeth so hard they splintered and scattered like wedding rice… her obese eyes *heaving* as a cord of coagulated blood and hair clots descended wriggling from her groin, an entomological discharge thick as mooring rope… the thing at the end of the rope resembling a humanoid, a diseased liver with twitching, deflating skeletal paws… Leta's face leering over the keys, spewing bearded plasma as she began to play a ragged tarantella using her nose and a tongue that had sprouted cartilaginous, knuckle-sized nubs... those jerky notes jabbed between Fayteyant's vertebrae like sharp needles, shocking him into action—grabbing his bag, opening the door—when a screeching behind him made him stop and turn around, against his will—she was singing while her mutated face hammered and flopped about the ivories:

"*You reap what you sow, doc and a lot of stuff you didn't...*
It all adds up to nothing – the arithmetic of living!
Your madness gets madder, your cracked brain will shatter,
roof sink into floor...
In the House Next to Nothing you'll always be lost, the exits
are never doors!"

At that point in the verse her face stopped playing the piano; it wagged like a tongue and Leta's ruined mouth belched gory foams festooned with silver pellets. The muck smothered the piano, rising so high as to completely censor the painted Daztgarham's lap dummies. It snuggled up to her bulbous waist where she knelt, corseting Leta in her own insides while churning toward a spanking-new Japanese screen—behind which Fayteyant glimpsed Vespertine's dainty feet rising on tiptoe in a dubious attempt to elude her sister's viscoid secretions...

Then—*finally*—Fayteyant bolted as the expanding marble echoes of Hextly, Bochkser—and others—stampeded toward him down the corridor. He fled like a man in a dream and almost tottered down a mile of paralyzing stairs—the dizzying central staircase to the first floor. Without thought—as the scared skunk spritzes—he straddled the broad, adipocerous banister, squeezed his bag between his plump thighs, and slid down at the glistening velocity of goat fat.

With ten or so feet to go he flew off and landed harshly on his side as though tossed from a speeding locomotive, the blow cushioned somewhat by a six-ply *Thylacine* rug. He was in any case so adrenalized, he was unaware of any bodily sensations. Fayteyant sprung to his feet, panting. Identical black clouds of Bochksers were rapidly descending... His life was over in one way or another—if not by excruciating, slow death, then the even slower, excruciating torture of new names, new assumed identities, new fugitive lives.

Hextly was like a roaring, objurgating Centaur God way up at the top of this many-storied nightmare… and then, skimming like one breath of air against another, bright like a ray of sun diving past his ear, came mad Vespertine's fragile exultation:

"Thank you, Doctor! Thank you! Thank you *so* much!"

And now all the troubling incidents of the past two days had been leading up to what happened next, the most profound, beautifully disturbing moment of Fayteyant's life: He looked up one last time before he escaped — why he took this unnecessary, time-wasting risk, he never knew — and saw that Hextly had thrown his dead daughter down to crush him, an act so desperate, so frighteningly pragmatic, that… that words failed…

She descended toward him wrapped in hushes that looked so awfully loud. Then her body missed him by mere inches, and it was midway through that thin but infinitely extended line between his possible death and the life that was to follow that her body seemed to slowly featherswoon past, as if gravity had a moment of indecision. Long fingernails tenderly sliced his face from cheekbone to jawline. They looked into each other's eyes… Leta's no longer monstrous but sidereal and warm. Somehow, she was still alive. Whatever hellish transformation she'd undergone, it was over. And while their eyes met Fayteyant felt an unfamiliar sadness. A heartache that didn't know its own strength, as though rings of happy children seeking his attention were tugging on his trouser-cuffs, not understanding how easily their collective efforts to share their happiness with him could just as easily make him topple, unintentionally bring him to serious harm or even —

— Love at Only Sight.

Her skull split into a wide, screaming mouth. The rest of her followed her like an infant born off the edge of an unattended butcher-block. Fayteyant glimpsed a bolus with skeletal arms arc through the air. It started mewing.

Doused in goat fat, blood and ambiguous humors, he

easily parted crowds across the full gamut of social classes down to the rowdiest. He looked like a newborn product of satanic magic, birthed clothed and fully-grown from Baphomet's cloaca. O, why had he looked in her eyes? He didn't slow down until the setting sun was a toxic orange, didn't stop running for hours until the darkness was continuous and inviolate as a moment of solemn memorial silence.

Fayteyant had miraculously eluded Hextly's brigade. Most likely the thing that had been Leta had somehow delayed them. But he was lost in the most subscrofulous quarter, in a narrow alley between a junk-shop and bakery. The world seemed worlds away. If only Leta had lived, if he could've been *her* hero—the wrong sister had been grateful to him, thanked him so effusively for such wrong reasons. His entire life must change. But it *had* been love at only sight. It must be real love, because he felt *guilty* when images of her gesticulating innards surfaced in his mind and he wanted to keep them there, to turn them over from all angles and examine her deepest gelatinous secrets... it was love because it was strong enough to chastise his fetish. To inculcate such intense shame. For the first time ever, he felt sickened over his constant preoccupation with biological revelation. Why, only a worm could think about such things while that precious woman lay murdered, cold as the cold marble floor that had opened her head...

But if he was going to learn to hate himself—and he desperately wanted to—he must leave Manhattan Island as quickly as possible. First, he had to determine where he was. The moon illuminated a sign nailed to the brick wall opposite:

GRAVELSPITZ LANE

PART #2
IS BLEEDING AN EXPLANATION?

VII. If it Ends in "–Itis"

Far too much is made of faces, and especially eyes, which – if only because they are built without blueprint – lack the communally informative meaning of windows. The human face is a dead-end, painted into a theatrical illusion of expansive road. Look away from conjuring tricks; turn your face from the face if you would learn that time is of the putrescence.

     – The Dark Wintering, Chapter VII.

Perceval woke in hoary darkness dimly smudged by the faltering light of several lanterns dispersed throughout a vast space, set at varying heights and distances from each other. Instinctively, he reached for the safety of the petrified horse penis, but his hand touched nothing but hard wood... then his bag, *Struwwelpeter* intact. As his eyes began adjusting to the ill-lit room, he saw some lanterns were paned with colored glass; on a table or shelf nearby sat a squat jar of leeches in purple water, impaled by beams of blue and red light. It was likely a makeshift barometer; Doctor Chapman used leeches for that purpose in his office at the orphanage...

Gradually Perceval understood he was laying on a thin mattress, uniformly crusty as with stale elephant menses, and this on the floor of a cavernous space. It didn't smell like terrified blood or carbolic or the unsalted swamp of orphanage soup; the air here was laced with a unique, all-penetrating corruption much finer than smell-particles.

He sat up and all at once felt like an asskicked, see-sawing pile of shit, and couldn't stifle a groan.

Suddenly a clear, bright lantern swung out of the darkness above him.

The man holding it was in his late twenties. His keen eyes were a difficult, screaming green. The right one was glass, and there was gold in it too, but Perceval couldn't tell where precisely. He smiled frequently; his mouth framed by parentheses indicating the many years over which he'd sustained this habit. He was thin as Egyptian papyrus god, erumpent hair the depthless black of ink-headed jackals. He wore black too, a chalkboard with inexhaustible capabilities to teach, deceive, praise, &c. He was funny ha-ha and he was funny strange. What had looked like a third eye glowing in his mouth turned out to be an expiring cigar; he exhaled smoke that brought tears to Perceval's eyes. That was almost magic — smoke birthing water...

This man grinned at Perceval.

"Boo," he said.

Perceval was unmoved.

"Stolid! You look as though you've seen no ghosts at all — are you a ghost?"

"No. Perceval Raptus."

"You're from the orphan asylum?"

"How do you know?"

"You need a good scrubbing, man. Even your shadow stinks... What made you come out in this — to *this*?"

"Where are you from? There's nobody from round here who isn't from round here."

"Scratchfyre factory. Not long in town. I'm a bit of a nomad you might say. Decided to get the hell out before my jaw conflagrated and collapsed. The storm rolled in and I sheltered here."

"You don't look like a Scratchfyre worker. Too smooth."

"All right, you got me, I'm afraid. No, you might say this place is in my blood. By the way, I gander you're insane, but it suits you — like heat to *Cordyline*, or similar jungle flower. You see, I spent more than a decade overseeing the treatment of roughly 6,849 lunatics, 457 idiots, 148 epileptics, and approximately 11,349 wrongly-committed victims of revenge on an annual basis. There were approximately 699 homicidal cases yearly; of these lunacy induced by inebriation represented just over 28%. I instituted a system of balneal treatments especially for insane, idiot, epileptic, and wrongly-committed females; the data is as yet incomplete. I perfected institutional usage of the *Fayteyant Scale of Lunacy, Degeneracy and Dissolution, &c.* I'm a progressive. I saved the *polis* $12,565.34 by replacing 1,333 straw mattresses with hair repurposed from deceased inmates. I could bore you with more statistics and details— which only proves I'm an expert in my field. So I know Stark-Raving when I see it. That, and I found you outside the building... let's just say you rode into town, so to speak, via a contrivance such as rarely is employed by the mentally sound... Now, I'm going to poke around a bit more. Haven't been here long myself. Want a cigar? I've one left."

"You're sure your name is Harold Chapman?"

"No. I saw it written in one of those journals over there. Speaking of lunatics—no offense, man, but whoever wrote this has the grandest delusions of medical genius. Why do you ask?"

"The doctor at the orphanage is named Harold Chapman."

"O? But what *is* a *name*? You know how the click of your key locking your door behind you gives false security—a sound that guarantees nothing? Well, a name is just that sort of pancake, too."

"You're not him."

"No. But finders keepers. I've taken his name and I'm sticking to it. Who knows—maybe he's not him anymore anyway. I've seen that happen... Here, another good lantern for you, go ahead and snoop... Be right back," he said, disappearing into library shadows, whistling no tune.

Why didn't Perceval dislike this man? He supposed it was much the way some dogs simply accept each other after one fleeting exchange of butt-sniffs.

Perceval explored. Everywhere his light shone he found worm-eaten books strewn in piles of esoteric arrangement, some stacked high as snow banks. Meanwhile the bookshelves were crammed with a confusion of apparatuses, of which gallipots, glass cannulas, bellows, burette-stands, Swedish spring-steel, rubber-tubed brass tambours, retorts, capsules, graduated glasses, strainers, bell-metal mortars, wool and asbestos filtering media were merely a suggestion of the whole tangle of vulnerary items (and these jumbled together among a motley collection of containers of curdled asses' milk, sugar of Sargasso mosses, cherry laurel oil, adulterated iodine, green poppy-headed morphia, bitumens, extensive volatile oils, unclassified, mucopurulents, cochineal of ararat, &c.).

On a deep window-sill: alembics, beakers, a broad crucible and countless specialized vessels. There was a blue-banded, chipped ewer and basin. The water was fresh — melted ice. Perceval splashed some on his face, drank the rest like a dog.

"Gander what I found in these old Calomel boxes," the stranger called.

Five crates, each filled with neat stacks of wax-sealed, brown paper pouches roughly the size of hip flasks. The crates and their contents looked the same but different notes were tacked to the lids. 1st: *Precursor 1*; the 2nd *Prolegomena Factors (strychnine, aconite)*; *Batch 8 (no mercury)*, and two crates were distinguished by seemingly random numerals.

Perceval examined a packet, feeling a finely-ground, powdery substance contained within. Centered on both sides was a deep black pentagram, with the ligature *&c!* printed in white letters at the center. Beneath this emblem, a phrase:

ETCETRACAINE

"What's this?"

"Patent medicine! A cure-all, a nostrum... people are monsters, and monsters are miserable, and will buy anything they're told will turn them back into princes... 190% pure quack... gives me an idea though..."

Perceval saw ghosts shamble out the aubergine shadows. That could only mean his new companion was planning to steal something material, or had done so already... The smallpox victims, histories of their final days in the flickering of their outstretched fingers:

They had gone cold, clammy, suffered through acute spasmodic eructation; cramps; extreme dehydration; prodigiously discharging their bowels while their ashy flesh shrunk three sizes too small. Cyanosis had cursed each pinched face, extremities livid. They looked poisoned by a monster out of Greek Mythology, with eyes sunk deep enough to catch rainwater.

They reminded Perceval just how tired he was. He felt he'd lost countless drams of blood. He had to lie down soon.

Even if this Harold Chapman (what else should he call him?) was planning to slit his throat, he nearly didn't care.

"We'll need a catchy slogan for it," Chapman said.

"What?"

"If we're going to sell it."

"Why?"

"Look, I can tell you're all right, and I need a right-hand man to do my grafting. There's got to be two. Only God and the Devil work alone, and as God-fearing a man I am, there's no mistaking me for the Creator. That leaves the possibility that I could be Saint Nick. But when's the last time you saw the devil with a sidekick?

See, a salesman shouldn't ever work by himself—don't want your marks associating you with the forces of evil. You obviously have less than no cash, and you can't stay in this place—especially not with your doctor friend using it for his secret laboratory. He's obviously insane—no offense... I've got to hit the road at sun-up. I've got a sweetheart meeting me in April in Rehobeth—that's only three towns from here, going east—New Toomes is the first and not far from Cirkle's Way. Come along. Get some cash and find yourself a sweetheart of your own."

"I thought you'd worked with... lunatics. What do you know about selling things?"

"Because it's about the same line of business. In fact, the best way to learn what the public wants is to observe the insane up close. And there can be no better training in salesmanship than to do the same—I've seen many a Moses or Heliogabalus I would've been willing to believe were the chosen of God or Emperor himself, if not for the context of our acquaintance-making—which was me locking them in cages.

"So, what do you think? No point dreaming with your eyes closed."

What the hell did that mean? Perceval had no idea. But faux Chapman had the confidence of the performer and the heckler in equal measure. He made you feel he was on your side and, at that same time *above* you, a privilege to watch him do his act.

"OK."

"I knew you were my man! Partners, eh. Wait, I've got it! *If it Ends in '–Itis' Why Not Try This?*"

"What if it ends in *pox*?"

"Doesn't matter. We'll convince them it does. People are just animals with money. They're so desperate to be happy monsters, you see. They just need to trust you and trust is nothing but wanting to trust somebody, and we'll make them want. We could even sell them the hokum in *that* over there."

Chapman nodded at a large, leather-bound book on a rusty operating table.

Perceval carefully removed the amber-corked bottle, a container of Kier's Rock Oil, some etidorpha spritzes and four entubed carminatives from the cover. He sat with the book and his lantern under the table.

The book creaked open. It stunk like tropical vivisection.

THE DARK WINTERING
BY OTTO JOHNGREATGRANDSON I

Perceval chose passages at random:

Read from right to left, we see embodied in the common typographic symbol for etcetera (&c.) an ontological sign illustrating three key stages of an alien evolution: A single point — an egg? Coal-chute to the underworld? Eye? The Void? — uncurls and rears up like a newly-hatched worm. This creature then stretches itself into a 3rd towering state — the infuriated lines and curves of its posture indicating a teleological design that is as highly specialized as it is ambiguous.

One must not tamper with &c. To do so could turn men and women into vicious Etceteracks. How would such metaphysically-immiscible lusus naturae appear?

They would each be absolutely unique, and yet simultaneously replicate each other precisely — like Leibniz's windowed monads perhaps, but with broken, filthy and rotting windows — each discrete and linked into an endless series of mistakes...

They would be the viscous, Dark Wintering of human kind.

Let me elucidate the apt meaning of this phrase to describe the &c. Principle.

Observe snowfall. It is a cliché that no two snowflakes are alike. But looking deeper at this commonplace, our attention is drawn to the fact that once fallen en masse, these sui generis units of snow appear absolutely identical. What is this snowfall, so atomically divergent and megascopically self-identical? The case of Etcetera bears family resemblance. Snow is a list in which you get lost in depth while trying to find the length of it.

Who can know how many entities are implied in a given instance of etcetera? The question can also be formulated: Who can know how many flakes are fallen with a storm?

In any case, these Etceteracks would conflate human biology with the impossibility of the catalogued-yet-unmentioned force of &c. Would such a thing even be alive?

Of course, the word "Alive" in fact means . .

Perceval stopped reading Johngreatgrandson's text to examine handwritten notes filling the wide margins, written with the crude verticality of amorous confessions carved in tree-trunks:

&c! (Etcetracaine) makes an absolute commitment to the unstated. This includes a commitment to that which it Does Not and Can-Not include. For my present purposes, the Does-Not consists of the entire possible list of maladies worldwide, which are too numerous to completely inventory. The Can-Not is that which has not yet been discovered or produced, all unknown, future pestilences – and those which will never be.

Etcetracaine does not suggest – but promises!

In time, the &c! principle will be adopted by the other branches of knowledge and practical life. For it is a universal force and not limited to the realm of medicine; but its use must begin in some concrete form, and so it will first incarnate in my medicine. Maybe this isn't a merely contingent event. Indeed, the physician's art is applicable to more phenomena than suspected. Even natural forces, classified as inviolate and impervious to disease, are tainted with the same failures characterizing the organic kingdom. For example, who can deny that the wind that combs the wheat and haircut, the breezes who tambourinate the leaves of the trees, are epileptic events?

I came to Cirkle's Way a physician without a practice. Had I been turned away from the orphanage, I doubt I'd be alive today for one reason or another. I was lucky to find shelter, let alone a place suitable to my experimentations in medicine, and penitence. If – but I must not write about myself – it's too painful. And who knows? Maybe I'm not myself anymore, anyway.

There was no room left for doubt: the doctor *was* the library ghost – the perfect place for clandestine activities. Nobody in town would go near it, and besides, people were afraid of anything to do with Otto Johngreatgrandson. Perceval saw the genius of the doctor's scheme: The more he frequented the library and the *less* effort he made to conceal his presence, the greater his chances of *not* being discovered – the lights he needed for his experiments only served to strengthen local belief that it was haunted... He'd always liked the doctor, because he refused to look directly in your eyes when examining you...

Perceval suddenly felt a room-temperature presence reading *The Dark Wintering* through his shoulder. It was a pale girl, mercury-poisoned gums eternally suppurating, ashy rectum forever scorched by tobacco-smoke enema.

She was nodding in agreement with the weird passages, as if it wasn't nonsense.

Perceval returned to Johngreatgrandson's text:

Of course, the word "Alive" in fact means –

– "A man's got to do what a man doesn't have to do, right Percy?" Chapman confused things, giving him a friendly slap on the back. "Heading east, tomorrow we hit New Toomes."

Perceval wondered how they were supposed to do that in the middle of a record-breaking blizzard. Then he fell asleep beneath the table, *The Dark Wintering* on his lap. His mouth hung slack all night, and he drooled on the pages like a holy man spewing so much prayer, you just *know* he's lost the fucking thread.

VIII. FOR THE GREATER GOOD RIDDANCE

Things seek to be equally random and fated. They want to move into a completely unexpected and predetermined moment. Think of playing cards: Although every shuffle is fated, still the players shuffle again and again and again, cards flashing whitely before they assume clear forms in their hands. Each time it seems a little different, and it is easy to mistake the happening of different things for freedom. Fate is like several shadows that overlap each other on a white field – do they make one big shadow or are they a collection of intersecting shades?

— The Dark Wintering, Chapter VIII.

Perceval doesn't know why, but he's got a peculiar, burning-noose/rope-burn feeling time has started running backward since what happened this morning didn't yet transpire. It's too hot and weird to think about... Anyway, it's impressive watching Chapman speak to the New Toomes crowd—he has the confidence of a monsoon. They all want to see what his green lightning-eyes see, no matter the price. His tongue extends quick lies as a centipede strolls a wall— effortless and never tripping.

Nobody who notices pays any mind to Perceval as he quits Chapman's side. They're too hypnotized by the grafter, and Chapman's so swept away in his glitzy performance that he isn't aware of his right-hand man quietly stepping backwards to disappear behind a barn. Chapman's radiating in the throes of his bamboozlegasm—*"WHETHER OR NOT IT ENDS IN – ITIS, WHY NOT TRY THIS?"* Their eyes are moistened with hopes that just a pinch of Etcetracaine powder is needed for their piles, catarrh, dyspepsia, consumption, self-pollution, neuralgia, ague, &c. to be forever cast out of their bodies...

Now Perceval's about two streets away. The crowd's started chanting some raucous shanty about a rattle-snake... the song ends in schadenfreude chortling. Coming up on his right he spots the:

NEW TOOMES WHOREHOUSE

Perceval walks up a short flight of rickety stairs. It's seems too quiet for a bordello, but a note tacked to the wall explains that today there's a special Two-for-One on Gaggings, illustrated by crude renditions of a variety of voluntary esophageal-obstructive acts. Two men are playing cards, sitting on barstools too high for the round table between them. They're constantly bending down to put hands down and choose new ones, and every time either one sits up straight again he groans.

"Do you have a room?"

They don't look up. The impatient sound of shuffling cards.

"All girls are occupied," the thinner one says. "On account of the Two-fer-One."

"And that snake-oil hawker," fatty spits more than mutters.

"You can wait outside, on the steps if you want. When a sweaty fella who ain't me or him comes out the front door, it's your turn."

"No it ain't," the fatter says. "You gotta go."

"Not talking to you. The fella newly arrived."

"What?"

"Not talking to you," the sour thin one repeats.

"I don't want a girl," Perceval says. "I'll pay — double — for a room. Just to sleep."

Neither has bothered to glance Perceval's way. The game continues, spines folding and straightening, the soft friction of the cards punctuated by grunts...Perceval stays where he's standing, awkward and blank-faced. This goes on for ten, fifteen minutes, maybe more. Skinny finally breaks the silence:

"Two dollars and third room on the left up those stairs."

"And nobody'll bother me."

"If you're gone tomorrow morn."

"And if anyone asks if you've seen me — you haven't. Deal?"

"Ain't you been payin' any attention," says Fatty, shuffling. "We haven't even tried."

Perceval reaches into his gray cloak. He tosses three or

four dollars on the table. This is just a small portion of the cash he'd stolen from Chapman's carpetbag this morning, which Chapman had entrusted to Perceval's care while he went to take a troubled, knollside shit. Of course, he did so while facing Perceval and their stuff, but the combination of cold wind in his eyes and the strain of evacuation forced Chapman's face into a squinty grimace, sustained mask-like over the considerable duration of his trial. Perceval recognized his chance. It had been five years since he'd pulled off this kind of brazen theft, but the required legerdemain came back easy. Like remembering how to fall off a bicycle.

The reason being that Perceval had changed his mind about Chapman when they set off from Johngreatgrandson's library this morning. This Etcetracaine racket wasn't for him, and neither were travelling companions. Chapman would just get in the way to Voice... It was difficult to explain; it was like when you risked falling through rotten floorboards, catching tetanus from upturned nails, to retrieve that sealed box from a shadowy corner of an abandoned house... You don't want anyone else there with you to stress the floorboards under you, or the rungs of the splintering ladder, and most importantly you must be alone when you pry the lid off... Anyway Perceval left Chapman about half of his cash. He did owe him something.

The room is seasonless with dust. Sepia-grained light struggles down from a high window... a bed, 3.5-legged table, a tall stool like downstairs, and a spirit-lamp. Perceval doesn't even consider the bed. He guesses the safest corner, lies down and spoons his carpetbag. Sleep comes fast.

After the Two-for-One period of the day is over, the passionless caterwauling of empty men and women doesn't wake him—nothing he hasn't heard a million times in the streets, among the WYMIN—it's an unrecognizable sound that jolts him awake in uneven blackness. It's an undefined but very late hour.

Perceval presses his ear to the thin wall: The unmistakably smooth, irrigated scrape of tongue licking against it, magnified ten-fold. Something trickles into his ear through the plank: Calid, steaming saliva, spiced with eyelashes or arachnid prosthetics... suddenly the wall bursts open like a bladder in an Inquisitorial vice. Perceval falls backwards, shuts his eyes, but the fluid crowds into his mouth. It tastes like sour tidal waves. The spit rises to his Adam's apple. It's full of rumors. Each drop whispers *pass it on* to the next... by the time Perceval gets the message it's been distorted from "*I am wet*" to "*No voice without spit, but much spit without voice. . .*" Perceval dives beneath the surface to find his carpetbag. It opens as he swims upward, and *Struwwelpeter* drifts out into the humid backwash. He grasps at the spine and the pages turn to little plankton-sized bits of pulp.

Now he blacks out...

...And now he regains consciousness. He's just a tad soaked and lying flat on his back. The ground beneath him wobbles between mass and incorporeality. He sort of remembers tumbling down a flight of stairs, and getting his nose picked by a pretty finger with black grains resembling roach-turds under its painted nail. His head feels like an untethered bathysphere... Everything is more rumor than real, yet more message than murmur. The thin and fat card players are there, only they're upside-down and making really funny faces, and swaying as though strung up like slaughterhouse hogs.

First, Perceval wonders why they're hanging upside-down.

Next, he thinks: *Waitaminute—I'm the one upside-down...* his back is pressed against the ceiling—then he falls from the grip of a pungent adhesive that had maybe leaked from his spine and glued him up there; his chin kicks the edge of the round cardplayers' table. His neck almost snaps off as he hits the swilly, sawdusty, tobacco-stained floor. . .

Somehow, Perceval stands up / down / in / out / back / nowhere. His veins buckle and writhe like sodomized worms, burrow deep until he feels them shiver refugee-knotted in his most xenophobic places... A vertical, foot-wide slit rises groggily to the surface of his abdomen, wakes up and yawns to greet the night... He collapses back to the floor, cold hemorrhages spume, and then he's up again, the slit vomiting his intestines, his wound sickened by whatever in him isn't damaged. A long strand hangs down from his belly to the misshapen thing that echoes a mishandled brain. Streams of bleeding gut just about everywhere. He loses balance again, slips falls into an increasingly hermetic mess… Krist, this up-and-down shit has got to stop already!

He's surprised to realize that nothing's being taken away from him. He feels fervid—no room-temperature sensation = no ghosts, which means *no theft in progress*—just maybe, even, some invaluable moment is being *given* to him in this unwrapping… opening a box without hubris…And then you find a good spot where you can be all alone. Your blood rushes—enough hesitation already—the lid pops off and…

A rifle fires point-blank in Perceval's face. A patch of black blood overtakes one eye, while the other gazes at whatever faraway place is brought into focus through the telescope of a Winchester barrel. One half of his head is gone and the other doesn't look remotely face-like. *Maybe* like a fucked-up shellfish. A twitchy Perceval-eye swings across his new mouth, dribbling incontinent cerebrospinal fluid that sizzles, evaporates on his burnt tongue. Like he's feeding himself with a dropper.

"Got him," someone says.

"He's standing again," says another.

"What in God's name…"

Perceval's chest and abdomen open wide. The men gathered in the New Toomes Whorehouse are startled to see the organs remaining within him have rearranged themselves, architecturalized into rickety steps that lead up into an abandoned attic.

Now they are running the wrong way.

IX. The Etceteracks are Coming!

The universe is organized according to a rational and harmonious principle: Things go from bad to worse, as well as worse to bad; these opposing forces ultimately balance so that one does not gain undue influence on our lives.

— The Dark Wintering, Chapter IX.

"Ready to make a fortune?"

Uhm? Perceval opened his eyes, lifted his head, knocked the crown of his skull on the underside of the library table.

"Careful!" Chapman said good-naturedly. "Food's up there."

Perceval had the oddest sense that time was running backward and all this was happening *after* what was yet to transpire. It was too weird to hold onto. *The Dark Wintering* slipped from his lap; he crawled past, stood and drowsily nodded at Faux Harold Chapman, who was insultingly well-rested.

Something smelled edible.

"Breakfast, Perceval. Help yourself—we've a long walk ahead."

Atop the table was a goblet of hot barley meal porridge, hot cornmeal pudding, one goblet of hot cocoa, a bowl of warm milk and cracked wheat, and two eggs. How Chapman had made this come to pass was a trifling mystery. Perceval wolfed it down and his body began to rejuvenate. He stretched sore legs, ambled to an oversized oriel window that faced the dead and living Datzgarhams, the Lithuanian Orphanage, the ruinous Scratchfyre factory and the rest of Cirkle's Way. The sky was blatantly missing, and beneath its disappearance an endless continent of snow seemed to deny the existence of human history.

"I found some good, leather bags in the back of the Library with wide straps," Chapman chirped behind him. "Easy to carry. I've loaded them up with Etcetracaine packets. two for each of us—they weigh almost nothing."

"How?" Perceval asked.

"Ah! Just follow me—You've got to think outside the

coffin…"

Chapman led Perceval through a maze of disorderly bookshelf corridors. Cots, stained sheets. He tripped over a masticated dolly. An alcove of burnt bibles, a clearing loaded with leather bags. Some were open; here and there a little eyesocket or skeletal gesture jutted into the pale light now pouring through the lofty windows.

"That's where I found ours," Chapman said.

"Here—go ahead, open that door."

Perceval turned the brass knob and saw the thinnest carpet of frost extending a mere twenty feet or so from the library, like a white shadow ending where a clear forest path of twigs and pine needles began.

"How?"

"I've seen this 1,000 times making the rounds of lunatic asylums. Inside, it's Babel and Babylon. Step through an everyday door in the wall and—bang!—it's Brooklyn. Everything needs a limit, even a blizzard. That path right there leads east to New Toomes. And you'll be fox-fucked if it isn't *exactly* where the snow stopped falling, am I right?"

They made good progress. By afternoon the sky had come back, shallow blue. Here and there white cumuli hung in discrete, unmoving clumps. The air was crisp, the trees were spindly, the old, narrow road had been trodden into a dead riverbed. They stopped only twice—once to eat, and again to deal with the consequences. They otherwise journeyed in silence. It seemed only a few chilly hours had passed when a flock of tilted houses spiked the horizon with belemnoid rooftops…

New Toomes was the kind of place pessimists went for reassurance and confirmation of their worst fears. The houses were gray-brown, gray-yellow, or gray-black, all maculated with lime-white bird-droppings. There were more narrow, deadweedy alleys between buildings than there were buildings. The New Toomies were a grum, squabby bunch. Half were drunks and the other half too melancholic or bored to drink. Nothing changed, perhaps because degeneration has an absolute pinnacle. God knows how this kind of thing goes on decade after decade… So when the two strangers came into town with their curious sacks of powdery pouches, people were mighty interested. It was the first novelty many could recall in forever…

A small crowd gathered in the ovoid town square to hear the travelling man with the screaming green eyes. Bland as any other congregation of anonymassholes, but for the clonic, fully-body spasms of a man holding a cane it would've benefited him to use. Chapman lured the New Toomies in like a psychopomp leading eager shades to Elysian fields. A few feet behind him, Perceval stood expressionless, exceedingly Perceval-like, with the two full bags of &c! at his side like a pair of well-trained, heeled mastiffs.

"… And so good people, a pinch of my powder puts that new *Coca-Cola* nonsense to shame. Etcetracaine curse neuralgia, hysteric melancholia, self-enervation, dwarfism, systole, quinsy, exophthamalia, Saint Anthony's Fire, hyperkeratosis, tenesmus, furuncluar conditions—and of course, catarrh and peritonitis! Even demonomania! It is a guaranteed product for any medical problem whatsoever and conducive to your neverending eucrasy—that's happiness…

"Now you might say, Dr. Chapman, I *know* happiness is not a product. You might say you know happiness is not a product and you would be right—you're smart folk, and if you weren't I wouldn't be talking to you on the level like this. On a high, scientific level. I'm explaining things because I know you are smart and smart people want explanations before they can accept something as true—or hokum. So you could come up to me and say I know you're a doctor but happiness is not some product like a lathe or a sack of flour. And we would say you are absolutely 115% right. Happiness is not a product. But it is a byproduct of this product here—*Chapman's Etcetracaine, A.K.A. Chapman's Omni-Cure Powder or Food or Solvent, &c.* It's got my name, but I know that's not enough to prove its worth. After all, every dead liar's tombstone's got their name on it! You're laughing because you got the joke—I can't tell you how many folks are too dim to figure that doozy out—but consider this, now: You might say to me, OK Doctor Why-Trust-You, it's impossible for happiness to be a byproduct of a product. That's shrewd, that's a good question. I'm glad you asked it. I could be a quack. It's OK; I know you're thinking that, too. Well if you want to call me a quack that's fine with me because I'm the goose that lays the golden eggs—you could say the golden-star eggs. But I shouldn't jest too much. This is serious; it's about your life and the lives of your children and all the generations to come. So let me ask you if you ever noticed something about the word Impossible. Let's think about that. Let's see what's hiding in there, in plain sight, like all good things—the Lord God Above and sunshine and fruitful crops, and you there—yes *you*, lovely little girl—my but that's a darling music box—O no, m'am let her play, it's lovely. I was saying, this is a town with fine blood. What is the word IMPOSSIBLE? You're right to point out that most of all it's made up of POSSIBLE. That's true. So people think that if you take the POSSIBLE out, well, that's called IMPOSSIBLE. In fact look closely now—can you all see this sign? The letters are magnetic—I slide POSSIBLE a little bit over there and we're left with what looks like two letters. Son, can you say them for me? That's right but a tiny louder please. You hear him? I-M. What's that sound like? 'I AM.' What did God say in the Bible—that's just it, 'I AM.' So where's that leave us? Just here: IMPOSSIBLE really means: I AM POSSIBLE. You might say, but you're just foolin' with words. 'I A-M' is not 'I-M,' it only sounds like it. But consider this: Does an accordion look like music, or does it sound like it? Does a fiddle look like an accordion? Does a fiddle look like music? Not until they are played right. What I'm doing here is playing the IMPOSSIBLE the way it should be, so you can hear the music of the truth. So, who will be first? Whether or not it ends in –itis… *why not try this?*"

The crowd threw back faces punctured with howling mouths and knowing, *wink-wink* laughter. In the palm of his sleight-of-hand.

"I know you're just itching to scratch your itches with this, but I just got three quick questions for you:

"You'd trust a good chap, right?"

"YEAH!"

"And you'd trust a good man?"

"YEAH!"

"So you can double-trust a good Chap-man, am I right?"

"YEAH! YEAH!"

"All right, then!" he said, laughing. "Come on down and get it, cheap! Chatty Percy over here will hand out the packets..."

Some of the crowd chuckled, others puzzled or peered. Chapman turned round to find Perceval gone...

Chapman wasn't confused for more than a second before he realized the gullible-looking orphan had fucked him, and good.

But there was no time to admire Perceval for this daring accomplishment. A half-assed line of New Toomies had formed. The first one up was the shaky man, probably younger than the 65 winters he seemed, stunted as though he'd lived his best years stuffed in a snuffbox. He had difficulty getting the cash from his pocket with his quivering "good" hand— the other being an alder prosthetic... Some men behind him began to laugh and sing (to the tune of the ancient *Ballad of the Sickle of Life*):

"I'm Stanford Grost and I shake, I shake, I shake like the ratt-le on a snake..."

One by one the others joined in, and before long Chapman himself was leading them through chorus after triumphant chorus.

X. The House Next to Nothing

Indeed, by the end of this chapter you should know in your marrow that there is no greater analogue for life than a cemetery; it encompasses both spheres of the human experiment. One half of it, built of stone and inerasable inscriptions, consists of the regularly expanding world of superstitious, solid and enduring objects; and beneath this hard, unyielding display lies the truer half of our lives — the objective, time-eaten world of decomposing reality.

— The Dark Wintering, Chapter X.

You are here.

— Blumenkrank's Condemnation.

The Sinking Season, 1888

I am nearly seventy years old. How is it that for the past 27 years I've been so completely empty and so full of guilt at the same time? Are these identical feelings, or am I multiple, or is there no such thing as simultaneity? Does the arithmetic of life really add up to nothing? These questions alone animate the dusty air of this new home:

The House Next to Nothing.

This place has been erected on the outskirts of not much, on the worst soil the south has to offer. It doesn't rise so much as peep above the rim of an extreme concavity of earth. When I first approached, I mistook the top floor for first story, puzzlestruck as to the purpose of such a squat structure. Then I found only a house after all; howsoever it reminded me of a bird stuck headfirst in an upended trumpet, a feathered gag blocking brass throat. But since moving in I've discovered the ground beneath is vaginal in elasticity, the house a mass stretching it toward the center of the earth, down toward an abyss over which it's more tarp than top. This place grows heavier with its own disappearance.

Why would I choose to live here? Because there is something that oh-so-perfectly should not be in this house: It is a fearsome, solid ghost — a real rhinoceros of a phantom. Yet I am afraid to touch it lest it vanish. That would mean it wasn't real.

When I saw it, I said to the owner — man named Shiel — how in God's name did that get in here? Who lived here? Why depart without this piano? He answered: Don't Know — Some Quiet Folk — What Piano? — just like that, the first consonant of each spoken word capitalized in a weird dialect; but he had the meek and downcast eyes of a horticulturist.

    I know this improbable piano. It is a Steinway & Sons Carved Rosewood Square grand. It belonged to Leta Hextly. Somehow it has followed me through a maze stretching nearly three decades and forty-eight states long: From The Goat King's Headquarters, his balls the size of Uranus and one finger knuckled with unblinking green eye, where I fell in love while Leta fell, to the fugitive's shameful road, to false names (I still don't know why I picked Harold Chapman), an orphanage in Cirkle's Way, where I thought I could hide in a library and change the world – atone for the death of my beloved – curse Otto Johngreatgrandson (I'd rather not wonder what became of him) – where all my unfinished &c! was stolen, where I finally gave up – DO NOT TEST IT – REJECT IT – back to the road, just after reports of those monstrous deaths across Connecticut. And now, sunk down to Kentucky – this South – urinal of the Yankee States.

    I haven't changed the world for the better. Committed Etcetricity never defeated Dismissive Etcetricity. Nobody has thanked me in years, not a soul has needed me. But at least I did uncover a hitherto unknown species, in the mirror: I am a creature sui generis – the 7-Sided Animal, or Belua Septfariam. You can easily identify Septfariam by taking the following inventory of dimensions: inside; outside; left side; right side; top side; bottom side; and homicide. Ha! Ha. I suppose I should've gone into cryptozoology.

    But I don't feel sorry for myself. I'm not even capable. Over the decades of running, my self-pity has metastasized from within to the people and whole world to whom and which I am so helplessly adjacent, until it's become an unbounded condolence without locus.

    Piano, piano.

    This ivory-grinned monster is my accuser and judge. And when the House Next to Nothing collapses at last, it will be my psychopomp, and then – who knows?

For the past week, Fayteyant had spent each day sitting by a dirty window, exhausted, resigned to ugly things, listening to sloppy, cymbal-shaped sounds of rain. Thus was he occupied the night the storm ended. Now and then he'd consult his improvised barometer, a bottle of leeches in ditchwater kept on the sill; well past midnight, they began convulsing, black tongues cunnilicting to their swampy world's surface—storm's peroration at hand. The rain wore thin; the final leech ascended while brindled skies fled, leaving muddied roads and flooded tarns and pools of quiet inside and out of his two-story clapboard. A practical-joke moon appeared unexpectedly and overbright, as if to mislead the wind and tides, confuse veins and seasons.

He quit the casement, entered the ill-lit study, sat on a wobbly chair of moldy, red silk brocade, facing the piano. As if it were real as a crime scene, as if his touch would tamper with crucial evidence, he simply stared at the bone keys in the dusty silence—

— — *Knock-Knock* — —

They were contrived woody-tolled blows, so unexpected as to seem hoax deliveries from other worlds—like the March 31, 1847 Wayne County, New York spirit-rappings with which the Fox sisters and their dining room table ushered in the modern Spiritualism nonsense...

— — *Knock-Knock* — —

The sound was an uneasy mix of *demand*, the firmly repeated striking of knuckle on wood, and an undermining of that urge to mandate a response—a palpably uncertain *hope*—heavily expressed in the hush that set one strike apart from its fellows. Someone was at the door.

The floors sagged severely, approaching the infundibuliform of a Calla Lily, and Fayteyant navigated the dark, funneling declivities of the floor with arthritic forbearance, holding aloft ha hissing lamp dimmer than a firefly's ass.

— — *Knock-Knock! Knock-Knock* — —

"Who's there?" he called, pulling the door inwards.

...Boo.

A slight, soaking breathless man from some dark-skinned, exploited land stood under the portico. His vague dark clothes were mud-drenched from boot to head. He looked shamed, dragged, dunked; disguised as his very own battered soul.

Boo Who?

Fayteyant immediately diagnosed the visitor as falling somewhere between the general classifications of Simpleton and Mongolian Idiot, with secondary Imbecilic and Religious traits, a tertiary Feeble-Minded marker, as per his own *Fayteyant Scale of Lunacy, Degeneracy and Dissolution, &c.* The stranger was harmless, possibly good-natured. Definitely moronic.

"Well?" Fayteyant demanded.

"You... are... a doctor," he panted.

Exactly...

"What's this? No, you are mistaken. What do you want?"

"Shiel told me you are a doctor...please help. My master is dying... His family, his beloved family is in danger..."

"And why did Shiel think me a medical man? The subject of my profession was never discussed during our short business transaction. Why, can't you see I'm just a retired piano de-tuner?"

Was that a gout of blood running down one side of the stranger's face? Or only slickening mud?

"He said you looked like a man who had watched many die in his day, but your eyes were too cold for a murderer, or a soldier."

Exactly...

Fayteyant was too tired to continue being foxy.

"... Where?"

"It is an estate over the hill, less than half a mile from here. Along the road to Fandango Camp Commons, past Palindrome Satyr Point. You know, near a Scratchfyre factory..."

The doctor's eyes telescoped remote. He gazed past the servant into the rustling night. It was run wild with leaves and grass and gusts in cold twiggy darkness, yet strangely hollow, very lonesome. A wave of nostalgic frustration washed over Fayteyant; it was like remembering an old, long-forgotten song and humming the melody perfectly—while being unable to recall the title or a single lyric.

"I'll go with you. Wait here."

Fayteyant felt the galvanizing thrill of a resurgent fetish: A visceral and chimerical emotion of danger and escape, distance and penetration. No need to dress, as he hadn't changed his clothing in a week. His medical bag sat upon a steamer trunk adjacent to the door, having faithfully waited two decades for its renascent necessity.

It was a bulky, tattered, leathery gallimaufry of items he'd managed to scrape together from the Otto Johngreatgrandson Library and here-and-there: phosphorous tablets, pouches of lobelia, tortoiseshell lancets and related venesectional cups, ampoules of *Tinctura Antiperiodica*, cyanide gauze, relatively unsullied scalpels, calomel bottles—better leave those behind—woolen strips, Tasmanian Tigerfur-threaded straight needles, diminutive ointment pots, graduated instruments, a flask of evaporating turpentine with ether, and troves of dust for inducing The Sneeze. No Etcetracaine. That had all been stolen from the smallpoxed nooks of Otto Johngreatgrandson's library.

The 7-Sided Animal gave the empty room a purposeless glance. The leeches were sinking again through the turbid moonlight.

The rain would soon return.

"Thank you sir," the man spluttered. Was he crying? "I am Mendasico, forever in your debt. Now please, *please*... This way... my master is dying..."

"Think before you thank—but lead on. By the way, who is my patient?"

"O! Harold Chapman—he is a great doctor, too. Perhaps you've heard of him?"

Fayteyant gripped one of Mendasico's arms while he carried the old man's bag in the other. Under the bright moon the doctor noticed a long sliver of mirror embedded in the side of his visitor's face. They trudged up the wet incline to the road, feet sinking inches with each step. They paused at the top for Fayteyant to catch his breath.

"Your employer—what's his name again?"

"Harold Chapman. Please let's hurry, now... I'll help you, the whole way. Doctor, why are you so pale?"

"What are the chances? I am... do you know my name?"

"No, Doctor. Tell me."

"It's a funny thing... terrible, perhaps... and a long story. If I tell you, it will be after our mission of mercy is over..."

They rushed along the landslide of a road. The Chapman Estate came into view as the rain began. The building towered over acres of unbroken woodland with the peaks and valleys of a natural landscape. To the east rose a fascicle of towers like taut nerves. Moving westward was a low country of widow's peaks and flat stone roof. Windows seemed flung randomly into the face of the house — triangles, decahedrons, squares, rhomboids, rectangles and circles of clear and stained glass, each darker and dustier than the last as things buried under things buried under things in cellars.

The tracks of an indeterminate number and size of footsteps ascended, descended and obliterated each other across the porch steps... As he tore up the stair, Fayteyant realized he hadn't even asked just why he was needed... carried away by what was either a gigantic, urgent moment or compilation of inextricable urgencies — is a fire made of flame or flames? — Mendasico violently pushed the neo-Grecian front doors open.

"Just to the left here, Doctor... the parlor..."

Several black kidskinned chairs, a ponderous rosewood table, and an étagère were strewn violently across the room. All were claw-footed, so that the overturned furniture resembled a scene of big-game slaughter more than any domestic chaos. A standing pier mirror had been shattered as though by a team of pugilists, flinging miniature, topsy-turvy parlor-views across the bewildering, 67-color oriental carpet... and no doubt, a wicked piece into Mendasico's face... Next to a massy, disarmed grandfather clock, a Parian bust of Heliogabalus had tumbled and rolled into the cold fireplace. It seemed to bleed from its decapitated neck, but Fayteyant soon saw the source of the sticky red pool: A man lay face-down on the glazed hearth tiles. Phalanxes of blood straight as sundial shadows reached out from beneath his body. It looked like ancient evidence; perhaps all blood, once spilled, has been spilled for centuries...

Was this Harold Chapman?

"How did this happen?" Fayteyant demanded.

"He is dying," Mendasico repeated, smiling nervously.

A muffled voice rose up from the wounded:

"Is bleeding an explanation?"

Fayteyant knelt down next to him.

"I suppose it is... Not a good one."

"Good *enough*?"

"Not really."

"O, can you really be so cuntdescending to a dying man?"

"Please," Mendasico begged. "You are both Harold Chapman, you are both doctors—you said yourself sir, *what are the chances?* It must mean something—you must help him as you would help yourself..."

Suddenly, from the next room came either an excessively masculine groan or the sound of a monument being dragged across flat rock.

"What was that?" Fayteyant asked.

"You say your name is Harold Chapman—Doctor Harold Chapman?" said the bleeding man, mostly into the Chinese rug.

"Who are you?" Fayteyant said, and yanked the man roughly onto his back.

The younger Harold Chapman, who had cheated the world with Etcetracaine, knew the flabby-faced man swaying above him was the one who'd wanted to save the world with it. Below him, the older Harold Chapman saw a bruised, pulp-nosed man with brilliant green eyes—one animal—one of glass. The prosthetic was severely cracked, anthracitic pupil cleft by some vicious assault; chandelier light scintillated in the crystalline fissures, bringing it to uncanny, overly-alive life—the real eye comatose in comparison... he was almost familiar... Suddenly:

Another enraged groan or monolithic displacement—

—Then the loud attack of a large slab of flesh against an unhinging door—

Silence... Mendasico's dusky face paled with anxiety. He picked up a fireplace poker and stood facing the noise, trembling a little.

"What is that?"

"What are you referring to?" slurred the wounded man.

"That babelcrashing in the next room! What's going on here?"

"O, that. I spent so much time, you know, around lunatics—in another life, believe it or not, I was Commissioner of Lunacy, my dear Doctor Chapman. One slept through such maniacal outbursts... ugh my head. Dizzy..."

"Please Doctor, can you save him now?" Mendasico asked—meek, irritated.

"Wha—O him? He's not dying. Just concussed, confused— but wait, Commissioner of Lunacy? Was this in New York City, by chance?"

"Yes, yes. Of course it was New York City. Didn't I just tell you that? Since you won't take bleeding as an explanation, will love do? Is love reason enough for all this?"

"Don't you mean Leta?" Fayteyant said coldly.

"Love. Yes, didn't I just say that? Wait, no, no, *no*... no *Leta*. She was *there*, pretty damn ugly, though that didn't stop me from knocking her upside the womb—they all look the same when they're crying. But Leta wasn't the one I loved, you know... could you hurry up and stanch the blood, Doctor? I believe it's exuding from this Heliogabalus-nose-sized hole in my crown—"

"—Wait. Mr. Mendasico, you mentioned that Mr. Chapman's family was in danger, too—where are they, then?

"I only meant, they will be in danger if my master dies... they are not hurt of themselves."

"That doesn't answer my question."

In a corner across the parlor, something damp and heavy fell to the floor, followed by the metallic discord of worried chains. Fayteyant whirled round to see a Japanese screen faintly vibrating... the room became unaccountably hot and humid.

"What the devil's that?" he said.

Nearby, a splintery complaint was followed by a crashing door.

Fayteyant stood, swiped a brass candlestick from the hearth, clutched it tight with a brave, liver-spotted hand.

Mendasico scrambled against his nerves to his wounded master, and dragged him behind the an upset settee. Chapman's head nodded, blood rilling down his forehead, off his nose... he was becoming increasingly intoxicated with its drainage. At a loss,

Fayteyant grabbed his medical bag and joined them on the mock-sheltering side of the settee, standing a few feet behind. The doorway on the opposite side of the room filled with seething blackness.

It was an exaggerated man in a kind of mourning uniform. One eye exceedingly large, the other scrunched, like a comparative anatomical display which shows the vagina crowning with infant's bulging head on the left, and its contracted, postpartum aspect on the right. His ears jug-handled, nose nubbed... The face sliced into crimson reticules of longitude and latitudes. One hand was clenched into a massive fist, mirror-punching knuckles torn to the bone and caked in tinseled blood. One of his knees was shattered and he shambled forward slowly. It was unbelievable he could move at all, and without a wince.

"Bochkser?" Fayteyant disbelieved. The doctor's heartbeats had gone *strigendo*, one coalescing into the next like an ominous drum roll.

"O, you know him too?" Younger Chapman said, upright and leaning against Mendasico, who held him so in a bear hug. He laughed, heckling, mirthless.

"I don't believe it," Bochkser said. "Doctor Nathaniel Fayteyant? Two birds."

"This is *not* Doctor Fay—whoever!" Mendasico snapped, as though personally offended. "That gentle man over there is Doctor Harold Chapman—just as *this* man in my arms is Doctor Harold Chapman. Don't you see, assassin? It is a sign. Try to kill *one* Dr. Harold Chapman, and *two* appear. Understand?"

"Dr. Fayteyant?" the master of the house said, chin on chest and eye still on Bochkser. "It is an honor! I just *love* your scale..."

Bochkser was momently confused. Then he giggled.

At his back Fayteyant heard an intestinal, poisonous, voiceless howl thrashing, choking throatless against chained confinement. He turned—nothing but the Japanese screen... Sweat flooded his wrinkled brow... the air almost tropical.

Bochkser unblocked the doorway, revealing The Goat King of Madison Avenue. He hadn't aged a greedy day, posed gloriously firm and free, as though urinating off a terrace.

"Ah, there you are, Eyeball! Did you really think you

could keep my man and I trapped behind a mere closet door? Who's that Geriatric Queefsniffer back there — wait, it can't. Is it?"

"They're both Harold Chapman, sir."

"What? That is rich," Hextly said with jolly snort.

"O God," Fayteyant said.

"God is just the oldest asshole in the room," Hextly said, "though you're a close second. But what are the chances, Doctor Faint-at-heart? I feared we'd lost your trail decades ago — you'd be dead in some gutter not worth owning. But we kept on after *this* one. Bochkser here determined he was snaking about under the alias Harold Chapman, and tracked him to this miserable pit. And now it turns out that you too are masquerading about as a Doctor Harold Chapman!"

Hextly walked over to the bar and poured two whiskeys. He brought one to Bochkser and straddled the only unmolested chair, sipping his own.

"Take your time, Bochkser, man. After twenty-seven years, what's a few minutes — hours? We're in no rush. Marshall your strength..."

"Listen, Father-in-law. How could I help it if Vespertine and I loved each other? So she ran away from you — why, I told you that just a moment ago — but she's happier here than on Madison Avenue. By the way you are welcome to stay for dinner... I can tell you all about my latest money-making venture. *You* inspired it and I want to thank you, and offer you a stake in the business. It's a cologne — distilled from goat fat! Smells like shit. I call it: *Sodomist*..."

"Shut up, Johngreatgrandson!" Hextly said, his blue eyes stinging Fayteyant. "Old man, you could've had this anonymasshole's job, man, if you hadn't let my Leta die... not to mention what you did to her career."

"The Commissioner of Lunacy," Fayteyant said. "*He's* Johngreatgrandson?"

"Otto Johngreatgrandson the Third, to *you*," Fayteyant's host said. "My grandfather was 300% mad-raving — but the library he'd built in Cirkle's Way was a good, out-of-the-way place to hole up, what with awful Bochkser on my trail."

"The library? You took my name — stole my life's work, my Etcetracaine..."

"But it wasn't your name, was it? Besides, I did you a favor, you walking corpse. You should've seen the side effects! I admit it helped me build my fortune, but I barely escaped New Toomes alive. And you should see what it did to my wife! I kept one as a memento. She mistook it for pepper... she always was a ninny, eh..."

"Where is my lovely daughter, hmn? Where is Vespertine now? I want to make up for disowning her. I'm going to disembowel her."

"I know you're going to kill me," Fayteyant said. "So be it. But you should know that you murdered Leta. She was *alive* when you dropped her like a bag of rocks."

Hextly snorted.

"Both my daughters were idiots, both thought they loved this idiot here. We're going to kill you, man, yes. But first I have to see an eyesocket about an empty ring. . ."

"My eye," Johngreatgrandson said, somehow more lucid. "I haven't seen that since you and the Bochkser Brigade corned me in Gravelspitz Lane..."

"You had amazing luck, last time, getting away before I could finish. Time for me to complete this pair of rings — see, asshole? And, I have a lovely glass locket too, just the right size for your seeing orb. I'll fill it with formaldehyde, wear it round my neck. I'll have all *three* of your eyes."

"Leave my Master alone," Mendasico said, saintly and imbecilic.

Hextly finished his whiskey in one gulp and drew a pistol from his coat. He put it in his mouth, then took it out and frowned, deliberating. Then he nodded to himself and shoved the barrel into one nostril. Holding the other closed with his finger, he blew his nose into the revolver.

"Greetings from my excretings," Hextly said, and fired it into Mendasico's face. The servant fell backwards, taking Johngreatgrandson down with him.

"I want to do this right so we will take our time, right, man?" Hextly said to Bochkser.

Johngreatgrandson III was whimpering, cruelly conscious.

"I feel much better," Bochkser said, adjusting the erection in his pants to a more comfortable, midnight angle. Just need to steady myself."

Hextly joined his servant in scanning the room.

"Don't see any canes, man."

"No need, sir," Bochkser said. He hobbled over to the étagère and sat on it. He gripped his leg with shattered knee and twisted it until it came off at the joint. Without a grimace, he tied the end of his trousers tightly round the stump and, reaching to the floor with a long arm, collected the exenterated pendulum of a grandfather clock. Bochkser then set his disconnected leg on the floor so that it stood by itself. He shoved the pendulum into the marrow of it until it was securely in place. Then he got up, and took a few steps. His amputated limb served as a perfect cane.

"Good, man!" Hextly said. "I must say, it really is you, Bochkser. Do attend to the doctor while I finalize my transaction with the triops."

Bochkser hobbled forward on his legs, a deadly cripple.

He approached Fayteyant with terrible slowness. The doctor stepped back, candlestick in hand, watching Hextly rifling through his medical bag for a surgical instrument, when a loud crash and something like a moan slathered in grave-wax turned his head to see the Japanese Screen on the floor; it buckled up and down as though a family of six was trapped and asphyxiating beneath.

Johngreatgrandson III began to cry in agony.

Bochsker's heavy, unsyncopated tread… Fayteyant ran to the screen, pulled it aside.

The brass candlestick dropped from his hand. Behind him, Hextly was pontificating about testicles and Magellan. Beneath him, a writhing Etceterack, adult-sized abortion tugging on umbilical cord of chain, one end staked to the floor by a railroad spike, the other affixed in a hole burned through its mid-section.

He recognized Vespertine at once. Even though her hair had fallen out, head to pubis, and her nails grown incredibly calcinated, piercing tips hanging down to what were either knees or labia… Her front teeth protruded past lower lip, which was disturbingly human, full and feminine. Her mouth opened wide, tongue a blackish-blue. Her eyes had caved into her head and slipped to the back of her mouth, vibrating with the uvula. Like her mouth, her eyes had remained strikingly unchanged from the last time he'd seen her.

Fayteyant caught a glimpse of blackness at the end of his tunnel, thrown into relief against the rest of the dark like red fire at the center of a rose.

Bochkser was a minute or so away now...

He couldn't flee this time and drew strength from the miraculously limited options available to him. Without hesitation he used up the last of his feeble strength to yank at the tethering spike, falling to his knees with the effort. He managed to loosen it a little, and Vespertine did the rest. She uncurled and reared up like a newly-hatched worm, stretching itself into its final towering state—the odd lines and curves of her limbs and hips designed for terrible, highly-specialized ends... the doctor looked up, seeing only Vespertine, arched over all like a rabid firmament, like a December 5th, 1868 blizzard-sky... Fayteyant felt the unusual heat disperse as a wave of room temperature air enveloped him and her gorgeous, human lips descended on insect strings to swing fish-luring before his old eyes.

She dripped closer. She said:

"*Thank you, Doctor. Thank you... thank you...*"

"My child!" Fayteyant said, his voice cracking with emotion. "You are welcome. You're so very, very welcome..."

And even as his sight ebbed away into darkness, Fayteyant's eyes misted. They filled with tears of gratitude, because he'd given someone a second chance. It didn't matter *who*; there was no time left for that. And he cried because it didn't matter who *he* was, either—only that someone had given a defeated old man this precious gift, to choose his last words, and he'd gotten them right... He'd made them beautiful—

—*Perfect!*

Because they were true.

Because there was no time left to think otherwise.

Epitaph #2 / Epilogue #2 / Fuck Me! It's —

...and so I must conclude that there is indeed life after death — the worms live richly on the corpse... And perhaps by now you have figured out that all this time you have been reading my suicide note. I apologize for the great length. Since you must have read past Chapter III, I hope you too were already on your way to Oblivion; otherwise I am sorry — All I can say is you're headed somewhere much worse — a place so terrible, there are no words for it.

— The Dark Wintering, Epilogue & Good-Bye.

I apologize for startling you — I'm not used to seeing anyone round these parts. Not any longer. What do you have there, that smells so good? O, cold sausages? Florida oranges and a goblet of cornmeal mush? No, thank you I ate — it seems I'm always eating. I couldn't. Such kindness is exceedingly rare. What? No, I'm sure we haven't met before. It's just that I look like several different ugly people at once, so I'm bound to remind you of some hideous acquaintance.

What's that book next to you? I see! Be careful... well, I only mean that books can inflict wounds far worse than papercuts... May I ask if you are feeling all right? I'm sorry if it's not my business but you appear burdened, under a dark cloud. No, I don't know if it's that obvious really, but I've done many things wrong in my life and know what it is to be troubled by regrets that send you to the road. So I've got more insight into your condition than most. Cheer up; things may always go from worse to bad. May I? Thank you, these legs do need a rest now and then... there. What was I saying? Yes: You seem to have been forever sitting, nibbling and thinking last thoughts in this obscure grove — indifferent and tense, waiting a turn that will either never come or arrive too soon. A grain of wondering sand on an hourglass floor.

May I ask where you're headed? No, don't go that way. Yes, it's true. New Toomes is a ghost town — literally and figuratively. What do I mean? There is something ocean-floor about the desolation, or like it's at the bottom of an alien vertical world. You feel you shouldn't even be able to *get* here. The idea you might ever be able to leave seems doubly ludicrous...

The gray buildings sway together like lynched men neck-hung off the great boughs of a single tree; the wind carries a curious salty, rotten stench that sets the brain against itself: Do you smell blood-drained corpses, their hard veins embalmed with purulent urine—or the sweet/formaldehyde aroma of chickens, pigs and woodcocks boiled in the cauldron of a cadaver's dissected chest cavity? And in that same wind lurk vivid approximations of things you've never heard before, faint but horribly imaginable: the unjust sodomy of velvet alphabet blocks on ruptured accordions; the increasingly compressed panting of a dog chained to the misaligned pistons of a machine, crushing its windpipe while running deranged circles round the faulty device; pneumatically triggered face-clacks; fork tines and dry beautymarks waltzing off East River bridges… Weird words, eh? Weird times…

Even the natural landscape has changed since those creatures came and went—if went they did. *Etceteracks* they called them round here—they say they were all wracked with pain and their eyes cried black powders. Their pupils scrambling around, like ghostly thought through the bizarre grooves, fissures and cul-de-sacs of the human brain… the ataxic trampling and prancing of monsters through the small world, stumpies dragged, the coffin-headed scraping wallpaper and bark off trees, knocking portraits from hallways and wasp nests from boughs, hoofed genitals moving forward through a series of failed attempts at masturbation—whispery garment-sounds of oleaginous facecreepers, whose every misstep exuded alien vocabularies… living, killing mistakes.

That's what I've heard…

If you go that way, you'll see the trees have grown—not up—but into obscene togetherness. Intertwined like severed fingers reassembling into some forbidden gesture. People say they leak sticky shadows, independent of the sun's movements in the sky. And the ground is softer; what was rocky is spongy and hard dirt is turning into a seeping mess. Perhaps that's why the buildings sway so. Or maybe, like the more fanciful say, those things eventually merged together and into the land itself. That New Toomes and its vicinity is one great living organism now, a beast part-human, part world, part something worse—but that's just speculation, and we'll never know.

Why?

O, because a dozen-or-so self-styled "Monster Hunters" went to catch them some Etceteracks—the toughest old salts I'd ever seen and all loaded up with rifles and sabers and knives and bravado. Only one ever came back from the vicinity of New Toomes. To him we owe the only description of what might still be darkening that accursed land and maybe even now spreading beneath the rind of that orange. And as for him, when he first returned he told them a bit:

All day he'd been lying on his belly in the mud at the edge of a field, waiting for something. He'd been hearing things: In the wind, indecipherable lamentations; laughter jagged and fast as lightning; the growling of empty-stomached brains; senescent musical gears tinkling, exactly like two streams of piss crossing over tambourines. But nothing he could see. No heads to mount on a wall... Night was near and he was close to giving up, when he saw a creature silhouetted against the depressing sun.

It was the size of a smallish man and roughly so-shaped. As it moved away from him into the west it held its arms out on either side. His fingernails were long, curved and indurate as obstetric specula, caked with sediments human, canine, and porcine; red ribbons of flesh tied round each as though it had ten things to remember. The hair on its head was grotesquely extended in every direction and seemed to hover over him like a saint with a dense cloud of flies for halo. This mane was moldy, sheathed in browns, dun, bistre, whites, ochres, greens, fuscous hues—of the entire spectrum of mammalian dung-hues. It was obvious that no water, no scissors had approached that musty mop for many years.

The hunter set his sights on the back of the thing's head. He was prepared to fire when it abruptly stopped moving; he was curious as to why... And at that point in the story he'd stop talking and just sit in the corner rocking himself to and fro. He'd jam his fingers in his ears, like trying to block out the sound of an explosion. And they stopped asking him to go on after that part, because he'd never tell and it only made him more agitated, the poor sod. He'd bury his face in his hands, like the muzzle of a starving hyena into deepest carrion.

Well, he started trying other things. In his ears, I mean. The fingers weren't enough to keep out whatever message only he could hear. He put sticks in there, forced in slugs with spoon handles. Eventually he moved on to screwdrivers.

He's dead these days.

Now you tell me, what in the name of Krist ought you make of that?

I know. Questions are crippled thoughts, aren't they? But I've got a theory. I think that Etceterack said something.

I think its voice was so monstrous, so overwhelming, that it drove him insane...

But it's getting late; I must be going. When you're done with your meal, take care to head west—through, believe it or not—yet *another* abandoned town. They used to call it Cirkle's Way. You can't miss it; you'll pass a great stone building on the way to the main road—a library. You might see a single old tombstone in the back with the curious epitaph:

DON'T GO

No idea. This library, it's decrepit but impassive and enduring as the sphinx. It'll be dark by the time you get there, and even I must own that at night it looks like a haunted charnel house...

I advise you to ignore these, keep your wits about you and don't stop until you see the road past the caved-in factory and clocktower. And even though it's so cold, if you see lights flickering back and forth across the library windows—don't be tempted to look there for lodging.

You just keep going.

You just keep going faster than you can...

What? O, never mind—I was mumbling to myself, hermit that I am. Of course! Yes, I was quite serious. You can unburden yourself to me without fear of judgment.

I'm listening...

My but that is a very sad story, my friend. And afterwards, did you quit her body or hold vigil? No, of course... you had to get away. They'd have snapped your neck damn quick. And the blood? The *glomerulus*? How did you manage without anyone noticing? But then where exactly had the breasts been misplaced? I see... O, so that was the *second* one. The third? I apologize if I lost track... but the details aren't so important anymore, are they?

I'm glad you told me. I hope our meeting has been of some help to you. At least know you are not alone. I've done far worse things than you, my poor friend...

Me? You're right, that's only fair. O no—I can answer that in a heartbeat. I don't need to think about it... I can tell you, with dead certainty that, looking back on my long life, the thing I regret most of all is that I read far too much.

Brooklyn, New York
December 30, 2011 – March 3, 2013

CHAPMAN THREE
THE REMAINS
ADAM P. LEWIS

Prologue
December 28, 1893

Chief Livingston ran up the church steps. He stopped at the large oaken doors and grabbed the door knocker, which squeaked as he lifted it. He rapped continuously against the metal plating. Inside, the distinctive sound echoed through the hallways.

Father McGuiness answered the door. "Ah, what a pleasant surprise," he said, smiling.

"I wish it were a pleasurable visit." Chief Livingston removed his police cap and held it over his chest. "I'm calling with a dire matter at hand. I must see Dr. Myerburg."

The priest's lips slowly faded from a heart-warming smile to a straight-faced expression. No one called for Dr. Myerburg, and with good reason. The horrors he had unleashed upon the city of Saratoga Springs over five years ago were still fresh in the minds of its residents. They wanted nothing to do with him, regardless of his former pass as the city's most trusted physician.

"Dear God." Father McGuiness covered his mouth with his hands. "Has it? It can't have happened again."

"I'm not sure whether it has or not. But Jane's grave was disturbed."

Father McGuiness stepped aside allowing Chief Livingston entry. "Doctor Myerburg will be angry with us for misleading him all these years."

"You and I both know it was for the best."

"Yes, we agreed upon it, but..." the priest paused.

"But what?"

"We should've kept Jane's body buried behind the church where the doctor could keep an eye on her."

"Just how many people stopped coming to your sermons, knowing there was only a stone façade between the buried and the congregation?"

The priest sighed. "Nearly half."

"And how many were too frightened to come because the doctor kept interrupting your sermons? I remember him flailing his arms and screaming that Jane had come back from the dead, that we all had to lock our doors if not flee the city before we were killed. And why was that? Because he had flashbacks of that nightmarish day at the Chapman Estate."

"I'm afraid..." the priest paused, not wanting to recall the diminishing attendance of his congregation, "...only a handful remained."

"Only a handful will *survive* if Jane—" Chief Livingston stopped, feeling he had said enough. "Where is the doctor?"

"Upstairs on the third floor." Father McGuiness pointed through the ceiling. "I'll bring you to him. Follow me."

They mounted the spiral staircase to the third floor. When they reached the top they hesitated, giving each other a worrisome look. They knew what they were about to tell the doctor might send him into hysterics. Worse yet, send him running into the streets as he had years ago, frightening the public.

The priest knocked on the door. "Doctor, can I speak with you?"

Inside, the doctor didn't answer. He kept his eyes fixed on the ground below his bedroom window and the mound of dirt dusted with snow, covering the remains of Jane's body.

The priest knocked again. "Doctor, please. Chief

Livingston and I would like to have a word with you."

They heard muffled shuffling from within the room. The handle clicked and the heavy oaken door inched open. Doctor Myerburg squinted at the men through the crack, only showing a quarter of his face.

"You're interrupting. Speak quickly," he ordered.

Doctor Myerburg had once been the most respected citizen of Saratoga Springs before he was forced into seclusion. Everyone considered him a friend. They invited him over for holiday dinners and family gatherings, as he had no immediate family in the area. They trusted him with all that ailed them: small pox, whooping cough, hay fever, influenza, cancer. They even trusted him to birth their children.

But now they shunned him. The citizens of Saratoga Springs discontinued seeking his medical advice and didn't dare speak his name, for it reminded them of the terror he had brought upon them half a decade earlier.

"I've come calling to..." Chief Livingston cleared his throat, working up the courage to tell Doctor Myerburg the horrific news.

"Out with it, I haven't time for this!" the doctor roared.

"Yes, well..." Chief Livingston adjusted his tie and cleared his throat again. This time Doctor Myerburg slammed the door shut.

"Jane's grave is empty," Father McGuiness called out.

Doctor Myerburg didn't respond.

The priest continued. "You were passed out drunk. It gave us time to remove her remains from the churchyard a few months after you buried her. The members of my congregation were bothered by your drunken interruptions. You scared them. We had no choice."

The door swung open. The air swished out from the room, smelling stale with body odor. Father McGuiness and Chief Livingston held their breath.

Doctor Myerburg rarely ventured from his room. He would've starved if it weren't for the hospitality of Sister Margret, who worried for him. She brought food and drink to his room during the morning and evening hours. Bathing was rare: once a month. A harsh standard for a doctor who preached to his

153

patients that bathing frequently would stave off disease.

"You removed Jane's remains?" Doctor Myerburg asked. A scowl pulled at his brows.

Both men felt their knees weaken. The glare from Doctor Myerburg and the grinding noise of his teeth warned they had made a terrible mistake.

Father McGuiness's voice shook while speaking. He paused and swallowed a lump in his throat. "Like I said, it was for the good of the congregation."

Doctor Myerburg bolted through the doorframe and clutched Father McGuiness by his cassock, slamming him against the wall.

"You old fool. Do you know what you've done?" His eyes turned to slants, his angered breath heaving in his chest.

Chief Livingston, a bulky man standing over six feet tall, half a foot taller than Doctor Myerburg, grabbed the doctor by the neck and pulled him off the priest. He slammed Doctor Myerburg into the opposite wall, restraining his shoulders.

"I'll have none of that," he said. "Do you understand?"

Doctor Myerburg sneered. "Did she rise? Because if I saw Jane rise from that grave I dug behind the church," he said, pointing in the general direction, "I could have stopped her, as I had years ago."

"We meant no harm," the chief replied. "We were only trying to put the townspeople at ease."

"All you've done is possibly allow that *thing* to rise up."

"There's more to the story," the priest said, standing behind Chief Livingston in case the doctor exploded again.

"What else?"

"Your replacement, Doctor Collins, made house calls to those who had fallen ill. Their symptoms were similar to what had affected Karen Chapman…"

"Stop mentioning her name in my presence," the doctor demanded.

"It's time you face the facts," the chief said. "You mustn't blame yourself for that poor girl's death. We all know Jane took her daughter's life."

The priest added, "But Doctor Collins saved them. So Jane might have never actually risen."

"There are explanations," Chief Livingston said. "One of the stricken claimed he was present when Jane's body was stolen. He could have been infected that way. But we have no evidence supporting that theory. And the others who fell sick aren't talking."

"*I'm* responsible for the dead, not anyone else—not you," Doctor Myerburg said, pointing to Chief Livingston, "not Father McGuiness, Harold Chapman, Jane or anyone else. It's my fault. I had the ability to stop Jane and I failed. I failed the whole town." He slid down the wall and sat on the floor, burying his face in his hands. His back undulated as he began to weep.

Father McGuiness formed a cross with his hands and prayed silently. Chief Livingston gave the men a moment to gather themselves before politely reminding them that there was the matter of a missing body to discuss.

"She was clearly stolen," the doctor said. "She's hasn't risen. No one is dying."

"Are you certain?" Chief Livingston asked.

Doctor Myerburg rose to his feet. "Without a doubt."

Father McGuiness sighed. "Then the horror is finally over."

"No," the doctor whispered. He pointed at both men. "You were there the night Jane walked into town and killed those men. Both of you were there. I saw you, Chief, cowering in the back of the crowd, not knowing what to do. You had your revolver drawn, but you were the only armed man who didn't pull the trigger. How can you think this is over? Neither of you helped to destroy what was trying to kill those people—the very people you both serve. The guilt you both should feel ought to keep you from thinking the pain is over."

"I tried to help," the chief said, "but I saw how the bullets passed through her. It was as if Jane were immune."

Doctor Myerburg ignored the response, turning his attention toward the priest. "And you, Father. You stood there on the church steps holding a cross close to your chest, with your eyes closed and your lips moving. But you didn't do a damn thing to stave off the evil. Neither of you moved until you knew it was safe."

"I was praying to my lord and savior that the demon

would meet her doom. What else is a man of my spiritual convictions to do?"

"Excuses, excuses. I risked my life for these people. A man of god and a public servant could not. You let your fears and values hinder your actions."

The doctor entered his room. Chief Livingston followed. Father McGuiness entered last.

The room was in disarray. The floor was littered with dirty clothes and moldy pieces of food. Mice and insects feeding on the food scraps scurried about the floor and ducked under the bed and into cracks in the walls.

Chief Livingston surveyed the furniture, all covered in dirty clothes atop piles of dusty books and scraps of paper scribbled with writing. He glanced at one of the papers and saw the handwriting was cursive and sloppy. He could only make out a few sentences, which repeated themselves: *You have to learn before you die young…*

Two candles lit the room, one of which snuffed itself out moments after the men entered. The other was nearly extinguished by a breeze as they walking by.

Doctor Myerburg stood at the window, looking down at Jane's empty plot. "I cannot live with these memories anymore."

"What are you talking about?"

He walked across the room and approached his bed, wedging his hand between mattress and box spring to remove a leather bound book. He tossed it toward the priest. It landed near his feet.

"My journal," he said. "Read it, and everything will be explained."

Father McGuiness bent and picked it up. "I don't understand."

"It's my confession."

The priest looked at the journal and nodded. Then he turned to Chief Livingston and said, "Come, let us leave the doctor alone. He needs time to reflect and heal."

The men exited. Halfway down the staircase a loud pop echoed, interrupting the serenity of the church. They stopped dead in their climb and turned back. They glanced up at the doctor's bedroom door.

"Please, God, no!" Father McGuiness shrieked.

They hurried back up the staircase, burst into the doctor's room, and froze. The doctor's right cheek rested on his desk. His right hand dangled by his side. The index finger of his left hand was still wrapped around the pistol trigger. Blood poured out and dripped off the desk onto the floor.

A female cry suddenly filled the room. Father McGuiness and Chief Livingston wheeled. Standing in the doorway, covering her mouth, was Sister Margret, tears streaming down her face.

Chief Livingston rushed to her. "This is no scene for a woman." He turned her around and escorted her from the bedroom, shutting the door behind them. Sister Margret's crying rang through the church halls, diminishing as she was led upstairs to her bedroom.

Father McGuiness removed a sheet from the doctor's bed and laid it over his body. While doing so, he noticed an envelope on the desk with his name on it. He opened. Inside was a hastily written note. He read it out loud:

"I cannot overcome my fear and my guilt. Consider my journal to be my confession of what transpired at the Chapman Estate. It tells the story in horrid detail. Please pray for my forgiveness."

Later that night, alone in his bedroom, Father McGuiness opened the journal and started reading…

Midmorning Friday, March 31, 1888

I heard the rumbling clops of horse hooves and the crackle of wagon wheels reverberating over the cobblestone road from my second floor office. The driver yelled, "Whoa there!" followed by muffled talking.

I pulled back the curtains and looked through the glass. I recognized the carriage driver and the overweight servant woman, Clarabelle, a former slave who moved north after the Civil War.

She jumped down from the carriage, ran up toward the house, and leaped up and over the steps. Her large frame landed atop the stoop and her unbalanced momentum pushed her into the heavy oaken door.

She pounded with her fists, screaming, "Doct'r Myerburg, come quick!"

I scurried from behind my desk and out of the office, down the staircase skipping steps. In one quick motion I stepped onto the landing, glided across the hardwood flooring to the door, and twisted the doorknob. The door swung open, but before I could invite Clarabelle inside she pushed me out of the way.

She spoke quickly while crying, her words accented by her flailing hands. I tried to piece together what she was saying, but her nose, dripping mucus over her lips and often blown into a handkerchief, made this difficult.

"Oh Lord, dat gal, dat gal!" she babbled.

I grabbed her hand and tried to console her. "Calm down. I can't help you unless you relax and tell me what brought you to me this morning."

"Heavenly Fath'r, watch wit' us o'er yo' child!"

As she rambled, she followed me to my study. She kept grabbing her chest and waving her arms, chanting prayers. Her eyes fixed on the ceiling as though she was looking through it to the clouds. She kept stumbling over her own feet, causing her shoulders to bang into the wall, where she'd fall down on her knees, the more proper form of prayer.

After entering my study, I handed her a glass of water and instructed her to breathe slow and deep between sips. She snatched it from my hands like a hungry dog and soon thereafter her hysterical praying subsided enough that she was comprehensible. And yet her southern drawl and broken English still made her difficult to follow.

"Karen … sick… Mr. Chapman … ordered me … to fetch you."

"Karen? What is wrong with her? Tell me of her symptoms," I ordered, leaving the study to gather my medical bag from the adjoining examination room.

Clarabelle calmed enough for me to understand. "I knocked on Miss Chapman's bedroom this mornin' because I 'eard her coughin'. It were a' awful coughin' fit, all filled wit' mucus dat makin' her throat clogged up a' all. I called through da door a' asked if she be okay. She answer me wit' a moan so I enter. I fell back through da doorframe when I seen her pale face an' dat blood 'round her mouth. Oh Lord, save da child, she done no one no harm!"

"Has she an appetite?" I asked while latching my medical bag. "Is she drinking plenty of liquids?"

Clarabelle grabbed my arm with all her might, yanked, and pulled me off balance. "No need fo' more questions, Doct'r Myerburg, hurry now!"

She nearly dislocated my shoulder. Annoyed, I jerked my arm from her grasp, grabbing her and pushing her to the floor. "I cannot help you unless you allow me to do my job correctly. Do we have an understanding?"

She cowered, pulling her legs and arms up in a fetal position, shaking her head yes. Her eyes closed tight and her lips quivered. She kept flinching at every move I made. It was obvious she was experiencing flashbacks of her former slave master beating her for not doing her job up to his standards.

I offered my hand and pulled her to her feet. I apologized. "I'm sorry, that was no manner for a doctor to act in. Especially to a lady."

She smiled, accepting my apology. 'S'all right. Wit me actin' all wild, I don't blame ya."

I returned her smile. "Come now. Take me to Karen so we can help her."

I picked up my medical bag, put on my overcoat, and headed out of the office. Clarabelle, still winded, lagged behind, so I waited on the porch for her. She was moving slow and breathing deeply. Her overweight body could barely handle the excitement and stress. I offered my arm for support, and she grabbed it and made it down the steps.

From behind, a male voice asked, "Hey, Doc Myerburg, you need some help?"

I turned to thank the carriage driver, but to my surprise it was Ben, the town blacksmith.

"No thank you, Ben, much obliged!" I said.

"Everything all right?" he asked.

I raised my eyebrows. "I hope so, Ben. I hope so."

Clarabelle climbed into the carriage and I followed. Before we sat down and the carriage door shut, the driver yelled, "Giddy up!" A loud crack of his reins broke the air as they whipped the horses, and the carriage lurched forward, causing us to fall into the seats. Clarabelle stumbled into my chest. Her obese body knocked the wind out of me. Flushed with embarrassment, she stood and apologized, straightening my clothes.

I stopped her. "Thank you, but I'll be fine."

The carriage sped away, the driver whipping the horses making them gallop faster down the street. "Hey there, clear out and get outta the way!" he warned the pedestrians, cursing those whom the horses nearly trampled.

The wheels dipped into potholes and bounced over loose cobblestones, making the ride bumpy and dangerous. The carriage tipped on two wheels each time the horses rounded a corner, causing the vehicle to careen violently.

Clarabelle came close to falling out. She would have if it weren't for her wide shoulders, which wouldn't fit through the window frame. When the carriage landed back on all four wheels our bodies bounced upon the seats, our heads striking the roof.

As we exited the town and entered the countryside, the ride began to settle down. I used the opportunity to ask Clarabelle questions pertaining to Karen's illness. But with each question, she became quieter, until finally she turned her face from me and stared blankly out the window.

My frustration grew as answers regarding Karen's affliction and the possibility of others being afflicted went ignored. The rest of the ride was done in silence. There was something she was not supposed to speak of, perhaps under direct penalty of her employer, Harold Chapman.

Upon entering the front gates of the Chapman Estate, the house created an overwhelming sense of awe. I had never visited the place, nor had I seen it. I've never ventured so far south, not even on a house call. My longest trips were always for hunting and fishing, but north to Canada.

The townspeople gossip and exaggerate about the size and appearance of the Chapman house, but those rumors are far from the truth. The house was bigger and more extravagant than any rumors hinted at. The Chapmans are wealthy but never did anyone or I figure their wealth to be so vast.

The house sat upon the eastern hilltop in a fifty-acre, gated estate and was architecturally styled in American Queen Anne. A style most popular among those worthy enough to afford the high construction price—which the Chapman family certainly could. Jealous people called the Chapmans spendthrifts and rightly so: the house was magnificent and the amenities extravagant.

The façade was asymmetrical, accented with two gables whose apexes complimented the bell-shaped tower between— tower being the dominant feature of the front elevation. A pediment porch cornered around the left side of the house, surrounding a large oriel window sectioned into thirds. The siding resembled fish scales and were painted light tan, with trim painted dark brown, as well as the dentils. The shingles were slate with a natural gray tint. Another tower constructed in the background eclipsed the size of the bell tower soaring approximately twenty feet higher in an octagonal shape. This open-air balcony resembled a gazebo, allowing those who stood within to get a clear view of the grounds, Saratoga Lake, and the mountainous region beyond.

As I gazed in wonderment, Clarabelle jumped from the carriage before the horse came to a stop. She landed on her side and tumbled onto the grass. Before I could ask if she was injured, she stood and ran up the stoop, skipping every other step. She then flung open the front door and yelled to her employer that she had returned with me.

An old, plump man with a gray, carroty mustache came down the steps. He hunched over and waddled as he walked. His dress, a morning suit, indicated that he was the Chapmans' butler.

"Welcome to the Chapman Estate," the butler said in a scratchy winded voice. "My name is George. If there is anything I can assist you with during your examination, do not hesitate to ask."

"Please, call me Doctor Myerburg."

He extended his arm to help me climb down from the carriage. "My apologies, Doctor Myerburg, and thank you for arriving on short notice."

"Much obliged, but there is no need to assist me. I can manage."

The butler smiled. He most likely never experienced respect from any visitor, nor perhaps from his employer. Harold Chapman had an unfavorable disposition toward the city of

Saratoga Springs, and one could assume it carried over to his employees.

George opened the front door and rushed me down a long hallway decorated with exotic paintings and statues. At the end was an oaken door leading into the parlor. Inside, kneeling by his daughter's side, was Harold Chapman. The man turned and greeted me. His lips were turned downward in a frown, his eyes watery. His arms shook, and his voice cracked with nervousness.

"Thank you for coming, doc," he said, shaking my hand. Then he motioned with his other hand to his daughter, sprawled on a couch and staring up at the ceiling.

Visuals gave me the first impression of her illness. Bloody spittle encrusted her chin and neck, trailing from the corners of her mouth. Her skin was ghostly white, giving her face a waxen complexion. Her eyes sunk into their optic canals, lips flushed in a crimson tone, and her body had turned frail, resembling a corpse.

"How long has she been in this condition?" I asked Harold, taking his daughter's wrist in my hand to check her pulse.

"Clarabelle heard Karen coughing this morning and checked on her," he answered. His voice cracked as he held back tears. His daughter's condition weighed heavily upon him, and he needed to relax before he broke down and upset his daughter further.

I smiled at him and said, "At first glance, I can tell she has tuberculosis. But just to make sure, I'll do a full examination. I can heal your daughter if the illness isn't too advanced, which it doesn't seem to be."

I lied. Her illness was in its last stages. But I didn't need Harold turning frantic on me or threatening. The parents of children I've examined in the past often turned violent upon hearing news their child would not recover.

Harold's voice became defensive and irate. "No, you are wrong, doc. She doesn't have tuberculosis, she is dying from..." He stopped, placing his hand near his mouth, as though he were keeping something secret.

My eyebrows rose at him in response. "Do you know something that would help me diagnose your daughter?" I demanded. "If so, you must tell me!"

He glanced at his servants, but they turned away. Some

looked at the floor; others turned toward the ceiling. They were obviously uncomfortable, wanting to ignore the situation.

"There is nothing anyone in this room needs to tell you, doc," he said. "Please continue."

I found it odd that he referred to *everyone*. It was clear by his servants' gestures and his own that they knew something. So I took a chance that one would speak and expose their secret. Directing my suspicions at them, I asked collectively, "If anyone knows something, you must tell me now — for Karen's sake."

No one said anything. A few of the servants' body language suggested they were eager to talk. They cleared their throats, eyes opening wide and lips separating, as if they were going to speak. But fear of the potential backlash kept them silent.

Frustrated, I continued my examination. I checked Karen's pulse and glanced at the clock and counted her heartbeats. While doing so the parlor turned into a theatrical event. The servants gathered around the couch looking on. Even as a professional their eyes felt uncomfortable, like they were prying. Being a public servant myself, I did not want to degrade Harold's employees by ordering them out of the parlor. But I did want to continue my evaluation in private.

"She must be moved to her bedroom," I said.

Harold snapped back. "In her condition she needs to stay where she is. It's written upon her face that she is in pain and moving her will only make it worse. You don't even know what her illness is. Moving her may kill her!"

"If she dies from being moved then I will take full responsibility for her death. But, as I stated before, your daughter needs to be comfortable. This couch is not meant for a sick person to recover or be examined on."

"She is fine where she is!" Harold snapped, mimicking the demanding tone of my voice with a sarcastic attitude.

"I haven't been able to perform a complete examination," I said. "I don't know if she has a communicable disease. It's possible that even before I diagnose the illness she's spreading it to you, me, and all of your servants."

Harold shook his head. He was stern with his words and tried to make it obvious who was in charge. "If everyone is already infected then your point in moving her is moot. She stays where she is!"

A plan to twist control in my favor struck me. "If you insist on the examination continuing in this parlor and on this couch then you'll not reject to your daughters breasts being exposed in front of you and your servants as I check her breathing?"

Harold walked to the door and opened it. "All servants must leave and return to your living quarters." The servants looked around at each other and at me without budging, until Harold yelled, "Now!"

But before they could reach the door I ran to it and ripped it from Harold's grip, slamming it shut. "If Karen cannot leave the room then nobody can. If everyone here is infected then the rest of the servants not present could contract the disease. They must not be allowed to freely roam. Not until I know what her illness is!"

I returned to Karen's side and started unbuttoning her nightshirt. From the corner of my eyes, I saw George staring at Karen's chest. My head turned to his. The left corner of his mouth curled up, his eyebrows crimping in toward the bridge of his nose. He rubbed his palms together over his groin as he licked his lips. My first impression of the little old man was a docile one, but indeed he was sexually perverted.

Harold noticed his butler's sudden giddiness and halted the examination before the third button on Karen's nightshirt could be undone.

"Stop, take her upstairs. She should be examined in private."

I rose and gave my orders. "Nobody leaves this room until I have concluded the exam, including a diagnosis. Is that understood?"

The servants muttered in agreement and Harold folded his arms in annoyance. He was incensed with the way I ordered his servants around. More aggravating to him, perhaps, was the way I exerted control over even him.

I helped Karen to her feet.

"I will be present while you examine my daughter," Harold said.

"I cannot allow that. I'm not sure if you're infected."

George rolled his eyes, let out a quick laugh, and muttered under his breath, "Like the others…"

Again my head turned to him. If he indeed said *like the others*, then their identities, whereabouts, and symptoms needed to be known. If their symptoms were the same as Karen's then a pandemic was starting, if it hadn't already.

Harold scowled at his butler with teeth pressed together, eyes nearly hidden under pulled down brows, cheek muscles twitching. This angry expression caused George's face to go blank and his head to droop. The old man knew something, but Harold's glance had caused George to keep that information locked away.

Whatever he knew, I had a feeling he was never going to tell me. Perhaps he knew the family's medical history; after all, he had been the Chapman's butler before the children were born. But my gut feeling told me he wasn't going to talk, not even in private.

Midday, Friday, March 31, 1888

Karen's knees buckled as she tried to push up the first step with her leg. For support, she draped her arm over my shoulder and held onto the railing. With each step, she let out a soft moan laden with coughing. The asthmatic attacks were suffocating her.

Midway up the staircase, she collapsed. Her arms were frail from sickness, making it difficult to brace her own weight. She fell into the wall and hit her head on the railing, almost knocking herself unconscious.

With all my strength, I lifted her up onto her feet and piggybacked her the rest of the way. But within two steps, my own legs weakened. I felt as though I were trekking through knee-deep snow. The climb was a struggle but we made it, and in a gentle motion I lowered her off my back and stood her up. She supported herself on the wall with her shoulder, fighting the flaccidity of her legs. Her shoulder slid along the wall as she shuffled toward her bedroom.

She paused and started choking, coughing black mucus from her lungs. Unable to wipe it from her lips, she let it drizzle down her chin and under her collar. When she finally slid the rest of the way to her buttocks, I lifted her again and helped her the remainder of the hallway to her bedroom.

Before reaching her bed, she clenched her stomach as the pain intensified. Tears started down her face. She doubled over and collapsed, her head jerking forward and her mouth opening to form an oval. She vomited so violently and extensively that her face turned blue. She fainted and fell onto her stomach until the vomiting ceased.

As she regained consciousness her body curled up into the fetal position, and without warning she was stricken with seizures. Her body thrashed on the floor and her head bucked against a nightstand, forming a deep gash across her forehead.

Appalled, I pulled her into the middle of the room, away from other furniture. Straddling her body and forcing her mouth open, I removed my belt, folded it in half, and shoved it between her teeth—a preventative measure against her biting her tongue off.

After a while, the fit of seizures abated. I bandaged her head and helped her to her feet. Removing her vomit-covered nightgown, she climbed into bed and pulled a sheet up to her chest, hiding her naked body. I retrieved a stethoscope from my medical bag and started the examination.

I examined her coronary functions and noted heart palpitations that were, in relation to healthy heartbeats, faint and erratic. Her respiratory function, which couldn't be evaluated through triangular auscultation of the lungs due to her body position, I examined through her chest. Her breathing was labored, shallow, and spotted with wheezing. Both tests indicated she was dying. Her illness was more advanced than even I had tried to mask downstairs in the parlor.

I turned to place the stethoscope back into my medical bag when her body shot up into a seated position. The quick lurch forward knocked me from the bed as her chest bumped into me.

She swatted at her arms, screaming, "Get them off of me!"

Her arms were bare.

"Please … get them … off … help me!" She thrashed her head in circles as if something was biting her scalp.

I jumped up and grabbed her upper arms between my hands. "Relax so I can help!"

Her head whipped forward and crashed into my jaw,

knocking me backwards. I lost grip of her shoulders and fell off the bed, onto my back. Her screams continued as she again pleaded with me to get *them* off. She scratched at her arms, drawing blood as she raked her fingernails across her skin.

I stood up and grabbed her left arm, looking for whatever was crawling across her skin. But still, her arms remained bare.

"What do you feel? What do you see?"

"The bugs, they are eating away at my skin. It hurts so much, please get them off of me, please!" She ripped her arm from my grasp and continued to claw. Her fingers dug deeper, peeling back layers of skin that curled under her fingernails.

"You're only hallucinating. There are no bugs on you. You must relax!" I yelled, holding her arms against the mattress. I tried to stop her from drawing more blood.

She whipped her head back and forth as she screamed, "My head is burning. I feel them slithering out from under my hair. Get them off!"

My fingers wormed through her hair spreading apart the follicles while searching for the bugs, but again I found nothing.

As her pain threshold reached its limit, she begged, "Please help me … kill me … end my pain!"

"I can cure you," I pleaded. "Just let me help."

With what little strength she retained, she pushed me off her body to the foot of the bed, then rose to her feet, opening a desk drawer and pulling out a letter opener. She put the point to her chest. The moment she pressed down, I lunged forward, grabbing her wrist. Her arm twisted, causing her to spin around. The letter opener fell to the floor. Before she could pick it up again, I opened the window and tossed it out.

She collapsed to the floor, too weak to claw at her arms. "Please, let me die."

I helped her stand and walked her back to the bed. I started cleaning and bandaging her self-inflicted wounds. Whatever images she was experiencing vanished. She no longer flailed her arms or kicked with her legs, so I felt the danger was over.

From outside her bedroom, we heard footsteps running up the staircase and down the hallway. Her father called out, "Karen — Karen, Daddy's coming, hold on!"

Seconds later Harold burst through the door, pushed me away, and held his daughter in his arms. Seeing the bandage on her head and her bloodied arms, he glared at me.

"What've you done to her? You're supposed to be saving her life, not making it worse. This is why I should've been allowed to be present during the examination!"

I pulled him away from his daughter. "I told you to stay downstairs. Look at yourself, you've got her blood on you and now you may have gotten yourself infected. Stop being a stupid hero and start listening."

He pushed me away and said, "Don't you come into my home and order me around like you're the man of my house!" He turned his back and folded his arms.

I walked around him, looking him square in the eyes. "You asked me here. I didn't come out of pleasure. As long as you want my medical advice, you've got to listen to me."

He seized the front of my shirt and slightly pulled me to him, stopping inches from his face. "Now you listen to me, doc. You're going to stay here and heal my daughter and then leave this house and never return. But until you do, you're going to listen to *me*. Do we have an understanding?"

Rage swept through me. I was angrier than I had ever been in my forty-five years of life. I wanted to drag him down the hallway and push him down the staircase, but the health of his daughter remained more important to me than releasing my anger. A fantasy of doing untold harm to Harold would have to suffice.

I took a deep breath and spoke calmly. "I understand. I will stay here if needed but if I'm called upon by another patient I will tend to them and come back later to check on your daughter. When she stabilizes I will need a carriage ride to my office to leave a note on the door explaining my whereabouts."

Harold shook his head in disagreement. "If no one else in this house can leave because they might be infected, then you stay as well. You may be infected. Those are your own words, doc, not mine!"

I didn't argue. He was right. I also knew that if I were going to save Karen's life, I would need help. I extended my hand in friendship and asked for his assistance. Seconds later he rushed out of the room to retrieve fresh water and clean bandages to rewrap Karen's wounds. The initial bandages were soaked with blood that was now staining the mattress. Once Harold returned, we rewrapped the wounds together and I continued my examination.

While counting heartbeats and tracking her pulse, I surveyed my surroundings. The room was Spartan compared to the extravagance of downstairs, except for a vase holding roses and a wall lined with Chapman family photographs. Harold and a much younger Karen stood next to a young boy and another girl, along with their wife and mother, Jane. The boy looked uncannily like Harold: tall, thick haired, but missing a beard. In the picture, Harold was much thinner than he was now, and the girls were a spitting image of their mother, which made for very attractive young women.

Jane and the other two children were absent from the house, which raised red flags as to their whereabouts. I couldn't remember the last time I'd seen them. If Harold sent them away in order to protect them from becoming ill then a pandemic could arise if they were indeed carrying some hazardous and highly contagious bacteria.

In a calm voice I said to Harold, "You have a beautiful family."

"Thank you."

"I haven't seen them around town in quite a long time, maybe a year or so. Are they on an extended vacation visiting her family in the south? I ran into Clarabelle a few weeks back at the market and she said they've been there a while because her father is ill."

Harold's voice trembled. "No, they didn't go south."

"Oh, I must have misunderstood. Then I'd like to examine them as well when they come home. Although I believe she has tuberculosis, I haven't definitely identified Karen's infliction yet, mainly because of her violent outbursts. Your wife and children may be carrying a bacterial infection, so I need to make sure they are healthy."

"You do not need to worry about my family spreading what has befallen Karen. My wife and children have passed on. They were afflicted with the same illness from which Karen suffers now."

Harold started to cry. I had nearly erupted in anger from what he'd said, but I refrained. For Karen's sake I needed to remain calm. But it was impossible to ignore the fact that he had not confided in me about his family.

"Why did you keep this information from me? It may be important. It could save your only surviving child's life!"

"I didn't want to explain to an educated person, especially a man of medicine, about the unseen and supernatural plague that affects my family."

"Unseen or seen, you must tell me what has killed your family. I am a doctor and open to multiple possibilities."

"The cause of their deaths isn't a disease that you or anyone else can cure with medicine. That is why I didn't tell you. That is why I told my servants to tell anybody who asked that they were away. I didn't want people to think I was a murderer or maybe a practitioner of witchcraft. My youngest daughter Maggie, like her brother David and their mother Jane before them, fell ill and died under the spell of an unearthly god."

"Whatever the case may be, you kept this a secret. You could have very well put a death sentence on the entire village of Saratoga Springs!"

"You know how the people of this town look at my family, especially me. They'd think I killed them for financial gain or by some scheme. If you were married and lost your family to an unseen force, you too would be targeted as the cause. This town is very religious. I might be put on trial for witchcraft!"

I became annoyed with him and almost collected my medical belongings to leave. He had failed to inform me of his family's medical history, which directly related to Karen's plight, and he had done it out of fear for his reputation.

But in respect of my medical practice, to which I had devoted my life, I set aside my complaints and decided to maintain professionalism by examining and watching over his daughter in an unbiased way. Neither my devotion to medicine nor my ill will toward Harold would construe my findings.

However, before the horror that we were going to experience is here described, I must briefly clarify my cynical regards toward Harold's social standing. In doing so, one will easily understand why a man such as Harold kept this secret to himself.

Harold, self-disparaged from high regards within the village of Saratoga Springs, distinguished himself unfavorably as a grifter. He swindled schoolchildren of mere cents and drunkards of whiskey bottles through dishonest schemes. Magical illusions, marked card decks, double-talking, and various aliases were his methods of stupefying the gullible and unsuspecting. Those citizens who displayed qualities of culture and learning were not dumbfounded by his tricks, nor were they easily corrupted into collaborating with him to commit similar schemes on unsuspecting travelers. Hence his disposition to surround himself with naïve schoolchildren and alcoholics.

Twenty-five years earlier, he tried to make his mark in Republican politics. He moved south—rather I should say he carpet-bagged and touted himself as trustworthy and sympathetic. Offering false promises to rebuild sections of the Civil War-ravaged south if elected to office, he solicited benefactions from disparaged, displaced, and needful Southerners. However he didn't use the donations for the good of a recovering nation, but instead indulged in countless bottles of alcohol and women. After wedding a wealthy southern belle named Jane Bottington, he returned north and was greeted indifferently by his countrymen.

Personally my only interactions with the Chapman family, aside from examining the children following birth, consisted of sidestepping Harold's alcohol-comatose body sprawled in front of taverns. Therefore, taking account of his known reputation and my own feelings, for him to falsify Karen's illness for personal gain and then attempt to dupe a rational doctor seems much too complex a scheme for a man of his level of ignorance.

I was staring out the bedroom window when Harold put his hand on my shoulder. "Doc, I apologize for not telling you about my family's past. I ask your forgiveness."

"I do not need an apology. I just need you to be straight with me from now on. If there is anything else you need to tell me then you must confess it at once."

"There is one more thing. Now is not the time or the place. You wouldn't believe me if I told you. You've got to see it for yourself. You've got to see it to *believe*."

"By all means, Harold, whatever it is, show it to me."

"After the sun sets meet me under the gazebo," he said, pointing out the window. "For the sake of believing my story, doc, I hope you experience the lights!"

Late Evening, Friday, March 31, 1888

Hours passed until the sun had settled over the horizon. Karen's condition stabilized, and she experienced no further hallucinations. I decided it was time for me to meet Harold outside and experience the lights.

Moments after I had joined him under the gazebo, George walked out from the house and supplied us with blue-veined cheese, two wine glasses, and a bottle of Port. We sat under the gazebo as a summer's breeze swished across our faces. The breeze was cool and created a mood of relaxation.

Harold sipped his port and sat quietly. For a moment my mind escaped from the stressful events of the house. I reclined in the Adirondack chair, outstretched my legs and closed my eyes, indulging in the tranquil moment.

Sometime later, I took pleasure in a second glass of port and third piece of cheese. Harold was sipping his third glass as he began to stimulate my imagination with tales about the mire just beyond his property. The stories were fantastic and frightening, featuring a cast of demons and ghosts. I did not interrupt him, assuming he was leading up to an explanation of the lights. After all, he had mentioned some supernatural cause behind his family's suffering just hours before.

"Have you heard of the Jersey Devil, doc?"

I shook my head while chewing a piece of cheese.

"Over a century ago, in the Pine Barrens of New Jersey, a woman named Leeds became pregnant with her thirteenth child. She said that child would be born the devil. On the baby's birthday, he was born normal but soon changed into a winged and hoofed creature with the head of a horse. The beast flew up to the ceiling and whipped a forked tail around the room, impaling the midwife with it. It's said that the mother was a witch and the father the devil himself!"

Sober, I would have scoffed at such stories. As a doctor, tales of the supernatural are automatically ruled out as imaginative explanations of events and sicknesses people don't understand. But, being my belly was full of port, my personality turned lighthearted and naïve.

"Do you suspect this... Jersey Devil, as you call it, has come for your family?"

He shook his head, proceeding to expound upon the ominous. He spoke of ghastly insecurities that induced phobias too intense to be cured by psychiatric therapies. He described demons whose evil minds constructed treacherous plights, through which no man could forge with sanity intact. His speech wavered in frightful intonations as he began speaking of the light that manifested within the mire, which he described as a torturing pestilence.

"The torturing pestilence is what attacked my family," he said. "Like the Jersey Devil, the pestilence is a horrific monster conjured up from the bowels of Hell." He held his wine glass out with his index finger pointing toward the general direction of the mire. "It can be seen clearly from this gazebo."

I sat up in the Adirondack chair and adjusted my posture to give Harold my full attention. I had never heard of the torturing pestilence during my years of study. And, my mind clouded by inebriation, he had successfully intrigued me.

"They are spectral lights that form over the marsh at nightfall. Small luminous balls that appear out of thin air, which can be seen drifting through the trees."

I interrupted with a soft snicker. "What you are seeing is only the natural discharges of swamp gas. Spectral lights, this torturing pestilence as you say, are nonexistent. It seems you've been tilting Port to your lips too often!"

He held his glass out before us and dropped it upon the maple tabletop. The glass base bounced and clinked as it spun and vibrated until it rested upright. He gave me an ill-tempered glare. He was not humored or convinced otherwise by my explanation of the lights.

But his abrupt anger, which scorned my scientific suggestions, withered under a sudden fear. His teeth chattered.

His brows rose, exposing the whites of his eyes. They stared deep into my own eyes, which were trustless to all paranormal subjects.

"As twilight sets," he whispered, "you can hear bullfrogs croaking and crickets chirping within Cole's Woods. Soon, however, they stop in unison as the torturing pestilence manifests. A small ball of blue light burbles from underneath the water's surface and rises into the air. Then the horrific light climbs to an approximate height of ten feet and contorts into the shape of a human being. I can hear its shrill, pain-stricken wails as it searches Cole's Woods for victims, and for the house it lived in when alive."

He turned, looking past me at his own house. "The one in which my family now resides. We were doomed from the moment the pestilence found us."

He glanced silently back into the woodlands. I took this moment of quietness to state my case once again. "Harold, if I may say, it is only swamp gas you are seeing. Trust me."

He stepped out from under the gazebo and pointed at the mire again. "I don't think it was a coincidence, the first time I saw those lights. It was just after Jane passed on. Soon after seeing them, Maggie died, followed by David a week later. On the eve of each death, I saw those lights form over the mire and float through Cole's Woods."

He cleared his throat. "The lights have no simple explanations such as natural swamp gas being discharged. It's the specter of my wife coming to feed on her own children, like a vampire. I laid Jane to rest in my family's burial grounds, just beyond the mire. I've dreaded her return for the past two years, fearing she would come for Karen. Now, being that the lights have returned, I believe she has come to claim her last child. If that's the case then I fear I'll fall soon thereafter."

I set my port on the table and said, "If I may ask, how did Jane die and why do you think she has come back for the rest of her family?"

Harold took a deep breath. "Two years ago I woke up to Jane moaning. She was holding her stomach, huddled over a vessel sink. I hurried out of bed and stood by her side, asking what was the matter. She did not answer me; instead she vomited blood. After she stopped vomiting, I insisted she call on you right away. I even had the driver get the carriage ready, but she refused help."

"Why didn't you make her come?" I asked.

He shrugged his shoulders. "I don't know. She said she was just too tired to go through an examination, and she didn't want the children to think something was wrong with her. All she wanted was to rest in bed. And so that is what she did for three days. I kept watch over her and remained ready to call on you if necessary. But she never asked me to. She just kept on getting worse. Then on the fourth day I awoke and found her dead. Blood was encrusted on her mouth and neck, so much that her nightgown collar was drenched. Her skin was white as a ghost, her eyes turned black."

I rose to my feet and stood next to him. "Who did she have contact with before she fell ill?"

Harold closed his eyes tight, trying to hold back his emotions. Through a voice broken and pained, he said, "She had just returned from her parents' plantation in the south. Her father was ill and wasn't expected to live more than a month. She arrived there a few days before he died and left two weeks after his burial. During that time, her mother fell ill also but recovered."

"What were her father's symptoms?"

"The same ones my entire family had—including Karen. David's was more severe and he died after only two days. Maggie lasted two weeks before perishing."

"Why didn't you ask me for help?"

"Their deaths were not caused from illness. They fell ill because of some evil entity," he said, banging his fist against the gazebo.

I placed my hand on his shoulder and squeezed in sympathy, which calmed him down. I then asked, "Why would you think that, Harold?"

His anger subsided and he started to cry. Wiping away the tears, he said, "When my wife returned home, she told me about a ritual she participated in a day after her father's death. This ritual started our family curse!"

"What kind of ritual?"

Harold paced around the gazebo without making eye contact. I could tell he was embarrassed. "Two months before she traveled to pay her last respects to her dying father," he said, "her brother Jack, who fought for the south in the Civil War, retired from military duty and returned home. He had been ill and received an immediate discharge. He had a terrible cough and was vomiting blood. The military doctors diagnosed him with tuberculosis. Many soldiers contracted it; it spread easily through the camps. Some of them got it during the war, but never died from it. Instead they carried it in their bodies and infected those around them. This went on for many years and the disease continued to kill soldiers. Jack happened to be one of many who got ill but didn't die — not right away, that is.

"His mother tried to nurse him back to health, but he died soon after arriving home. Jane received a message telling of her brother's death, and that she had missed his funeral. We were planning a trip south to visit his grave when another message arrived telling of her father's illness. Without giving it a second thought, she hurried south without me or the children."

Harold sat down, crying again. I gave him a moment to collect his thoughts.

A while later he continued. "After her father's funeral, a family friend who attended pulled Jane and her mother aside and expressed his concern for their loss. More importantly, he was concerned for *their* health now. He filled their heads with superstitions of souls rising from their graves to feed on the living and drain the life from them. He convinced them to exhume her brother and father, remove their hearts, burn them, and drink the ashes to ward off evil spirits. He said that if they didn't, the spirits of the deceased would return for them and continue to feed. So they did it, and I believe that was how my wife fell ill. Maybe something went awry during the ritual... maybe they missed some important preliminary step...

"At any rate, when Jane returned home she wasn't herself. She stopped talking and kept to herself. She loved reading books and riding her horses, but she did none of those things. She became withdrawn. I figured she was just grieving so I gave her time to herself, but as the days went by she never came around. That is when I forced it out of her and upon hearing her confess that she had cannibalized her own family members, I was shocked and sickened. She told me that her father looked like a vampire and her brother a ghoul. Their bodies had grown fat, as if they were still eating and drinking, and their hair and fingernails continued growing. I'm not a man to believe in the supernatural, and so I found her story absurd. It wasn't until after she died that I began to think maybe there was something to her story. After David died, I became a believer."

He turned from me and covered his face, obviously embarrassed over what his wife had done. To him, Jane was a southern lass filled with charm, manners, and highly respectful toward the Catholic Church. He couldn't face me and stood up and walked out from under the gazebo. I could hear him sniffling and I felt uncomfortable in his presence.

I wanted to explain the situation to him from a doctor's point of view. I wanted to say that to the uneducated, the victims merely appeared to be vampires. Their bodies lost their pigmentation, similar to a vampire's complexion, and after death they began to bloat as if they were still feeding. But actually their bodies naturally released gases during decomposition. The skin would shrivel back from the fingernails, giving the appearance of new growth. The skin around the skull also shrink, giving the effect of hair growth.

He didn't need to tell me her story in full detail, but out of respect I didn't stop him. I understood what he was explaining to me. I already knew of such a ritual from colleagues who witnessed such events first hand. Victims showed the first signs of their illness by blood trailing from their mouths, ghostly skin, and sunken eyes. During the night, they woke up coughing, their throats clogged with mucus, and by morning relatives would find their loved ones either dead or at death's door. Superstitious people called this disease the vampires' consumption. As a medical doctor, however, I knew they died from tuberculosis—which was sometimes treatable depending on the stage and severity of the illness.

To stave off infection and protect themselves from the consumption, surviving family members exhumed those who died from the disease. Then the family would remove and burn the heart and feed the ashes to the sick to cure them. This ritual also stopped the nightly visits and drainage of life from the living. The healthy also consumed the ashes in order to ward off the supernatural affliction. Then the family members would mutilate the corpse by decapitation, removing limbs, and arranging them to confuse the evil spirits, rendering the corpse unless.

It was that final step—the removal of limbs and their rearrangement—that I figured his family had forgotten to do. Because of this, they had allowed the cause of their plight to rise from the grave and commit its hellish acts. I kept this theory to myself; I didn't want to upset Harold any further. I decided that seeing the lights he spoke of was the least important detail of the night. His grieving, his daughter, and his own mental wellbeing were more important.

I rose beside Harold and stared with him down the Cole's Woods trail leading toward the mire. I thought about the conditions his family took upon falling ill: the blood trails, ghostly skin, sunken eyes, and quick deaths. I could no longer mock him or try to convince him otherwise. He had swayed my opinion of the subject at hand. I decided to leave him be so he could mourn in peace, rather than try and will him into disbelieving in the supernatural.

"I must check on my patient before I turn in," I said through a drawn-out yawn. "Thank you for the cheese and port, your hospitality today has turned very cordial..."

Before I could finish, he covered my mouth with his hand and placed his index finger in front of his lips. He pointed into the woods and said nothing. He didn't have to; the visuals that I laid my eyes upon spoke on his behalf.

Drifting about the woods was a dim light. I had to focus my eyes away from it to see it clearly. A ball-shape formed, and for five minutes it remained suspended in one spot about five feet above the ground. Its brightness intensified slowly, and it began rising higher as its shape distorted into a full-bodied apparition of a human being. It then moved parallel to the property.

"The torturing pestilence," Harold whispered. "It has risen!"

Shocked, we did nothing more than stare and watch it. We affixed our eyes on the light as it illuminated the surrounding trees and bushes. To our surprise, the light metamorphosed into a vaporous, winged creature. It soared above the braches, taking the shape of the Jersey Devil that Harold spoke of. At least I figured the form to be the Jersey Devil. However, my own imagination formed the image from the thought of the creature that had been implanted in my subconscious. The creature's appearance, more than likely, was just a coincidence.

We stood and watched the specter's form contort into shapes that looked like arms and legs, which grasped at movements created by the breeze thinking, as if it had intelligence, there were victims within its reach. As it scoured the woods, its disembodied voice groaned in drawn-out, repetitious tones, "Harold...Karen...Harold...Karen..."

Neither of us dared to move an inch, nor did our heads turn to follow the light; only our eyes kept constant contact with it. We muttered not a single word, fearing the light would hear us. We drew not a single breath, fearing the light would smell the port in our exhalations. Scared to death, we stood petrified that the light would attempt to possess our souls or worse.

Then all of a sudden, without warning, the light dematerialized and vanished. Harold and I breathed a sigh of relief. After figuring it was safe to move, we turned and walked to the house in long, quick strides, glancing over our shoulders into the woods. We hoped the light didn't detect us and double back.

Neither of us muttered a single sentence. My mind ran wild and I became overwhelmed with various thoughts pertaining to the paranormal and more importantly the torturing pestilence. Nothing I said at that moment would've sounded sane. And to Harold, everything I wanted to say would've sounded merely rational.

Upon entering the house, we checked on Karen. She was still in dire condition. I checked her vital signs but they hadn't changed. This gave me hope that she could be nursed back to health—unless what we'd just seen in the woods was indeed coming to take her life.

I performed my quick examination, and Harold's spirits rose when I determined that his daughter could survive. He ordered Clarabelle to keep vigil and to retrieve us if his daughter's conditions changed. We then said our goodnights and retired to our respective bedrooms.

Midnight, Saturday, April 1, 1888

With Harold's permission, I dressed in nightclothes worn by his late son, David. After climbing into bed, I pulled the blankets up to my chest and hoped to take full advantage of the comfort until morning. My eyes fluttered closed but opened as thoughts of what had transpired within the woods plagued me. It seemed like an eternity trying to fall asleep, but in reality it was no longer than an hour.

Redirecting my attention on sleeping rather than the light's haunting aura was difficult. Its ghastly vocal pattern and overall terrifying presence turned my state of mind to paranoia. All shadows of tree branches shifting across the bedroom walls became monsters coming to take my life. The shadows reminded me of the light and how it moved through the woods as it swooped, changed shape, and floated to dizzying heights.

I felt lethargic from the alcohol I'd consumed. My inebriated mind was clouded and any attempt to confront the true origin and meaning of the light remained impossible. I had lost my ability to reason soundly. Furthermore, the alcohol fueled my emotional state. The visions of the light were too dreadful to think about, and too mystifying to understand.

With much relief, I finally fell asleep and awoke just as the sun was climbing over the horizon. The questions about the light still circled through my head. How could a body rise from the grave in the form of an apparition, without it being some illusion?

To me it seemed impossible, but I saw it with my own eyes. How could this ghost think, speak, attack, and feed on the living? This was a deep mystery which would never be uncovered by mere brainstorming. To uncover the answers I'd have to examine Jane's body or at least her grave. And exhuming her body was out of the question, as asking for permission at this time would infuriate Harold against me once again. We managed to set aside our differences and I didn't want anything to ruin it for Karen's sake. She didn't need the added stress of two grown men continuing to argue right from wrong, bark orders at each other, and fight like toddlers over a toy.

I laid in bed thinking, but after a short time decided there was no explanation for what I'd seen. It could not possibly have been a hallucination. If it were a mirage created by alcohol or an overactive imagination, then only I would have witnessed the spirit. Therefore, I would not have shared the experience with Harold. What I saw was real.

At last I got out of bed and splashed cold water on my face. I dressed accordingly for the weather in David's clothes; outside a hard, steady rainfall pelted the roof, creating quick muffled thumps. The air was chilly and a fog blanketed the property. Visibility was poor. The edge of the Cole's Woods and the trail entrance leading into it could not even be seen. The gazebo was eighty yards away, give or take, and silhouetted by fog. Only an outline of its masterful construction could be deciphered.

The decision was made the night before that it was better for Karen to get plenty of rest, rather than me waking her up in the morning. Clarabelle was supposed to fetch me to check on her condition at the proper time, but neither Harold nor his servants were up and about the house, so I took it upon myself to prepare coffee, in hopes of assuaging my hangover.

While the water heated, I heard Clarabelle's voice through the house: "Mis'er Chapman, come quick! Karen gone an' be attacked. Da child been attacked!"

I raced up the staircase and down the hallway to Karen's bedroom. Clarabelle sped past me, weeping with her head buried in her hands. "Forgive me, forgive me," she shouted. "I done da best I could've, oh Lord!"

In the bedroom I found Harold kneeling at his daughter's bedside with his head pressed against the mattress. At first glance, it was clear that Karen was close to death.

On her face dried, bloody spittle encrusted the corners of her mouth and over her chin. Her skin had turned pale, lips crimson-flushed, and her eyes sunken in. Her labored breathing suggested fluid in her lungs. It was obvious to both Harold and I that our worst fears had come true: the spirit we saw drifting about the woods had returned to claim Karen, and now she was in serious trouble.

I ran from Karen's bedroom into David's room to collect my medical bag. Before settling into bed I'd placed it on the windowsill. When I reached for it, I glanced out the window and saw no trees growing near the house. The nearest tree was growing far away at the edge of the woods. Those shadows I'd seen drifting across the wall last night weren't made by any branches. They were made by that damn floating light.

I turned from the window and left the room, blaming myself for Karen's condition. If I hadn't been drinking, I would have thought with a sober mind and checked in on Karen. I could have kept her from being attacked.

Harold, upon hearing me re-enter the room, cried through his hands: "That demonic light, it—it circled around and entered into my house. I'm losing my last child to it. You have to help me reverse this plague before it takes her from me. You have to help me destroy the cause of this torturing pestilence, the corpse of my wife!"

To make sure I understood his request, I asked, "You want to exhume your wife and disturb her resting body?"

"It is not disturbing the peace of the dead when the dead rise and commit devilish deeds!"

Without further hesitation or thought upon the matter, I obliged to his gruesome request. I knew what we were to do, and I did not find it objectionable. If we had not seen the light in the woods and heard that eerie voice then I would have called him mad. But I *had* seen the light, and the deed he was asking me to commit would give me the opportunity to examine her corpse.

That afternoon Harold led me into the basement where we collected a crowbar, spaded shovels, a large knife, oil lanterns, and other supplies necessary to complete our task.

While placing the smaller tools into a large sack, Harold turned to me and said, "If by chance something were to happen to me, I want you to run away. Do not hesitate, do not turn back, and just continue to run. Come back to the house and leave the property with Karen. Do what you can for her."

"Do not talk in such a grim manner," I said, pulling the drawstring on the sack tight. I had my doubts anything horrible would happen. But at the same time, I was reluctant to go into this situation haphazard. "I think we are both going to return safely."

"I could only hope. But if you were to die and I survived then I would feel a great amount of guilt. This is my family's curse. Not yours."

"As long as a patient of mine is dying, then it is my ordeal as well."

Harold shook his head in agreement. "Then make this deal with me, doc, if one of us is to parish then the other must return to the house without regret to save Karen. As a father, I will give my own to save my child."

"As a doctor, I will give my own to save my patient."

Harold extended his hand and we shook in agreement.

George appeared at the bottom step of the cellar staircase and cleared his throat. "Excuse me, sirs, I have your boots and coats laid out by the backdoor, as you requested."

"Thank you, George, and please keep an eye on Clarabelle. She seems stressed from the situation. If she cannot watch and care for Karen as the doc has instructed, then relieve her until our return."

"As you wish." George bowed his head, turned, and climbed upstairs.

We followed behind and headed for the back of the house. There, we laced up the boots and pulled on our jackets. The heavy sack of tools rested over my shoulder. Harold carried the shovels and pickaxe under his arms.

We walked across his backyard. Behind us, the dew that clung to the blades of grass left impressions of our footsteps. The rain that had fallen throughout the day was now a mist, which dampened our clothes and slicked the tool handles. Harold kept dropping the shovels, and the sack over my shoulder became heavier from the moisture soaking through the fabric. The fog failed to lift, keeping visibility down to about the same distance it had been during the morning. We passed the gazebo, and soon we came to the entrance of the trail leading into Cole's Woods and Harold's family plot.

Visibility slimmed to barely ten yards between the trunks. The trees looked like skeletons as their branches reached through the fog, turning into crippled boney arms, contorting in various directions. As we brushed up against them, they teased and tapped our shoulders, bedeviling our minds with tricks and images of monsters. The tree bark, highlighted by murky shadows, formed faces with eyes that followed our every step.

We heard the crackling of brush and froze in our tracks.

Hairs stood on the backs our necks and goose bumps popped up over every inch of our bodies. We confided in each other that neither of us had been this frightened our entire lives. We listened in the direction of the noises and stared into the fog. Something unseen and horrific lurked in the woods. But we managed to shirk our apprehension and hike on.

For the next twenty minutes, we cautiously kept our ears poised to detect the slightest noise. Every now and then we heard a twig snap and a dead leaf crunch in the distance. Whatever we had sensed earlier was gaining on us; nay, *tracking* us. We said nothing as we continued hiking, for we were both too frightened to speak.

Harold stopped and sat on a fallen tree. I dropped the sack of tools and rubbed the pain out of my shoulders. "Are you okay?" I asked.

"I need a few minutes of rest. I haven't hiked through these woods since I buried my wife. I forgot how hard it is. The fallen trees, the sharp drops and steep hills, are a bit too much on my old body. Since my wife died, I stopped taking care of myself. I've gained many pounds from drinking and eating too much."

I sat down next to him. "We should not rest long, though. I fear we are being followed."

I opened the sack and removed a canteen, unscrewed the cap, and handed it to Harold. He sipped the water and handed it back. I sipped as well and screwed on the cap. We sat for another ten minutes not speaking, keeping our ears to the woods around us. The silence was broken when Harold jerked his head to the left, grabbing my forearm with such force that I almost screamed.

"What is it?" I snapped.

He pointed into the woods. "See those two boulders?"

"Yes."

"Just to the left there is a bush. I saw something dart behind it. If you look close you can see a dark figure crouched behind it through the branches."

I stared at the bush but saw nothing. "I don't see it. What did the figure look like?"

"Human."

I squinted, studied the bush, then saw it, a short figure trying to keep still. It was hiding from us and waiting for us to move, possibly in order to attack.

"I see it now. It is curled up in a ball."

Harold stood and held the pickaxe up over his head, ready to strike anything that lunged forward. "It's the corpse of my wife. She is trying to sneak up on us from behind. But we must get her before she gets us!"

I pressed my hand against his chest, holding him back. Then I lowered the pickaxe with my other hand. "That isn't her. It's something else."

"What else could it be?"

"I don't know, but we have to find out. If we let our guard down it could attack and we'll never save Karen."

I opened the sack and removed the crowbar, brandished it like a sword, and crept toward the bush. Behind me, Harold held the pickaxe in front of his body. The head of the axe was level with his shoulders, the end of the handle at his waist. Through the fog we saw the dark figure dart out from the bush and hobble behind a tree. It was short and pudgy, a limp causing it to dip to the right, arms flailing to keep balanced. Behind, a tail whipped in the air and flapped in the draft as it ran, breathing heavily.

Without speaking I motioned for Harold to go right. I went left. We circled around to the tree and raised our weapons. I held up my fingers and counted down from five, and as my thumb curled in to zero we jumped from behind the tree, bringing our weapons down. Harold let out a violent scream and closed his eyes.

"Wait, Harold, no!" I yelled, looking down at our target. In one swift motion I turned my wrists up and redirected the crowbar skyward, into the pickaxe head Harold was thrusting down. With all my strength I pushed on the pickaxe and broke it from Harold's grip. The weapon spiraled through the air, coming to rest in some nearby trees.

I looked at man on the ground that we were about to kill and asked, "George, what are you doing here? You almost got yourself killed!"

Before he could speak, Harold lifted him to his feet and started scolding him. "You old fool, you're supposed to be watching over my daughter and Clarabelle."

George's voice shook as he raised his hands, pressed his

palms together, and interlocked his fingers. "I...I...I'm sorry. I just needed to tell you that most of the servants have fled. There aren't many of us left. The ones who stayed fear you won't be returning, and they demanded an update on your progress. Even Clarabelle is threatening to leave if I did not check. She needed to know you were still alive. So I came here to find you."

"Why did you hide behind that bush?" Harold asked angrily.

George favored his ankle, bowed his head like a scolded child, and said, "I could not tell if that was you. The fog is too thick to make anything out. That is why I hid. Then I ran because I saw someone coming toward me. I twisted my ankle and fell."

"You could have been killed if I didn't recognize you," I said, placing a consoling hand on his shoulder.

George looked at me with an apologetic smile. "I'm sorry, sir. I didn't want the remaining staff to leave."

I sat George on the ground and pulled off his shoes and socks then felt his ankle for breaks. "Nothing broken here, but is your ankle strong enough to make it back to the house?"

He replaced his shoe and sock, stood, and walked for several paces. "It is, doctor, and I do apologize again!" Then he was off just as suddenly as he'd appeared, hobbling back toward the house.

We reached the mire minutes later without further incident. The fog churned over the water and thinned, making for clearer visibility and allowing us to see across. Alarmed bullfrogs, aware of strangers amongst them, hopped from their peat moss perches. Rotted trees, whose trunks were implanted in the murky slush comprising the mire's bottom, leaned out of the water. Some snapped off midway up their trunks, while others broke off at the surface. From one of the trees a spooked owl quickly spun his head around, caught sight of us, flew off and disappeared into the fog. Beyond the water, the fog re-thickened, cloaking the rest of the foliage.

We walked around the water's perimeter and found the opposite side of the trail. We continued another fifty yards until the path came to a dead end.

"Where do we go from here?" I asked, placing the sack of tools on the ground to give my shoulder a rest.

Harold pointed into the mangled brush. "My family's plot is beyond that thicket. My great-grandfather created it here to hide it from grave robbers. It worked. Not a single grave has ever been disturbed. We will have to crawl under this thicket to get to the plots. I'll go first, you hand me the tools after I make it through."

The thicket was dense, intertwined with vines that wove through the wild raspberry and burning bushes, both displaying their fruits and flowers. Sections were comprised of fallen tree branches. With our imaginations running rampant, the branches looked like broken and strewn bones. The ground, thus littered with broken-off braches and dead rotten berries, resembled the scattered remnants of deceased humans in various stages of decay.

For those whose bravery would labor at this suggestive and ominous sight, they would have turned back. For us, however, it was an encouraging sign to complete our task.

Harold dropped to his knees and onto his stomach. He jostled his body through and under the entangled brush, contorting his torso around the curvature of each limb and trunk. Upon reaching the opposite side, he called for the tools. I pushed them along the ground beneath the bushes. Then I followed suit.

After crawling through, I stood, brushed my clothes free of dirt, and gazed upon the cemetery's unfortunate condition. Its dilapidation was to the extent that future burials, under normal circumstances, would be banned until renovation had deemed the site safe. Sinkholes sporadically pockmarked the ground. Weeds and wild flowers sprouted between thigh-high patches of sunburned crabgrass. Fallen trees had crumbled to the ground and become stricken with swarms of insects.

A dozen wooden crosses marked the deceased family members' resting places. However, no visible inscriptions were carved upon them. Only the apparent rate of decomposition gave clues as to who occupied the graves, and for how long. The weeds and grasses grew over and wrapped around the older crosses, encasing them within a chrysalis of rotted stems and leaves. Some were ridden with termite mud tunnels. Thin wooden strips peeled from their façades and flapped in the breeze. The more recent crosses were merely sun bleached, blemished with small crusty bird droppings.

"Which grave is your wife's?" I asked.

Harold pointed to the far left corner. "That one."

We approached the grave and examined the ground around it. The turned, darkened soil, void of weeds and grass, indicated that something or someone had recently visited the plot. Knowing something could be lurching about, possibly ready to trounce, I felt a tingle of fright drizzle down my spine, as though fondling skeletons had crept their cold, boney fingers across my skin. At that instant, I wanted nothing more than to exhume and exterminate the corpse of its demented and slaughtering plague, then flee the gravesite for good.

But instead Harold handed me a shovel and spoke in an apprehensive voice. "We better hurry. The sun will be down soon. We will not wish to disturb the grave after nightfall and allow the corpse's body access to the world."

Sunset, Saturday, April 1, 1888

We dug into the grave, with the sun still high above the horizon. Yet the thickness of the mire's vegetation shadowed the gravesite, giving the impression of a premature dusk. The dig was harsh on our old bodies, and numerous times we had to stop to rest our muscles and catch our breath.

Harold complained of his back cramping. My back held up well under the strain, but my shoulders tired and burned from carrying the sack all that distance. The skin on my hands turned raw as the wooden shovel handle twisted within my palms. Torn strips of cloth from the jacket I wore served as gloves, but the idea came too late as the rawness of my palms soon blistered over.

We took alternating breaks to replenish ourselves. Harold took the first digging shift, as I rested on the ground and sipped water from the canteen. I took time to rewrap my hands and rub the cramps from my shoulders. With each break, however, we stalled our advancement through the soil to the coffin. As did the roots that had grown over the coffin lid, which we chopped away with our shovels. We also removed rocks of various shapes and weights, creating a bigger strain on our bodies. Because of this, the dig took longer than expected and induced consequences and terrors unforeseen at the onset.

Harold dug at a pace that was hurried and worrisome. I feared he would overexert himself and pull his back muscles. I encouraged him to slow down, to allow his muscles recovery time between shovelfuls, and to conserve energy. But he scoffed at my suggestion, smile that he was *all right*. He also stated that the dig must be completed before the sun set and before the monster buried within awoke.

He continued digging rapidly, tossing dirt from the grave, but moments later he stopped to lean on his shovel handle. "I'm starting to feel lightheaded and weak!" he exclaimed.

"You must rest," I said. "I fear the digging and stress of the situation at hand is too much for you. It may sound selfish of me but I do not wish to continue this ritual without you. A family member of the deceased is needed to break the spell."

He looked at me and smiled. "It's not selfish, doc. It's the truth."

With my help, he climbed out from the grave and sat upon the ground. He unscrewed the canteen cap, took a sip. As he rested, I continued the dig and after a few shovelfuls, I examined his condition. His breathing became deeper and his eyes restabilized. His health seemed to be improving.

About ten minutes later, weakness settled into my own body. My breathing turned into a struggle. My lungs felt empty with each drawn breath, and my diaphragm started to spasm. My heart rate dropped and I felt as though I was spinning in circles.

I stopped digging as Harold had moments before, propped myself up on the shovel handle, and closed my eyes to stop the spinning. Whatever affliction weakened Harold's body had started to hinder me as well. This was not a coincidence but some sort of unseen plague.

I opened my eyes and gazed into the ground, hoping my vertigo would cease, but it only worsened. The soil churned with frightening images of ghouls. The faces of victims past wilted into human-serpent hybrids, feeding and mating upon mounds of dead carcasses, rotting and floating in pools of blood. These carrion dreams exploded into liquefied sparks that burbled from within the dirt.

Sensing something was wrong, Harold asked, "Are you all right, doc?"

"I've become weak," I said through short, choppy breaths. "I'm experiencing transitory deliriums."

"Deliriums? I do not understand."

"Short hallucinations," I said, then collapsed onto my knees without warning.

I could feel the stench of the carcasses filling and clogging my lungs, forming into a sphere that expanded and constricted my trachea. The sphere continued growing until it vibrated and tore as if hatching. Then I felt a small serpentine creature propelling in vertical undulations as it slithered down to the end of my trachea. I gasped for air, but the girth of the creature suffocated me. It wiggled and split into two separate serpents, both slithering into my bronchial tubes, where they intruded into my bloodstream.

I looked at my arms and saw my skin bulge and wiggle from the serpents traveling through my veins. I felt them burst through the vein walls, burrow underneath, and disappear into my muscles. My skin stretched as the creatures grew in size, multiplying in the same manner as before: one serpent becoming two, two becoming four, four eight, and so on. I soon lost count as the serpents reached triple digits.

I collapsed onto my stomach and thrashed about. My stomach went sour as bile sizzled the flesh off the serpents' bodies. My diaphragm violently constricted, forcing the creatures to be vomited out through my mouth.

The heads of the creatures were void of eyes. Their mouths opened with forked tongues. Their skin was covered in black and red scales with patches of raw skin where my stomach acid had boiled away their hides. They had no appendages and the tail end formed a segmented point with a scorpion-like stinger with serrated edges.

The creatures slithered toward me and hooked their tails over their heads, thrusting their stingers into my skin. The tails sliced and punctured me until they formed a hole large enough to burrow back inside.

The pain was horrific. It felt as though hundreds of knives

were stabbing and slicing at my skin. I could not move my arms to swat them away because I was too weak. All I could do was lay and watch their bodies slither into mine. My heart raced as the first serpent wriggled its head into the wound. I felt every inch of its length burrowing into my flesh until its serrated stinger disappeared into my body. One after another the serpents entered through the holes carved in my arm and torso.

One serpent entered through my ear. Its body became wedged within the canal and it bucked about trying to get free. It bellowed an angry squeal between hot, breathy hisses. I could feel it stretching its body out, then contorting thinner, hoping to free itself and navigate deeper into the tiny crevasse of my ear.

Suddenly a loud popping and tearing sound exploded, followed by the feeling of the serpent dissipating into smaller serpents as its body ripped in half. The tiny creatures slithered deep into my ear and fed upon my eardrum. The last thing I heard for that brief moment before I went deaf was their biting, gnashing, and tearing.

The other serpents traversed my arms, bent around my shoulders, and gnawed their way into my chest. As they gathered around my heart, immense pain radiated throughout my chest. In an instant, my torso tightened and my heartbeat ceased as the creatures ravaged it. The light from the lanterns diminished and my eyes flickered closed. The pain in my chest subsided as I started losing consciousness. I realized I was dying.

Then a soft thump vibrated through the dirt inside the grave. My body lifted off the ground, drifting out of the grave. I began to lower and felt the stiff blades of dead grass crumble under my weight. Within seconds, I felt my muscles strengthen, my heart beating, and the rest of my respiratory systems begin to function normally. My eyes opened. The heat and the light from the lanterns blinded me, and I rubbed my eyes until I could see again. Harold was crouched over me, unsure of how to handle my sudden collapse.

"Tell me how to care for you, doc!" he insisted, panicked.

I tried to sit up but the trees and grave markers spun around me. I collapsed to my side and closed my eyes while everything continued to spin. The pain and sensation of the serpents consuming my body disappeared.

"I do not require you to care for me," I said. "Whatever is buried in that grave drained my energy through visions of torment, but it seems there is nothing physically wrong with me. I'll be fine soon enough."

"What did you see?"

"Serpents. They hatched inside of me and started devouring my body and soul. The same would have befallen you if I had not noticed your body becoming weak and pulled you from the grave. I now know why Karen was hallucinating. The torturing pestilence was controlling her."

"I'm sorry. I should have helped you before you collapsed."

"No need to apologize. When I felt my body succumb to the torturing pestilence, I should have climbed out of the grave on my own."

He turned and looked into the grave. "If it is true that you experienced the plague that has attacked my family, then I will finish digging and sacrifice myself before allowing you to die."

"If you collapse then I will pull you from the grave."

He shook his head. "Do not rescue me. Leave the area and tell the remaining servants to flee and take Karen with you. We made a pact and now you must own up to it."

I did not argue.

He jumped into the grave and continued digging. He dug fast and with the intention of reaching the casket before he was overcome. Minutes later, he pushed the shovel into the ground and we heard a hollow thud. It was just in time. The sun washing over the treetops had lowered beneath the canopy, and only our lanterns illuminated the gravesite. The torturing pestilence's witching hour was drawing nigh.

Harold scraped dirt from the casket lid. The wood had rotted from lying underground for two years. It had turned dark from the moisture seeping through, caused by rainfall and the mire flooding over during the spring thaw. It was apparent by the small crevices and holes decorating the coffin that insects had also festered inside.

"Prepare for the worst if she is alive," Harold said.

I nodded and held the pickaxe tight in my hands. My fingers wrapping around the handle turned white as I shook in fear. I positioned my body so my right foot was pointing to the thicket. If I had to run, I wanted to be ready.

Harold dug into the side of the coffin with a crowbar and pried off the lid. The wood was weak and the rusted nails made access to the contents effortless. The lid crackled and creaked as he lifted it. A whish of decayed air flushed over our faces, creating the feeling of asphyxiation, which in turn produced a dizzying effect. I pulled up my shirt collar to block the smell, but it was concentrated with fumes too intense to filter. My eyes dried, and they felt like they were burning.

I stared down, blinking in pain, into the opened casket. The sight of the corpse itself was horrifying—though as a doctor it was engrossing in a morbid sense. I never saw a human body in such a state of decay or any type of flesh in such a condition, other than carrion serving as a meal for scavengers. The body was riddled with unrecognizable worms and insects, which had eaten through the wood and into the corpse, using it as a breeding ground and an abundant food source.

The corpse's skin was gray, leathery, and shriveled around the bones. The skull, accented by clinging skin around its jaw line and cheekbones, looked waiflike. The eye sockets were deflated, giving the impression of large, vacant pupils that never blinked or broke contact with us. This voyeuristic feeling made me uneasy, as though the corpse was studying our movements and timing an attack at an opportune moment. Its chin was dropped, mouth opened, creating the sense of an undying, silent scream ... some of which I thought I could hear. But it was only my imagination, or the residual effects of the hallucination I'd suffered.

The burial clothes were tattered, lying loose around the body. Underneath the corpse was a thin layer of sludge, with an oily light spectrum floating about.

Harold knelt and whispered into his wife's shriveled ear. The words were mumbled and quiet. What little could be understood and heard was assumed to be an apology. He then pulled a knife from his boot and sliced into the corpse's chest. The dry skin crackled as the blade cut through. I handed Harold a hatchet and he rammed it down upon her sternum. The blow, though weak, was enough to break through the brittle bones and crumple them into small fragments.

He pushed his hands into the entrails, extracting the heart. It resembled that of a thriving human heart, for it possessed a healthy hue and muscular tones, which surprised the both of us. A corpse buried this long should have had a decayed heart that was shriveled and discolored. This corpse was not then dead; it was alive and had in recent times consumed the blood and soul of a man.

I shivered in disgust, and Harold turned, climbing out of the grave. He placed the heart in a shallow bowl fashioned from stone. With a wooden mallet, he ground up the vital organ into pieces. Using lantern oil, he doused the heart, then struck a match and dropped it into the bowl. The heart burned quickly and radiated a bluish glow. The smell of the burning flesh was dry and reminded me of venison.

Seconds later the fire smothered itself. Harold ground up the larger pieces with a rock and turned the ashen remains into a fine powder. He carefully shook the contents from the bowl into a small glass vial of water. He stirred it by twirling the vial, creating a concoction that, if drank, would ward off the torturing pestilence … or so we hoped.

"Here's to your health!" he said in a sarcastic yet hopeful tone, holding the vial over his head. He swigged a portion of the liquid. His face cringed and he gagged and almost coughed up the mixture. His face cringed, but eventually turned into a smile.

He handed the vial to me and I looked through the glass into the mixture. I shook it and watched the suspended, undissolved powder swirling within. The more I watched it, the more apprehensive I became. I thought about what the mixture was and found myself arguing over the morality of consuming it. But then again, the desecration of the grave, removal and cremation of the heart, seemed to negate any potential for morality.

I closed my eyes, held the vial to my lips, and smiled. "Cheers!" I said, kicking back the liquid like a whiskey shot.

The taste was dry and smoky. My eyes clasped together and my head jerked back, forcing the mixture down. I gagged, not from the taste, but from knowing I consumed ash derived from a human heart. Pieces of ash trickled down my throat as others remained in my mouth. I scrapped my tongue on the backs and fronts of my teeth, wiping away pieces of burnt and ground up heart that lingered within my mouth. I swished a bit of my saliva around and swallowed the remaining particles.

Harold took the vial from me. He capped it and tucked it deep within his coat pocket for safe keeping until we could return to Karen's bedside and have her drink from it as well.

We waited several minutes to allow the mixture's healing capabilities to take effect. My stomach turned as my bile's acidity digested it. I belched and regurgitated the mixture into the back of my mouth. I gagged and came close to vomiting but held back while breathing in deep, hoping the nausea would subside.

"You okay, doc?"

I looked at Harold and smiled. "I'll be fine. I'm not sure if it's the idea of drinking the elixir or the ingredients itself making me ill."

He held his stomach and said, "I feel sick, too. Maybe it's the pestilence within the mixture that we feel. We may have swallowed the infliction voluntarily."

"If that is the case then we have committed suicide!" I said.

Nightfall, Saturday, April 1, 1888

After several minutes the nauseous feeling eased, but my stomach kept churning. Because of my medical training, my own aches and pains went ignored as I kept an observant eye on Harold. By the way he was standing — upright with his hands by his sides, rather than hunched over holding his stomach — I decided he was feeling better.

He leapt into the grave with a sudden confidence heightened by the consumption of the elixir. "Hand me the hatchet," he said, holding his hand out for the tool.

I lowered it to him, but before I let go I looked him in the eyes to express my concern. "Be careful. We may have drunk the remedy, but it might not have taken effect yet."

Harold jerked the hatchet from my grasp. I took no offense knowing full well he was eager to execute the deed. He pushed the corpse's head to the right, exposing a large portion of the neck, and raised the hatchet high. His hand waved back and forth inches at a time as he lined up the blade with the target. He glanced over his shoulder, and by the look on his face it was clear he was worried. The deed he was about to commit would either fail entirely, or else cure his family of the torturing pestilence. I shook my head in a slow approving manner, signaling to him I understood his apprehension and guilt.

He lowered the hatchet to the corpse's neck again, positioning his arm to strike the target cleanly. He then lifted his arm in a quick, jerking backswing and plunged the hatchet toward the corpse with a scream of anger.

But a second before the moment of impact, Jane's corpse sprang to life. The extremities Harold was about to detach and arrange in corresponding positions wrapped around his torso, and he dropped the hatchet. He struggled, trying to free himself and grab the hatchet again, but it was out of reach. He kicked and punched ineffectively. Jane's grip was strong and constricting, and her arms pulled her husband closer, the pressure bending his spine.

Surprised, I jumped backwards and fell onto my back. I pushed myself up and grabbed the pickaxe and held it over my head. I sprang forward, ready to bury one of the points deep in her skull.

But before I could strike the pickaxe down, Harold cried out, "No—save yourself!"

My rage ceased abruptly and I dropped the pickaxe to the ground, reaching into the grave to grab Harold's arm and yank him free of his wife's clutches.

"You fool … let go … save yourself … save Karen!" Harold's voice struggled to speak, as he ordered me to flee and uphold our agreement.

I let go of his arm and turned to run, but my body became stiff and I stopped dead in my tracks. My feet sunk into the earth under a tremendous weight of dread. The leathery, eye-voided skull stared over Harold's shoulders, into my eyes.

Black cataracts clouded the lenses of my pupils, and a dark cloud formed about my head. I could feel my life draining and collecting within Jane's soul. My extremities went limp, my muscles flaccid, and my senses dulled while becoming deprived of all their perceptiveness.

Jane cackled in joy. Her laughter was high-pitched and broke the bond that mesmerized me and linked my soul to her. I blinked as my eyes focused through the cataracts and my knees buckled. Black clouds swarmed around Harold's entire body, but thin enough for me to watch the torturing pestilence ravage away his life.

He was alive when his body started decaying. His complexion turned gray and his muscles wilted. His skin broke apart like a crack upon a frozen pond. Through the crack a cloud of red dissipated into the air as the blood boiled within his veins. His head flopped over on his shoulder and his pupils stared back at me. I saw nothing as I stared through the eyes of his dead body. His wife had drained him of life within seconds.

Jane dropped her husband's body then stood over him, absorbing, feeding off the lingering vapors. The corpse of Jane, a shriveled bag of bones and decomposed entrails, started rejuvenating through a progression of evil. Her muscles twitched and expanded under the skin of her expressionless face, forming eyes that glowed red. Dry strands of hair thickened and glossed over her head with a healthy sheen. Her fingers, stiff and boney, stretched and popped, making a sound like twigs being stepped on and broken.

Jane walked over her husband's body and reached for me. With what little strength I still possessed, I turned and ran headstrong from the burial ground. The light from the lantern faded into the dark abyss of the night, barely illuminating the thicket, but I leapt and burst through to the trial on the opposite side. My body sliced open with small lacerations made by the jagged braches, though my pain soon subsided under a greater agony and fear.

Running down the dark trail unable to see, I tripped over a rock protruding from the soil and fell into the brisk waters of the mire. My heart, stricken with heavy and erratic palpitations, and whose pressure was great, worked as an anticoagulant, allowing the blood to seep from my body. Blood dissipated in the water. This bloodletting lured leeches and dozens of slimy bodies attached their suckers to my skin: to my arms, legs, back, and upon my neck. The mucus worked like an anesthetic, numbing my skin. It was difficult to determine how many leeches had latched onto me to feast upon my blood.

I forced myself to wade, my head above the water, and try to swim. But my muscles had become weak. I decided to float instead, hoping I would regain enough strength to swim and run back to the estate.

At the end of the trail where it met the thicket, Jane rustled through the branches. They snapped as the leaves on the ground crunched beneath her feet. She was coming for me, and I needed to escape. But I was too weak to swim. By chance, my body drifted toward water's edge where I could crawl out and flee. But fearing Jane would hear me sloshing and capture me, I remained in the water with the leeches. This to me seemed a better option than being tortured by a ghoul.

Jane's footsteps grew louder with each step as she neared the mire. My heart pounded harder in my chest and louder in my ears. The water was cold but sweat started trickling down my forehead. My lips quivered and my arms shook, causing ripples to form a target around my body.

I gazed toward the trail, waiting for Jane to emerge. Seconds later, she appeared in an atmosphere of death-walking terror, her joints creaking, her arms swaying at her sides. Her back was hunched over, giving the appearance of an old woman. Her rigid gait, created by her knees' range of motion, remained inflexible, but loosened with each stride as she slowly regained her land legs. Her head drooped, her chin resting on her chest, as if her weak neck could not support the skull's weight. She moaned and gurgled the names of her children: Karen, David, and Maggie.

Dead bugs and worms dripped from her body as each footfall pounded the earth. Swamp flies buzzed and landed on her, instantly dying as their life force was drained away.

Divots along the path tripped her up, causing her to roll her brittle ankle. Her bones snapped and cracked as she stumbled to the ground. She lay on her stomach a moment before pushing up on her hands. She rose to her feet and continued advancing along the trail, dragging her broken ankle and foot behind her, searching for me.

I tried to remain calm. I forced my arms still to avoid making ripples in the water, which she would see. My body began sinking and my ears dipped below the surface. The water touched my lips and I tasted its flavor in my mouth: dirt and raw fish. Panic set in as I sank deeper.

Tilting my head back, I kept my nose above the surface and swallowed the remaining water down my throat. I breathed normal but could feel droplets clinging to my nose hairs. In my new position, I could not see, hear, or smell Jane. All I could see was the fog rolling over the mire, all I could hear was the elevated blood pressure beating in my ears, and all I could smell was the fishy odor. I sensed no waves rippling against my skin, to tell me whether or not she had entered the water.

Then I saw her eyes. They were glowing red and staring into the water near where I was floating. I stared back while projecting positive thoughts, hoping to make her turn away in some form of extrasensory persuasion. Unfortunately she felt me penetrating her mind with unwanted thoughts, and she turned her head to fix her eyes on me. I could feel her stare penetrating my soul, filling it up with her demands.

She persuaded me toward the water's edge, and I unwillingly obliged. I lifted my feet from the bottom of the pond, paddling my hands through the water. When I was five feet from her, she waded in and lifted me out. She slumped me over her shoulder, walked me to dry land, and dropped me on my stomach. My legs still dangled in the water, and I felt more leeches squirming into my shoes. But leeches were the least of my concerns, for I was at the mercy of the dead.

Feeling water dripping on my back, I opened my eyes and looked over my shoulder. Jane was straddling me. I shut my eyes again, giving into the fact I was about to die. I was too weak to run or fight. All I could do was hope I would die quickly.

But as I waited, a black cloud filtered from Jane's mouth. Its pungent death stench singed my nostrils and chocked my lungs as it engulfed my head. My eyes slowly closed, and I slipped into unconsciousness.

Daybreak, Sunday, April 2, 1888

I do not know what transpired between the moment the black cloud filled my lungs and the instant my eyelids fluttered open. When I awoke, I found myself still lying at the water's edge of the mire. Small cuts and circular bite marks littered my body where the leeches had latched on, and my skin was pale from the blood loss. Dozens of these leeches lay scattered about, their tiny bodies shriveled up like burnt bacon.

My arms and legs felt weak, my head dizzy. For nearly an hour I tried to stand but all I could do was crawl away from the water onto the pebbles and sand lining the trail.

As I rested, I wondered if everything I had experienced was a nightmare. But the leech wounds covering my body told otherwise. I realized my luck the night before when Jane found me, for I had feared I was as good as dead and had resigned to the fact. My body had been hers for the taking, my soul for her pleasure. But a miracle had occurred and she left the mire without bringing me further harm. All I could figure was that when I passed out, she had considered me dead, and what little blood and energy she fed off from the leeches attached to my body, she had thought to be mine.

My throat was dry and I was tempted to sip from the mire. But the thought of contracting cholera, typhoid, or any other diseases carried by the microorganisms, such as dysentery, stopped me doing so. I forced myself to stand and gained enough strength to stagger down the trail back to the thicket. Jane had cleared a path through the brush about the width of a doorway. I walked through and into the cemetery.

With a great deal of caution, I approached Jane's open grave, unsure if she had returned to her resting place before sunrise. I expected to see her within and the appearance of her body back to its normal state. But, if that wasn't the case, then she might have wandered into the population and begun attacking Saratoga Springs citizens.

I snuck toward the grave keeping one eye focused on it and another on my surroundings. The tools were still scattered about, the lanterns burned out. Ten feet from the grave, I heard a crunching sound under my feet. I lifted my foot and bent down.

The vial that held the mixture we hoped could save our lives was shattered into pieces. The elixir had not saved Harold but I still held hope for it, as it could very well have worked on Karen.

I continued to the grave, leaned over, and peered in. At the bottom, Harold's dead body lay twisted and white. His clothes were torn off his body and his shoes flung from the grave. His skin clung tightly to the bones. His eyelids were open, exposing eyeballs that had turned gray and deflated. Insects scurried from his ears, while worms wiggled between his teeth and curled under his tongue.

I looked away, picked up a shovel, and prepared to bury Harold's corpse within his wife's grave. My body's weakness had vanished upon seeing him lying lifeless, the shell of a man misunderstood by his community. A man who gave his life to save me, those he employed, and his fellow citizens. Whatever opinions I had of him in the past were now gone, and I held him in the highest esteem. I decided at that moment I could not leave the gravesite until I buried him, a final thank you and a show of respect, of which he was deserving.

Filling in the grave took only twenty minutes. My body felt no fatigue for the pestilence that drained my strength the night before was gone. I was sore from blood loss, but the pain was only noticeable when I focused on it.

Visions of Karen being killed washed over my mind. The shovel fell from my hands and I ran from the gravesite, through the thicket, following Cole's Woods Trail back to the Chapman house. I pushed myself to the limit, Karen, George, Clarabelle and the rest of the servants in my thoughts. I had to save them if they weren't already dead.

The fog of the previous day had lifted and sunshine pelted my face between tree branches and shadows. The eerie anxiety the woods induced was now replaced by a feeling of serenity. I felt the presence of woodland animals rather than fearsome, invisible demons. I smelled flowers and heard birds chirping. These feelings gave me bravery, which I would need upon reaching the house.

I emerged from Cole's Woods, ran through the backyard, and stopped at the Gazebo. I leaned against it catching my breath. My chest heaved, my stomach coiled in, and I coughed and spit saliva from my mouth.

While resting, I glanced up at the house. The once beautifully designed home was turned into a dilapidated shack. Slate shingles lay in piles at the foundation, window glass littered the grass, shutters tilted and hung from single nails, and the porch railing had toppled over and was resting on the ground.

My back slid down the gazebo post. My eyes started to blur as I looked at the grass. The blades morphed into bones and then into fingers and then into hands. The army of skeletal hands crawled toward my body like spiderlings emerging from silken egg sacs. My pupils started to blacken and the feeling of dread swept over me. That pestilence I felt in the grave had invaded me once again, albeit in a weaker state.

Jane was near and felt my presence. If she was not, her aura lingered behind enough to slow my advancement to the house. The skeletal hands grabbed at me and climbed up my pant legs. This time, however, I fought off the hallucination and rose to my feet and staggered on to the house.

Lying next to the back porch was a letter opener I had tossed out the window two days before. I picked it up and held it like a dagger, ready to trust it deep into Jane's chest if I found her lurking inside.

The back door was locked, just as we left it the previous day. Leaning against the house to support my weight, I shuffled around to the front door, but upon laying eyes on it, I froze. The door was ripped off its hinges and strewn about the lawn.

I approached the entrance and peeked through the doorway. Inside, lying on the landing of the staircase, was George's body. His internal organs and muscles were removed, and his flesh had shriveled into deep crevasses that folded over one another. His clothes hung loose around his limbs. His face retained his last expression—fright—and his eyes were wide open, his jaw slack. His tongue was curled back and his plump nose crinkled and narrowed and drooped off his skull.

I searched the house for other victims and, more importantly, survivors. I forced myself to run up the staircase and into Karen's room. Her dead body was gone and the bedroom was in disarray. The top mattress had been pushed off and lay on the floor below the footboard. The sheets were torn to shreds and the feather pillow stuffing was strewn about. The vanity mirror was shattered, as were the glass picture frames. With each step, shards of glass crumbled beneath my feet. All the clothes in the closest and dresser were tossed about the room. The windows were open with the curtains dangling over the siding, as if someone had tried to climb out to safety or something horrific had entered, murdered, and used the window to escape.

Bloody handprints were smeared everywhere, and by following each print I could reenact the struggle. Karen had first been standing on top of her bed, for the handprints were inches from the ceiling. Then the prints moved downward at a sharp angle to the floor molding, and then onto the floor itself, where they disappeared under the toppled mattress.

Underneath the mattress, I noticed curled up toes. I flipped it over and found Clarabelle lying face down on the floor. The handprints were hers, not Karen's. Having been exhausted of life, her black skin had faded into a light tan with patches of white. Her body had collapsed in on itself from being drained of organs, blood, and muscle. Excess skin pooled about two feet from her bones, like a bunched up blanket. I could not see her face, but I could tell by the outline of her jaw that her expression was the same as George's — fright.

Karen's body was missing. I could only speculate about what had happened. First, Karen rose from the dead and attacked Clarabelle. Or second, Jane attacked and killed Clarabelle and then took her daughter's body with her to turn her into the same creature Jane had become. If the second was true, then that meant two demons walked the Earth, stalking, attacking and preying on the innocent.

I tore down a curtain from the window, covered Clarabelle's body, and left the room to continue my search. With all the noise I made I would have drawn attention to myself, and whatever demons lurking within the house would have attacked me if any were present. So I felt safe for the time being.

The rest of the house was ransacked. Drawers turned over and contents tossed across the rooms. Clothes, shoes, and personal effects strewn from closets and dressers. The kitchen was toppled with utensils, with bowls and food littering the floor and countertops and trailing out into the dining room. Throw rugs were torn, curtains ripped to the floor, more holes pelted into walls and more glasses crackling under my feet.

But a family portrait of the Chapmans hung untouched on the living room wall. This effigy displayed the healthy, living, and loving group before it fell to the torment of some evil entity. I stared at their faces and into their eyes, wishing I could have saved them. I whispered an apology to them, then walked away.

Continuing my search, I found more victims who had been unable to escape Jane's wrath. I found the cook in the pantry, tailor in the nook, and seamstress in the parlor, each laying in a mass of deflated skin. All met the same fate, all were killed in the same manner, and all because Harold and I had been unable to complete our task the night before and destroy the root of evil, the torturing pestilence, Jane Chapman.

I wandered outside to the carriage house to retrieve a horse to ride back into town and warn the townspeople. The large oak doors were closed tight and the windows covered over with dust and particles of hay. I could not see inside to determine whether or not the lurking fear that was Jane or Karen hid inside. I pressed my ear to the side of the carriage house and listened for sounds, but heard nothing. I walked to the front of the stable and pulled open the heavy doors and stood in the entrance. The smell of stale horse urine and feces swept over my face, diluting the bittersweet scent of hay.

I surveyed around and underneath the carriage. There were no signs that a single body was hiding or lying dead, and this latter came as a relief. I had grown immune to mutilated bodies over the past twenty-four hours, but still I did not want to find another victim. I hoped someone had survived.

I took one step inside the carriage house and paused. It was quiet, which made me nervous. I figured I had not heard any of the horses because the walls were built thick, but now that I was inside their lack of presence alarmed me. I crouched and looked under the small gap of the stalls for the horses and anyone or anything else. Each of the six stalls was empty except the last. Underneath that gap, I could see a black mass of what looked like a pile of remains from a distance, blocking my view into the stall.

I stood up and crept forward. The top of the door to the stall was level with my neck, making it hard to see inside unless I hoisted myself up onto the side wall or opened the door. Not wanting to put myself in a compromising position where my body was not able to flee, I opted to open the door. With a slight push, it creaked open enough to peek inside. When I gazed upon the stall floor I pushed it open the rest of the way and stared at a gutted horse lying atop a bedding of blood-soaked hay.

Its head was intact, as were its legs and hindquarters. Its mane was dampened with blood, along with the tail hairs. The belly was slit from neck to anus, though the ribs were still attached, leaving the rounded shape of the torso. Strewn about the stall were all the organs.

Without averting my eyes, I backed out and started shutting the door—when I saw what looked like human toes or pieces of intestine poking out from under the horse's hide. I pushed open the door again and removed a horseshoe hammer from the wall, put the hammerhead under the torn lip of the belly, and pulled up on the skin to look inside the horse's body cavity. Curled up in a fetal position was the carriage driver, alive. Sensing he was found he began weeping and shaking in fear.

I whispered to him, "It's me. Doctor Myerburg."

He turned his head away from the spinal column. His eyes were opened wide and stained red from the horse's blood. His face was covered in blood, along with red and gray organ tissue, and his clothes were drenched as well.

"I've came back," I said. "I thought you were killed like the others."

I reached out and pulled him from within the horse, helping him to his feet. His once curly hair was matted with blood and chunks of flesh that glided down his cheeks.

He stepped from the stall and muttered, "I killed the horse. I killed it to save myself."

"I'm sorry..."

He interrupted and spoke louder. "I killed the horse!"

"I know. I'm sorry I did not return sooner to help..."

Again he interrupted, pushing past me. "It was all I could do to save myself from that monster."

"Monster? Do you mean Jane?"

He turned and grabbed my arms, shaking me while yelling between laughter. "That—that wasn't Jane; no...no, no, no...that was a monster. I heard screaming and I—I rushed through the back door and into the kitchen where the screams came from. I stopped dead in my... in my tracks when I saw it kneeling on the floor sucking blood from the hole that it made in the cook's chest. I screamed and the monster looked up at me. It stood and stepped over the cook to reach its arms out... You see, it was coming for me. And that was when I ran out of the house—to the stables."

He paused and looked around. He leaned forward and placed his face inches from mine, whispering, "I don't know why I ran out here."

He paused again and his body shivered as he drew a breath. His talking became less wild and more straightforward as he continued whispering, though his eyes never broke from mine. "I suppose my only thought was to save the horses and not anyone in the house. I then opened each stall and shooed the horses away, except one. I meant it no harm. I was going to ride away on it, but in all the commotion its old heart must have gave out and it collapsed. Maybe it would have lived, but I panicked. And that... that is when I did the unthinkable. I took a knife and I cut open its belly!"

I looked down at his hand; the knife he used to open the horse was still clutched in his palm. His hand twitched as he continued his graphic story, raising the knife and stepping away from me. "I—I heard that thing, that monster enter and look for me. But it only found an empty carriage house and a dead horse. I saved myself by hiding inside the animal."

He then began creeping toward me with the knife raised. "Did you hear that? I hid inside the horse, the horse that I craved up like a jack-o-lantern. If it weren't for you and Mr. Chapman, wandering the woods and doing acts only the devil himself would cherish, then I would never've butchered that poor, defenseless animal!"

With each step, I backed up and tried convincing him that what he had done was right. "You did what anyone would have in your situation. You needed to survive and tell the world that a monster is loose."

An evil smile came over his face. "You don't understand, Doc Myerburg, a monster that has been lurking inside of me has burst out. Not everyone would have done what I did to survive.

Only a monster could do to an animal what that monster inside Jane did to the helpless cook, and as far as I'm concerned, you are the direct cause of this monster becoming unleashed. And before you cause me anymore hell, my monster is going to end your life!"

He lunged at me, knife slashing through the air. I put my hand in my back pocket to retrieve the letter opener to defend myself, but fumbled and dropped it. He jumped and I ducked and rolled out of the knife's path, landing against a carriage wheel. My head hit the wheel and I was almost knocked unconscious. I felt dizzy and could not stand. I pulled myself up on the wheel, leaned against it, and looked behind me. The driver was lying on a small haystack. Protruding from his back, dripping with blood, were four prongs from a pitchfork that was lying atop the hay.

I staggered over to the letter opener and picked it up, just in case he was still alive. I once kept a man who had accidentally fallen on a pitchfork alive for almost a week some years ago. The prongs had only embedded a few inches and had not impaled him. This instance was similar so I kept my guard up, knowing that he could try and attack me again. I turned him over and the knife that he was going to stab me with was embedded in his throat. If the pitchfork had not killed him, then the steel blade certainly had.

I removed the knife and the pitchfork and placed him back into the stall with the horse. I walked back inside the house and wrapped the other victims up in blankets and curtains that were not torn to shreds. I then carried their dead bodies out and placed them into the same stall. With the pitchfork, I buried their bodies in hay. Before they returned to life like Jane—if they were to at all—I decided to cremate them and prevent any such resurrection. Then I searched the carriage house for lantern oil to use as an accelerant, but found none. I remembered that in the basement there was more oil that we had not brought into the mire. I left the stable and headed for the house.

Late Afternoon, Sunday, April 2, 1888

I found the oil in the basement and was about to leave when I heard a scratching noise and began smelling roses. The sound was like someone dragging their foot across a dirty floor, and it was coming from behind a stack of trunks. The rose smell reminded me of what Harold told me about Jane in the cemetery: that roses were her favorite flower.

I pulled the letter opener from my pocket and crept like a spider across its web, quiet and slow in a horizontal path along the trunks, keeping a safe distance. I trained my eyes along walls, searching for shadowy movement. And there poking out from behind one of the trunks I saw the shadows of feet. Jane or possibly Karen. If I was lucky, I had found both. If indeed luck was on my side, I could kill them both, too, before they killed me.

Adrenaline still rushed through my veins from my brush with death in the carriage house. I felt jittery and on high alert. I was not going to wait for another close call that might send me to my grave. I resolved to keep on the offense, rather than try and defend myself again.

As I moved toward the trunks, I heard breathing coming from whomever and whatever was hiding behind them. I raised the letter opener in a striking position and placed my hand on the nearest trunk. I swallowed hard. My heart pounded through my chest and my hands shook. I felt my knees wobble to the extent they were knocking together. I counted to three and pulled down the trunk. In that instance the figure stood up, I closed my eyes, and with all my might I buried the letter opener deep in its chest.

I released the letter opener and opened my eyes. "God, what have I d-done. Please, no!"

With the letter opener implanted into her chest, Clarabelle staggered back away from the trunks, crashing into the wall and onto her side. I pushed down the remaining trunks, scrambling over them, then dropped to my knees and held up her head.

"I'm sorry," I said, tears forming. "I thought you were..."

Clarabelle interrupted, looking me straight in the eyes. Coughing, she said, "I figure you was too!"

Her left arm fell to the floor and her hand uncurled. A large, serrated knife clanked to the floor. I looked at the blade, knowing that if I had not stabbed Clarabelle first, I would be the one lying there. Next to her were two roses, the ones from the vase in Karen's room.

My hands shook. "I thought you were dead. I saw your body lying on Karen's bedroom floor."

"That is Karen. I was prunin' her roses when she woke an' started screamin'." Clarabelle's head rolled to the side and she coughed up blood.

I wiped her mouth clean, and she continued. "A horrible thing were a standin' over Karen and I runned from da room an' hid in a hallway closet. I return later when all da screamin' inside went quite an' I found her body torn apart. I found all da others too. I then 'eard someone enter into da house, so I runs into da basement and have been hidin' here ever since. I now know it were you dat entered..."

"I can save you," I said. "All I need to do is find my medical bag."

"Please, sir, lemme die. Help me remove da blade from my chest." Again she coughed up blood, her chest muscles tightening.

"You don't deserve to die this way."

"Please, sir, lemme die."

I stood up. "I think I know where my bag is. I'll be right back. Just hold on."

But before I made it to the staircase, I heard the metal letter opener clank to the floor. I wheeled, hurled over the trunks, and dropped to my knees. She had yanked the blade from her chest. I tore a large section of fabric from her shirt and pressed it against the wound. The blood popped and burbled as the air in her lungs escaped. Her chest spasms increased and her legs and arms flailed. Her neck stretched back and the remaining air passed through her mouth.

"Stay with me, Clarabelle, stay with me!"

She looked up into my eyes and spoke her final sentence. "You have to learn before you die young."

The words repeated inside my head, and I knew what she meant. She meant I had to learn from the deaths of others, before I died too.

Her head flopped to one side. A slight trickle of blood drizzled from her mouth and nose as she let out a final cough.

Then her arms went limp and her heart rate dropped. Her eyes looked into mine as her eyelids fluttered closed. She let out a moan, no longer breathing.

Then Clarabelle died.

I whispered my final apologies, pulled her body out from behind her hiding spot, and dragged her up from the basement. In the carriage house, I place Clarabelle next to the others and spread hay over her body. I poured the oil and lit the pyre ablaze. The flames spread and shot up to the ceiling. Fumes of burning flesh were a welcome scent compared to the decayed stench that drifted throughout the house.

As the pyre burned, I stuck the pitchfork in, removed a pile of burning hay, carried it to the house, and tossed it through the backdoor. The fire spread and within minutes the roof was engulfed. An hour later the house, weakened by fire, collapsed in on itself. If there was a curse lurking behind the façade, it burnt away with the house. I walked from the property to the front gate. Embers drifted, fell, and landed on the ground around me like snowflakes. The smoke was making it hard to breathe. To escape, I started jogging across the property toward the road. Off in the distance, I heard yelling and crying that a monster was loose. The townspeople, they were in danger. I started running.

Sunset, Sunday, April 2, 1888

From the outskirts of town, lights flickered from oil lamps and torches. The echoing of screams and cries from the remaining women and children filled my ears with anguish, as I feared Harold and me had spawned a monster no man could destroy. The men were yelling also, but in anger. I sprinted, eventually making it into town some minutes later.

The men were gathered in a large circle that was six bodies deep. In their hands they held torches ablaze with red-hot fire and pistols and rifles pointing at the circle's center. Men without firearms held onto sickles, axes, and other tools they would use to fight, maim, and kill.

"Devil woman!" one man shouted.

"Burn her—burn her back to hell!" another yelled,

throwing a torch toward the center of the circle, followed by a unity of cheers, as if the torch had struck its target.

Pushing my way through the crowd, my eyes caught hold of Jane in the middle of the circle. She still resembled a corpse but had rejuvenated more since our frightful encounter in the mire. Her eyes were glowing and foam burbled out of her mouth. Playfully, she stroked the hair of a young man who was propped against her leg. The man appeared motionless, but he was still breathing. What little life he retained was being drained, I could tell. His body withered before the mob's eyes, as he was turned into an old man. His skin wrinkled and cracked from dryness. His black hair turned gray and fell from his scalp in clumps.

Jane snatched the man up and held him by his shirt collar. She opened her mouth and a black cloud drifted forth, engulfing his head, which snapped back as his arms tried to break free from Jane's grasp. His chest heaved, his legs kicked. He tried to yell out but was suffocated from the black cloud.

Jane breathed in deep, inhaling the cloud into her lungs. Her chest began to expand as her breasts ballooned under her ragged clothing. Her cheeks filled, flushing over with pink as her natural skin tone was replenished. Her torso filled out her clothes, and her thighs began to expand.

The man's body flapped like a flag in the breeze. His skin had now turned black and any human resemblance was gone.

"Burn her at the stake!" a man yelled from the crowd.

Then, in unison, the crowd began chanting, "Witch, witch, witch!"

I stepped out from the perimeter into Jane's view. My movement caught her eye and she squared her body to mine. She raised her left arm, extended her fingers as if reaching out for me. I could tell by the way her hand shook that she was still weak, but strong enough to kill each of us one by one if need be. And by the look of the man she had turned into a bag of bones, she was well on her way.

"My maker!" Jane gurgled. Her voice sounded guttural and winded.

A loud murmur rolled over the crowd upon hearing her speak.

Ben, the blacksmith who had offered his help days before,

yelled from the crowd, "It's true. I saw Doc Myerburg a few days ago. I saw him; he was climbing into a carriage with one of the Chapman servants. He did this to Jane Chapman. He turned her into this demon!"

The crowd grew angry and started shouting, pointing their firearms in my direction. They all chanted, "Devil-man. Devil-man!"

Two grabbed me from behind. One held a knife to my throat, holding me captive. "You'll burn at the stake with the witch for this, devil man!"

"Please, let me go," I begged, stretching my neck and lifting my chin, trying to pull away from the knife. "You don't understand. Let me explain!"

"Slice his throat," one of the men said. "Then we'll burn him. Make the devil man suffer!"

The knife started raking across my neck. The blade cut through my skin, but just before it could slit my jugular, a new man galloped toward the mob on horseback, calling out, "Fire, fire! The Chapman Estate is on fire!"

Mercifully, my executioner lowered the knife and I ripped my body free. I fell to the ground and crawled away, clutching my neck. The blade had cut into my skin but not deep enough to be fatal. I tore a strip of cloth from my shirt and wrapped it around to absorb the blood.

The man on horseback leaped from the saddle, pushing his way through the crowd and into the circle. "I just arrived back from the Chapman Estate," he said. "The property is burning. The house has been destroyed by fire as well as the carriage house. There is a pile of bones smoldering in the yard. Someone murdered everyone there and tried to hide the deed by burning their corpses!"

The man's imagination was far from the truth, indeed. I had been trying to save their souls from coming back to life, a monster like Jane. I was anything but a killer trying to conceal his murderous rampage.

Ben raised his pistol at me and cocked the hammer. "Whatever it was you have done there has brought hell upon our town. You spawned this demon. You're a murderer," he said, pointing his finger behind him at Jane.

"Please, let me explain!" I begged, falling to my knees with my hands clasped together.

"Explain your actions to the devil!" Ben barked.

In my mind, his finger pulling the trigger moved in slow motion. My heartbeat rose in my chest and felt as if my heart muscles were tearing apart. The hammer dropped onto the bullet, followed by a flash exiting the muzzle chamber. I closed my eyes, not waiting to see the bullet enter my body, but I never felt it. A loud pop echoed into the night and the bullet flew over my head, ricocheting off the metal sign hanging over the gunsmith's shop door.

I opened my eyes and saw Ben hoisted into the air. His legs were kicking and his arms were trying to reach around him to grab onto Jane. In the confusion of the moment Ben had forgot, as had the crowd, that she was still standing there, waiting and feeling the insatiable urge to attack.

Gunfire exploded around me and the expelled gunpowder singed my neck hair. The unending pistol and rifle reports were deafening. It sounded like dozens of stringed-firecrackers were hung, lit, and then detonated around my head. I covered my ears, dropped to the ground, and watched in horror as the rain of bullets pelted Ben's body. With each bullet that entered into him he twitched, his face wrung into grimace.

The bullets passed through Ben and entered into Jane, but they were ineffective. Jane continued holding him up in the air, opening her mouth to engulf his head in that black cloud.

"Hold your fire!" I yelled over the crowd, rising to my feet and waving my arms.

The reports ceased one by one until all was quiet. Fumes of gunpowder dried my nostrils and a loud ringing bludgeoned my ears.

The men watched, horror-stricken, as Jane filtered the life from Ben. His body aged and shriveled—just as the last man had who met his fate within Jane's grasp.

While she fed off Ben, I grabbed a torch from one of the men and circled around her. I inched forward, making sure she could not sense my movement. Whenever she turned, I lurched to stay out of her line of sight. Closer and closer, I came upon her back. My heart raced and rose into my throat. The force of its beating within my ears drowned out the yelling of the men and the random gunshots. I was within arm's reach when she tossed Ben away, and her arm swung around and hit me across the chest. I lost my footing and fell to the ground. The torch fell from my grasp, rolling out of reach.

Jane turned and lifted my body up from the ground. Only this time there were no leeches sacrificing their bodies to save my own. I was hers for the taking, for the leeching of my soul, for her to possess for all eternity.

I glanced away from her and yelled over the crowd, "Run away! Leave before she kills every last one of you!" Like Harold before me, I had to sacrifice myself for the good of mankind.

The majority of the men scattered like scared mice before an opening barn door. But some remained because they were either too scared to run or because they were too stupid. In order that those who were running got away to a safe distance, I fought Jane. I kicked my legs and pounded my fists into her head and chest. But my blows proved weak and ineffective.

She slammed me into the ground, crouched over me, picked me back up and slammed me again, shoulder first this time, following with my face and then implanting me in the dirt. She was playing with me, torturing me before she opened her mouth and engulfed my head in the black cloud.

My shoulder was dislocated, my nose broken. I heard a gunshot and saw the bullet exit through her chest. She turned and looked at the man who fired the gun. She staggered toward him, but he dropped his weapon and ran. She managed to follow him about ten feet before another bullet entered into her arm, followed by more bullets.

I crawled to the torch, picked it up, and stood. After gaining my footing, I ran at Jane but before I could thrust it through her back and into her body, another bullet pelted her. She turned, caught sight of me, and started walking. I stood my ground and fought the pain of my dislocated shoulder, holding the torch in both hands like an axe.

She grabbed me and lifted me off the ground and opened her mouth. The black cloud dispersed from within. It smelled of rotten fish and carrion. The smoke burned my eyes and suffocated my lungs. It was now or never. I had to kill her.

I raised the blazing torch over my head like a dagger. The heat began melting my skin and the flames scorched my knuckles. I withstood the pain and rammed the torch down into her mouth. With all my strength, I held it in place and pushed the fire deep into her throat. I could hear her body tissues crackling and igniting.

She held onto me while stumbling until she fell onto her back. As we landed, I held the torch in place and continued pushing. Smoke billowed out from her nostrils followed by sparking flames. Her eyes melted, popping and exploding with black liquid onto my hands and face. She bucked, trying to kick me off. Her arms flailed trying to grasp the torch and when her arms found it, she tried wrenching it from my grasp.

She failed.

Seconds later she stopped moving. I stood and staggered back, regaining my footing and turning to look at the remaining men who were all silent. Their jaws were dropped, their firearms still aimed upon Jane.

I walked over to the closest man and reached for his axe. He let me take it from him.

I turned, watching Jane as she burned. The flames used her bones as a wick and her body fat as candle wax, cremating her inside out. Her skin bubbled and popped like a witch's cauldron over an open fire. Her skin began to crack open and smoke seeped from the fissures. Soon after, her clothes caught fire and flames engulfed the rest of her. Her hair curled up as it began to burn and her teeth jumped from her mouth. Embers made of pieces of her clothes and skin floated into the air, drifting about like snow.

I walked over and raised the axe. Swinging it through the air, I rammed it down into her right shoulder. Embers plumed from her body as if a log was tossed into a roaring fire. I wiggled the axe free; her melted skin had fused to the cold metal axe head. I heaved and her arm slid off and dropped to the ground. It made a splashing sound as it landed. I drove the blade into her left shoulder, followed by her head, right leg and finally her left leg. With each chop from the axe, more embers plumed into the air.

"She's dead." An arm grabbed mine from behind, and I turned. It was Father McGuiness.

Chief Livingston grabbed the axe handle and pulled it

from my grip without resistance. "She'd dead," he said, echoing the priest. "She'll haunt us no more."

Exhausted, I collapsed into Father McGuiness's arms and began crying.

"Chief Livingston," the priest said.

"Yes, Father?"

"Retrieve a coffin. The doctor has more work to do."

Father McGuiness lowered my aching body to the ground. Through tears, I looked at the flames dying down across Jane's body. When they had died out, I raised the axe a final time and quartered Jane's smoldering remains.

Chief Livingston dragged a coffin behind him, along with a shovel. He bent to scoop up Jane's arm. Before he could lift it from the ground, I grabbed the shovel handle. "No, I've got to do this."

"You've been through too much already, doctor. Please allow me to help."

"No, this is all on my head. I've let this happen. I've got to do this. It's the only way to stop Jane from returning from the grave again."

Without argument, Chief Livingston's fingers uncoiled from around the shovel handle. He stepped back, giving me room to finish what I set out to do days before with Harold.

This time, I succeeded.

Jane's body lay in the coffin, her limbs rearranged in opposite positions, legs folded over her chest, arms outstretched at the hips — all done to confuse her if she once more resurrected.

After I hammered the lid shut, Father McGuiness asked, "What are you going to do now, doctor?"

I sighed, wiping sweat from my brow. "I can't go back to medicine. You each saw how these men looked at me tonight. They all stood around me, watching in horror as I killed Jane. They weren't as afraid of her as they were of me. They'll never trust me again."

"In due time, they'll trust you," Chief Livingston said.

"There's no time to wait for forgiveness for what I've allowed to happen to his town. It's my fault. I won't fail them again. I'll keep watch over Jane's grave for the remainder of my life. I'll wait for her to rise again should this solution, this dismemberment, fail to work."

"I cannot allow her to be buried in the city's cemetery; people will be trying to dig her up for years to come," Father McGuiness said. "They'll try to make sure she is truly dead. They'll do more to her than you've done here tonight. She'll never rest in peace."

"I'll leave the city with her. I'll bury her in the countryside. I can build a shack. There I can keep an eye on her."

"You're in no shape mentally to live alone. You'll need care. You've cared for this town for years. Allow someone to care for you."

"What do you suggest?"

"We'll secretly bury Jane behind the church tonight. There is an extra room used for storage. We can clean it out and you can live there. Sister Margret will help care for you. She's young and God is with her. There's nothing she won't do to help those who have given so much to help others."

I nodded in agreement.

Together we lifted the coffin. We carried it through town to the church. The streets were empty and silent. The citizens who hadn't fled Saratoga Springs went from scared spectators to people in hiding. Even dogs and cats were absent. Each living soul feared they'd be killed, same as Jane.

We set the coffin down behind the church and Father McGuiness said, "There," pointing to a window on the third floor. "There is where your room will be. You'll have an unobstructed view of Jane's grave."

"Good," I said, turning and pressing the point of the shovel onto the ground. I pushed it through the soil with the remaining strength of my foot. "Excuse me, I've got to have Jane buried before sunrise. Word will get out soon that it's safe. People will be returning to their homes. They don't need to see where she is buried."

"If you need a break from digging, I'll help," Father McGuiness offered.

"As will I," added Chief Livingston.

"No, thank you," I said, without hesitation. "This is still something I need to do myself. Like I said before, this is my responsibility. But you two gentlemen can help in another way."

"Anything. What do you want us to do?" Chief Livingston asked.

"Make a pact with me." I stopped shoveling and extended my hand. "Everything that we're doing in secret tonight is never to be spoken of again. People will try, like you said they'd do in the cemetery, to destroy Jane's body. It'll be best if they think she's buried in the countryside."

Chief Livingston took the doctor's hand and shook, sealing the pact. "Agreed."

"Agreed," Father McGuiness echoed, and shook the doctor's hand, nodding in approval.

Epilogue
New Year's Day, 1900

Father McGuiness watched the Snook Hill groundskeeper pat down the dirt on Chief Livingston's grave. He had been killed the night before, breaking up a bar fight that erupted moments before the century's end. The barkeep had drawn a pistol on two brawling men and pointed it at the instigator, a burly looking fellow wearing tattered farm clothes and a roughed up slouch hat. The barkeep didn't mean to pull the trigger; he merely wanted to stop the men fighting.

Chief Livingston had become too old for breaking up bar fights. Neither of the men listened to him. The chief was now in his sixties and limped due to being thrown from his horse the year prior, after the steed was bitten on the ankle by a rattlesnake. He couldn't get the men to stop throwing punches, especially with a rowdy crowd egging them on to fight regardless of police presence.

So Chief Livingston's demands to cease fighting went ignored. To intervene, he grabbed the arm of the farmer to halt another punch. Figuring it was one of his opponent's friends, the farmer spun around and without hesitation, punched and pushed Chief Livingston across the barroom into the barkeep.

The barkeep tried catching him by hooking his arms under the chief's armpits. But the jolt of body weight shoved the barkeep back into the bar railing. The shock nudged his arm, causing his finger to pull the trigger, discharging the bullet from the gun barrel. The bullet struck the chief behind his left ear and exited through his right eye. Chief Livingston died before he had collapsed on the hardwood floor.

Father McGuiness sighed. He bowed his head as he walked away from his friend's grave. The first snowfall of the year started sputtering from the gray clouds above. Snowflakes landed upon his face and quickly melted. Before he reached his carriage, he paused and looked across the dirt path bisecting the cemetery. In the far corner he saw a small headstone and walked over to it. He stood in front of the headstone, which was inscribed only with Doctor Myerburg's last name and his date of death.

Father McGuiness stopped by the doctor's grave each time he was in the cemetery. He found it to be his duty to read a protective passage from his Bible. While Doctor Myerburg was alive, Father McGuiness never saw it as a necessity to recite any passages to the doctor. As years passed and Jane remained in her grave it made sense to allow the doctor to continue to believe he was protecting the city. After all, he had done so while practicing medicine. If the doctor had been unable to rest peacefully alive and was always on edge, his soul needed to feel some rest and security now.

Father McGuiness opened his Bible and began to read:

"Isaiah 57:1-2 Good people pass away; the godly often die before their time. But no one seems to care or wonder why. No one seems to understand that God is protecting them from the evil to come. For those who follow godly paths will rest in peace when they die."

Father McGuiness sighed heavily through his nose and whispered, "I wish you died knowing Jane's remains were stolen to rid the town of her memory, and nothing more. Then you would have understood the sense of security it brought to the townspeople. You would've lived your life happily ever after." Father McGuiness nodded. "Yes, I do believe you finally would've smiled again."

The priest closed his Bible. The winter storm picked up from a flurry to a dense snowfall. Before he walked away, he took a final look at Doctor Myerburg's grave. "Rest peacefully, my friend," he said. And then he was gone.

ACKNOWLEDGMENTS

Aaron J. French: Thanks to Adam Lewis for bringing this project to my attention, to Erik for joining the team, and to you both for sticking with me as we sought publication. Also thank you to Andrew and Uncanny Books for the excellent work. To John Taff for his awesome blurb. And to my friends, brothers, and companions who inspire and assist me always; you know who you are.

Erik T. Johnson: Most of all I'd like to thank Erica for not killing me while I was killing myself trying to get this story right. I also must thank Aaron J. French and Adam P. Lewis, for the invite and the honor of including me in this crazy endeavor; Michael Bailey, for believing in my work, putting it out there, and many more reasons; and, last but headlining, my amazing friend and fantastic author John F.D. Taff for innumerable kinds of support, both personal and professional.

Adam P. Lewis: First and foremost, I wish to extend my gracious appreciation to those directly involved in *The Chapman Books*. Andrew Byers, founder of Uncanny Books, for offering to publish this unique collection. Without his professionalism this project would not have fulfilled my expectations. Aaron J. French, who shared numerous alcoholic beverages with me and listened to me ramble, half in-the-bag no less, about the Chapman Family's history. Aaron also deserves special kudos for bringing aboard Erik T. Johnson, who brought to this project his eclectic enthusiasms and oddities. To my writing colleague and accomplice, Ty Schwamberger, for the past several years he's offered advice, inspiration, and opportunities within this sometimes unfulfilling business authoring fiction. Without his support, the Chapman Family and their unfortunate history would've stayed buried within my Aunt's dusty attic. By means of shock and awe, Bloodbath, Cannibal Corpse, Skinless, and Obituary battered my eardrums through headphones while researching for and writing my portion of *The Chapman Books*. Without inspiration from those mentioned bands much of the written imagery within my contributed pages would have been tame and rated for general audiences. Last but not least, closer to heart I thank my family—my boys, Daniel and Gehrig, and my wife, Dianne—to whom this project is dedicated, for their patience while I hogged the computer writing and researching and ignoring housework.

ABOUT THE AUTHORS

Aaron J. French (a.k.a. A. J. French) is currently a book editor for JournalStone Publishing and the Editor-in-Chief for *Dark Discoveries* magazine—a professional, internationally distributed print magazine specializing in dark fiction, currently on its tenth year of continuous publication and distribution. He has worked with and edited such authors as David Liss, Norman Partridge, Gary A. Braunbeck, Thomas Ligotti, Steve Rasnic Tem, Jonathan Maberry, F. Paul Wilson, and many others. In 2011 he edited *Monk Punk*, an anthology of monk-themed speculative fiction and *The Shadow of the Unknown*, an anthology of nü-Lovecraftian fiction. His latest anthology *Songs of the Satyrs* will be published in 2014 and features a brand new novella from New York Times best-selling author David Farland. Aaron also served as co-editor for *The Lovecraft eZine* for several months in 2012. Aaron's fiction has appeared in many publications including *Dark Discoveries, Black Ink Horror, Something Wicked, After Death..., Bedlam, Beware the Dark, Chiral Mad, The Lovecraft eZine*, and others. His zombie collection *Up From Soil Fresh* was published by Hazardous Press in 2013. Also in 2013 "The Order," Aaron's occult thriller novella about a Lovecraftian secret society, was published in the *Dreaming in Darkness* collection. His single-author collection, *Aberrations of Reality*, will be released mid-2014 by Crowded Quarantine Publications. He is currently an active member of the Horror Writers Association. Aaron is pursuing a Religious Studies degree from the University of Arizona, where his main areas of interest and research include Anthroposophy, Western Esotericism, Freemasonry and Esoteric Orders, and Esoteric Christianity. His nonfiction articles on Thomas Ligotti, Alejandro Jodorowsky, and Karl Edward Wagner have appeared in *Dark Discoveries* magazine, while his online column "Letters from the Edge," focusing on the occult, spirituality, rogue scholarship, esotericism, and speculative fiction, is featured regularly on the *Nameless Digest* website. His academic paper "Toward Christian Renewal," which explores potential contributions of esoteric Christianity within mainstream Christianity, was published in 2013 by the peer-reviewed journal

The Esoteric Quarterly. He is currently a member of the ESSWE, the European Society for the Study of Western Esotericism.

Erik T. Johnson writes FS/FHH (Funny-Strange, Funny Ha-Ha) fiction. His work has appeared in many fine periodicals such as *Space & Time Magazine*, *Tales of the Unanticipated*, *Electric Velocipede*, British Fantasy Society's *BFS Journal*, and *Shimmer*; and anthologies including multi-award winning *Chiral Mad*, *Chiral Mad 2*, *The Shadow of the Unknown*, *Box of Delights*, and *Dead but Dreaming 2*. A complete bibliography, blog, scrawling, news, doodles and all that, can be found by visiting YES TRESPASSING (www.erikTjohnson.net).

Adam P. Lewis immersed himself within the world of horror at an early age. While growing up and snowed in at the foothills of the Adirondacks, he read the likes of Edgar Allan Poe, H.P. Lovecraft, and Ambrose Bierce. These authors, along with many others, inspired him to write his own horror, sci-fi, and mysterious fiction. Adam's work isn't merely based on fictional monsters, but also historical figures such as Lizzy Borden, Edgar Allan Poe, Lewis and Clark, and Sacagawea. Adam is also credited for book reviews, movie reviews, essays on true crime, and song publishing credits; musically and lyrically. Currently, Adam is working on historical horror novellas, short stories, true crime, and collaborations. When not writing, Adam resides in the heart of the Adirondacks reading, watching baseball, and being a husband and father. For more information, publications and questions, visit www.byadamlewis.weebly.com, follow Adam on Twitter @adamhorror, or on Facebook (www.facebook.com/byadamlewis).

www.ingramcontent.com/pod-product-compliance
Lightning Source LLC
Chambersburg PA
CBHW030301200626